Caroline,

Time you started to read more!
Enjoy!

Jack Temple Guilty

Bob Moss
xx
3.1.2020

Bob Moss

Copyright © 2019 Bob Moss

All rights reserved.

ISBN: 9781711705408

The rights of Bob Moss to be identified as the Author of the work has been asserted by him in accordance with the Copyright, Design and Patents Act 1988

To Valerie Andrew and James

CONTENTS

1	Jack's Mentor	1
2	The Red Lion Tap Room	20
3	The Three "R"s	31
4	The Extra Mile	45
5	Speculation	64
6	An extraordinary meeting	81
7	The bodyguard	96
8	"Hail Caesar!"	111
9	Rising Star	125
10	Negotiating Tactics	136
11	The Detective	150
12	First Date	161
13	The Letter	173
14	The Escort	183
15	Cointreau On Ice	195
16	The Candidates	207
17	Breaking News	221
18	House of Lords	231
19	The Agenda	238
20	Cause for Concern	251
21	The Girlfriend	261
22	The Verdict	274

ACKNOWLEDGMENTS

Not many people know that James Bond is my brother-in-law. He is not the fictional character we all know despite sharing many of 007's finer characteristics. I will spare James's blushes by not listing them, save to mention his meticulous attention to detail when reviewing this book. Thanks James.

Author Tim Kevin has given me sound advice on several book-related matters and offered solid encouragement matched by enormous enthusiasm which was much appreciated.

I thank David Goddard Senior Clerk at 4 Stone Buildings and President of the Institute of Barristers' Clerks for finding the time in his ridiculously busy schedule to offer some helpful advice and also Jackie Ginty Deputy Senior Clerk at One Essex Court who offered kind words of encouragement.

Gill Butchard has been a secret publishing friend for many years, helping me on numerous occasions with ideas for the Clerksroom magazine and this book. The banter was inspiring.

I should also thank all those in the legal profession I have had dealings with over a career spanning more than 40 years, and who unknowingly sparked my imagination.

To anyone who thinks they may be in the book just remember it is all fiction. And it is no good asking me as my reply will always be "You might very well think that; I couldn't possibly comment"!

1 JACK'S MENTOR

Jack could hear a phone ringing but nobody was answering it. Everyone in his clerks' room knew he expected the phone to be picked up within three rings. It was one of his commandments. The twelfth to be exact, after the usual ten and his eleventh: "Thou shall not presume".

He heard himself shout "For God's sake somebody answer that!" At this point Jack awoke to realise his mobile was getting louder and louder on the bedside table. "Bugger!" he mumbled to himself as he untwined his arms and legs from what seemed like a long silky smooth octopus asleep around him. He answered his mobile with a grumpy "Yeh".

"Jack, its Nathan. Sorry to bother you but I need your credit card." Now the last two words got Jack's attention. "What time is it?" he asked. "I'm not sure" replied Nathan, "But it must be after one. Look, thing is I've left my wallet in chambers. Be a good fellow and speak to this nice waiter will you. He wants his bill paying. Can you sort him out?"

"Where are you?" asked Jack.

Nathan Blake, a junior barrister of seven years call and member of Barcourt chambers where Jack Temple was the senior clerk, was not one immediately thought of by his peers as a geek. The clerks considered he was rather more a fake geek with no common sense.

Nathan replied: "Chez Lamps. We were working late in chambers and a few of us popped out for a bite and one thing led to another."

Chez Lamps was the nickname for a regular haunt just off Chancery Lane used by Nathan and his cronies. The restaurant's nickname was short for Lampard's.

Jack was supposed to be impressed by Nathan's reference to working late so it would somehow make him more amenable to the suggestion that he use his own credit card to fund Nathan's boozy night out. He was not impressed, but was always mindful of when he might want a favour, perhaps covering a case in the Carlisle County Court or some other distant outpost of the legal empire.

As Jack asked Nathan how much the restaurant bill was his attention became focused on one slightly more pressing question he asked himself.

"Where's my wallet?"

The pale white torso he had been lying next to turned over and in the half-light he saw the vision of beauty that had held his attention all evening until they had both fallen asleep exhausted. Another satisfied client he thought as he remembered where he had left his jacket and wallet.

Jack sat on the edge of the double bed and spoke again to Nathan referring to the waiter: "Put him on".

He dealt with Nathan's bill and the waiter seemed delighted with the tip. Jack was always a generous tipper in case he needed a favour in the future and he knew he would recoup every penny including the tip through Nathan's chambers expenses. What annoyed him as he settled back amongst the arms and legs of Octopussy was that Chez Lamps was only round the corner from Chambers. Nathan was perfectly capable of walking to get his wallet. "Lazy git" he thought as he closed his eyes.

Jack usually woke automatically at 6.30am sharp. It did not matter whether it was summer or winter time, his body clock knew when to stir him. The tube journey and walk down Chancery Lane to Chambers was 45 minutes on a good day, and he always liked to be in for 8.00am despite the fact that chambers was not officially open until 8.30. His former senior clerk and mentor Ralph had taught him:

"The early bird always catches the worm Jack", and by and large Jack found this to be true.

If there was going to be an early doors crisis, it was too late to win the day by 9.00 o'clock. Jack understood that anyone could handle the good times, but a clerk was judged on how he or she dealt with a crisis. And as senior clerk, Jack had dealt with all sorts of tricky situations. That's why he had the job, and loved it.

He never took solids on board before leaving for chambers as he did not really want to wake up and pull himself together until he got out of the underground. Once in the relatively fresh London morning air he would take a hot croissant filled with scrambled egg and crispy bacon plus a large cappuccino at the coffee shop at the top of Chancery Lane tube station before walking the last few hundred yards to chambers.

Today was a little different. Jack would argue that there was no such thing as a normal every day routine, which was what most clerks found so exciting. The routine on this Friday morning was broken by Octopussy.

Jack had given Beth the nickname "Octopussy" because of her long arms and legs. Actually her personality demanded a better name but he never changed a nickname once chosen. It was bad luck. Elizabeth Richardson was demanding enough in all aspects of her life. This was a lady who knew what she wanted, and she usually enjoyed it.

Beth was an experienced personal injury solicitor. When it came to instructing counsel, she expected them to deliver a first class service and on time. She prided herself on delivering for her clients exactly what she promised, and that was how she had built an excellent reputation in the personal injury field. Everyone knew her as Beth. She had a well-proportioned tall body that had been toned up by regular visits to the gym, light skin colour and long black hair.

Fighting her corner for her equity partnership had produced a hard smile and cost her one marriage. She was not about to step into another binding matrimonial agreement and always knew Jack had responsibilities at home. Last night was not the first time they had hooked up, and probably would not be the last. As she saw it the arrangement was a win-win for them both.

Her firm had to date been selective about who they instructed and spread the work around which meant there were three chambers currently in favour. Jack was after all the work. Personal Injury cases were on the increase, partly fueled by the increasing claim culture. He wanted a reputation for excellence, and getting all of the work from Beth's firm would send a strong message to other firms as well as to barristers who might be looking for a new home.

Beth's firm was Crompton and Ashdown based in Birmingham. They had been created by the current senior partner Geoffrey Ashdown and John Crompton who had retired two years before. His retirement had been the opportunity for Beth to get her equity partnership. She had raised enough capital to buy part of Crompton's share. She could buy the rest over several years. Her initial cash injection was used to fund the planned expansion. They now employed 50 solicitors and legal executives doing mostly claimant work. Beth and Geoffrey invested heavily in computer technology and their turnover had trebled in the last three years.

The problem Jack had was twofold. He knew that the senior partner Geoffrey Ashdown dealt with the bigger claims, the sort of work which needed a junior and a QC. He favoured chambers with several top silks, the posh name for Queen's Counsel, and Jack knew he did not have enough QCs at Barcourt chambers with the right standing in this specialist field to attract the best work.

Secondly, he knew that Beth could turn against him which would happen if he cocked up either because a barrister did not deliver or made a mistake, or he blew their personal relationship. That would leave him exposed to criticism, and then potentially to an exodus from chambers of those members who would follow the work. That could ultimately lead to Jack's sacking. He was playing a risky game, but that was part of the attraction.

Beth stayed in London for the trials of her cases which usually lasted several days. On this occasion her case in which she had briefed Sarah Ryman, a personal injury specialist in Jack's chambers, finished on the Thursday afternoon so Beth chose to stay on in London for one last night. Her client, an ex-miner, had won a substantial six figure award which would act as a precedent to open the door to many more claims for similarly injured miners.

More important to Jack, costs followed the event, meaning the Defendant's insurers would be picking up the bill. The agreed fees, which were generous to say the least, would not need renegotiating down but be paid in full. So Beth and Jack had good cause to splash out on an expensive meal, plus a couple of bottles of top bubbly.

Looking at Beth in the morning was a rare treat for Jack, even if she reminded him of the risks he was taking. It was true he had woken early at his appointed hour, but was prevented from getting his entire body to rise until gone eight o'clock by the ever present female tentacles. All his senses, especially the lovely early morning perfume from warm satisfied flesh, told him to stay put for as long as possible. "Why not?" he thought, and then proceeded to remind Beth of why he was the right man for the task.

Beth had been in no hurry to get to Euston Station for her train back to Birmingham, until she realised that her office was open and she would have to let her secretary know she would be late in. She would not offer any explanation as she was an equity partner and could do as she pleased. Jack ordered a taxi which they shared. He dropped her off at Euston Station and then carried on to Chambers.

He had logged into the chambers' computerised diary system from his other mobile phone, a Blackberry, during Beth's short bedroom adjournment for a call of nature. So he was reasonably relaxed about his late arrival in his clerks' room. As nobody had any inclination to question his time keeping, in part for fear of upsetting him, he was able to take up his customary position at the head of the team for another exhilarating day. Plus it was Friday and the weekend was just on the horizon.

To describe Jack as "old school" was a little misleading. Hardly at school would have been closer to the mark. Exam qualifications were conspicuous by their absence from his CV. This was his one and only employer to date. He had got the job he would say on personality but actually it was by recommendation via a friend whose father was a clerk. Anyway, as Jack said: "what do I need a CV for? I'm not going anywhere."

Like many of his senior clerk colleagues around the Temple in London, Jack left school at 16 with a truancy record as long as his arm. He wanted to get on with life but did not know how to go about it. His peers went into factories or industrial units close to home and set about developing the beer gut before they were legally entitled to. He felt he wanted to work with clean hands inside a crisp white shirt held together by a silk tie and some classy cuff links. He often showed his dry sense of humour by his choice of cuff links. His pair of "Guilty" and "Not Guilty" links from The Carbolic Smoke Ball Company were his favourites.

Jack's hair was always immaculate as if every strand grew at just the right amount each day to be in the right place on his otherwise sun tanned head. At six foot tall he felt in proportion and well balanced. Even at 35 he could still but only just get into the same football kit on a Sunday morning as he had ten years ago, but the legs felt a little heavier in the second half. He would never admit that, but instead barked orders to the youngsters to do the hard yards.

He had a small wardrobe in chambers containing a selection of suits for every occasion. Each one cost four figures and looked like it had never been worn before. His colleagues thought he must have shares in Emporium Armani. There were the matching shirts and ties plus a selection of Church brogues you could see your face in. Of course such displays of apparent wealth didn't please everyone. There were those at the Bar Jack worked for and the poorer solicitors who instructed members of his chambers who thought they are paying too much for his appearance, and those who just admired and aspired.

Chambers was like a ship at sea. On board there was only one captain. There were the owners [barristers] but they were just travellers like the rest of those on board including the crew [clerks] of the good ship "Chambers". And make no mistake, at Barcourt Chambers, Jack Temple was the skipper. He knew everything there was to know about life in chambers, and then some.

The face of youth had given way to lines of experience, but Jack was still adored by the ladies who could sometimes just take one look at him and know they would be offered a good time. Jack did not disappoint anyone. He always went the extra mile. It was part of his nature.

In his early years as a clerk Jack often sat down to listen to some of the senior clerks sorting the legal world over a beer after the day was over and the diary had been put to bed at The Wiltshire Inn, a regular watering hole opposite the Royal Courts of Justice just off the Strand. They would often bemoan the antics and stupidity of their counsel. Sometimes they would try and work out how they would describe their job to a complete stranger with no connection with the law or lawyers. This involved quite a few beers and some heated debate.

The role of a clerk had been traditionally associated with an East End barrow boy with a suit on. There were very few female clerks. The young lads were taken into small sets where there might only be a handful of barristers and one senior clerk who operated on his own and took in a junior to run errands and deliver briefs when the volume of work demanded. So that junior would have to wait a long time for dead men's shoes and promotion, but they felt lucky and grateful for the work. They held members of their chambers up on a pedestal, and never questioned what they were told to do. No task was too small. They were just happy to oblige.

Although times were moving on, some senior clerks had still come from similar origins. Jack listened to the stories his seniors told of their youth. One of them suggested that a good senior clerk was really a cross between a theatrical agent, a nanny and a pimp. The others thought this an unfair description of their talents, although Jack saw the funny side, including his willingness to get his hands dirty as would the nanny when the situation demanded. That is what he expected of his clerking team. That was why he always appeared to be willing to change the toner cartridge in the chambers photocopier.

As he entered the clerks' room in Barcourt Chambers that Friday morning, Jack threw out the customary "Morning" to his team who to a man pinged back "Morning Jack" almost but not quite in unison. There was no need for further greetings as everyone was focused on getting all the barristers sorted for the day. That involved making sure that each member of chambers had their brief, were on their way to court and there were no last minute problems. There would be time for chatter and a coffee once chambers was empty until counsel wandered back at lunchtime.

Having checked his inbox and delegated what he could, Jack looked to see who was in the diary for lunch and early evening drinks. Some in his senior clerking world did not work on a Friday afternoon, so a networking lunch had a habit of dragging on until the early evening shift in one or more of the drinking houses centred on the Temple, Chancery lane and around the Strand. Clients expected to be entertained and Jack's role included being chief social secretary. An away fixture might involve travelling with solicitor clients as far as

Soho, but such trips were more frowned upon.

It was impossible for Jack to wine and dine all the solicitors who sent in work to chambers, so he would target the big wigs and those with valuable briefs or a lot of work. Then he would use the full waterfall of experience in his clerking team to entertain solicitors and their legal executives, right down to the junior clerks buying a glass of wine for the secretaries who sometimes came to conferences in chambers. Everyone had a role to play, and that was how young relationships were nurtured to forge strong links when the young became the mature solicitor or paralegal with lots of valuable work.

Socialising came second to one golden rule at the end of each day. No clerk could leave the clerks' room until the diary for the whole of chambers for the next working day was sorted. "You are only as good as tomorrow's diary" was a phrase only understood and appreciated by bar clerks. Jack often heard it used in the Wiltshire Inn, and his own clerking team lived by the rule.

So when it came to tough questions about a barrister's career, why they were no longer getting work from a particular solicitor, or any work at all, counsel would only look at the clerks. It was never their own fault, and the person to point a finger at was the clerk who looked after their work. So if there was no work in their diary for tomorrow, then it was time to complain, sometimes to the Head of Chambers, but more often than not to the senior clerk.

Once the diary was sorted, there was never any shortage of volunteers to entertain clients as everyone got to dip into petty cash. Jack used to fund some of the sessions himself, partly to avoid any debate by the management committee about a percentage cut to his income and he was enthusiastic about putting his hand into his own pocket for the benefit of others. It also enabled him to have his own slush fund to use at his sole discretion.

This was Jack's first and he hoped only job as senior clerk. A few months before he got the job, chambers had elected a new head of chambers. After that election, Jack had unwittingly been part of a mini internal revolution within Barcourt Chambers that led to his appointment.

The previous year he had been going about his business as first junior clerk without too much thought for his long term future or that of chambers. He was just getting on with the job day by day, keeping his head down. After all he was still only in his early thirties and not looking to make the step up to senior clerk just yet.

He had been guided thus far by his mentor Ralph, their senior clerk with over 25 years' experience. Ralph had his critics, but knew everyone, especially the judges, including those in the judiciary who had not been elevated from within Barcourt chambers. But the younger stags in chambers, particularly those who specialised in civil law and saw what was happening in their expanding market, wanted more from their senior clerk, someone who would go out and get the work in for them.

About 6 months before his appointment Jack had what he at the time thought was a chance meeting with Morgan Carpenter. Morgan was a recruitment consultant, the nearest thing to a head-hunter for clerking staff. With only about 500 chambers in England and Wales, and between 2,000 and 3,000 staff in total, the market was too small for any of the big human resource companies to get involved as anyone selling to or within this sector of the legal market knew it was notoriously difficult. Jack's meeting with Morgan was for the latter to assess if he thought Jack was ready for the big time as a senior clerk.

Morgan knew his way around. He was always in the various watering holes in the Temple. A former senior clerk himself he knew how to sniff out a job opportunity. He was just as happy to place a new junior clerk as find a new home for a team of disillusioned counsel hell bent on fresh and greener pastures.

Unknown to Jack, Morgan had been involved in several clandestine meetings with the unhappy juniors in Barcourt chambers, including Nathan Blake, who had convinced themselves that Ralph was not up to the challenge any more. The old guard in chambers would be unlikely to sack Ralph and the junior members seriously risked an internal war. The blame for such an event would fall on their shoulders, and they would not expect sympathy from other chambers when they needed to find a new home. They would be classed as trouble makers, and shown the door. Morgan's plan did not involve any such risk.

At the last of his secret meetings, Morgan convinced the juniors that the way forward was for Ralph to be offered a sideways move to another set, so leaving the way clear for the election of Jack. The youngsters had grown up with Jack and felt he was the man for the job and capable of stepping up to the plate.

Jack would also be a lot cheaper by taking one or two percent off his commission at least for the first few years. It would appear to the rest of chambers and the outside world as a natural progression for Ralph rather than a coup by the feisty youngsters. It would be seen as Ralph's choice to leave.

The juniors, led by Nathan Blake, regarded Morgan's idea as the perfect solution, but were sceptical of its success. How on earth was Morgan going to persuade Ralph to leave chambers? He was part of the furniture and proud of his achievements. Morgan felt Ralph should be asked by him alone, in a private meeting, the existence of which could be vehemently denied by Nathan and his cronies later if it failed and the story got out.

Morgan asked in return that he be appointed by chambers as sole consultant to provide Ralph's replacement when the time came. Everyone agreed, even suggesting that there would be no challenge to his published commission rate. As Morgan often had to curb his fees percentage, he left the pub in high spirits.

Morgan thought it was going to be a difficult conversation with Ralph to persuade him to jump his ship. He had asked Nathan Blake and the others at Barcourt for three months to allow time for a suitable alternative position to become available and to pick the right moment to convince Ralph to move chambers. He would need to dangle a big carrot to have any chance of success.

He knew that Ralph had occasionally talked of one day retiring to Devon, but he was not one to resort to slippers and a pipe until his health demanded it. So when two months later Morgan heard of a job in Bristol running a smaller common law set, he decided now was the right time to make the approach.

Ralph was a West Ham supporter. He had been all his life, taking up his fathers' season tickets. They shared a passion for the game played the right way, and so did Morgan. They met in a bar not far from West Ham's ground at Upton Park so Morgan could have the chat he wanted without fear of interruption or recognition.

He started the conversation playing on Ralph's dislike of his long commute, leading gently towards the idea of a stepping stone to retirement in the form of running a provincial set. Ralph however was far too alert as to where the conversation was going, and after a few minutes Morgan realised he was being rumbled.

"You know how rare a good senior clerk's job out of London is, Ralph. Finding the right one could take years. But it could just be the right stepping stone to retirement for you. Let's face it, Ralph, you could do the job standing on your head. An easy short local commute each day and more control of your time. The money is not as much, but neither are the costs of living in the West Country. What do you think?"

It was the commute bit that appealed to Ralph as much as the job itself. 40 years of an hour each way on the underground was more than enough for anyone. But being the good negotiator he was, he played hard to get. He knew the Bristol set would jump at the chance of securing a top London senior clerk. It would not only attract quality recruits to their chambers, which would mean more income for Ralph, it would send out the right message to local solicitors that Bristol could attract the best in clerking.

Ralph said he would give it some thought, but knew he could not hang about. If he was going to move himself and his wife to Devon, they needed to make a decision soon.

After a couple more meetings behind closed doors with Morgan, Ralph took the bait. He allowed his CV to go to Bristol, and travelled one Saturday morning for an interview at 11.00 am. He was on the train back to Paddington by 2.0pm having secured the job. He looked forward to a few more years as the big fish in a smaller pond.

Nathan Blake and his cronies were ecstatic. They got what they wanted at no risk to themselves. All they had to do was persuade the old guard in chambers to elect Jack Temple as their new senior clerk, and they could all look forward to a prosperous future.

To begin with the older members of chambers were in favour of head-hunting an existing senior clerk and got Morgan to approach off the record Richard Murray senior clerk at Carey Street chambers. Richard fancied the job.

But it was not to be as the junior members of chambers persuaded the old guard that Jack was the bright new future, and Jack was ready to step up to the plate, and would be cheaper. Promotion from within their clerks' room appealed as Jack was the devil they knew.

There was a big party to thank Ralph for his work and wish him well. Nobody feared him taking much if any of their work to Bristol. Jack needed little encouragement to speak personally to as many solicitors as possible. He did not want any client walking away on his watch.

Jack attended the chambers' Extraordinary Chambers Meeting

[ECM] when he was elected as senior clerk. He was over the moon. Life had just taken a big step forward, and he was determined to make a success of himself and his chambers. Woe betide anyone who stood in his way.

So there he was. Jack Temple: Senior Clerk Barcourt Chambers Temple London WC1R 4FS. He regarded himself as a modern traditionalist with a grasp of the future, whatever that meant.

The Long Vacation was the summer holiday period which ran from the 1st August to the 30th September each year. This was the traditional period dating back to the 17th century when the major courts would be closed. It was the time when many young members of the bar got their first brief, usually a return from another member of chambers who was away.

It was also responsible for the birth of jealousy amongst the junior members. The gestation period through pupillage would turn to full on jealousy that would grow and mature over many years, occasionally manifesting itself during a blazing row. Sometimes it would spawn revenge, and then hell had no fury like counsel scorned.

Jealousy was mixed up in the competitive world of the sole practitioner. Solicitors in a partnership culture did not have the same rivalry. Anyone who got pupillage and then a tenancy in chambers was amongst the very elite anyway.

Being in the top five percent was never enough. They wanted to be in the top one percent, then top of the tree. And if that meant walking over the bodies of colleagues, then so be it. Getting to the top was what it was all about, whatever their upbringing or background.

These sole traders only came together to seek work, have their cases and diaries managed, fees negotiated and then collected in. For all those services each counsel paid a percentage of their total fees per month to contribute to the running of chambers. There was no other collective purpose and little corporate identity, hence no collegiate atmosphere unless plotting with mates for their own benefit, often in the tap room of the Red Lion pub.

Consequently whilst each sole practitioner made a living, chambers as a whole made no profit. The aim was to break even each year by balancing the money collected from each barrister with the costs of running the business. That was Jack's responsibility.

For each young member of chambers hovering around the clerks' room, it was always their new pigeonhole as opposed to anyone else's which merited filling first when the clerks had briefs to reallocate, especially in the Long Vacation. And if another youngster got a bigger brief, or one from a more prestigious firm of solicitors, or marked with a higher brief fee, jealousy was born. Every time it happened, the resentment grew a little stronger. A jealous counsel was unhappy and angry because someone had something they wanted, indeed firmly believed they were more entitled to.

The sharp wit and banter of these professionals was on display in the barristers' robing room at the courts and the social gatherings in the various restaurants, pubs and wine bars around the Temple. There was rarely open hostility. Such comments and behaviour would be vented on the clerks.

"Why did Mr X get a brief from Y firm? I would have thought my skills were more appropriate?" The clerk questioned would mentally turn to his standard answers to standard questions, and answer:" The solicitor asked for him by name sir." The clerk knew that nobody could argue with such a request from a solicitor, so for now the matter would be dropped. Counsel would make a mental note to raise it with Jack if it happened again. He would want to know why he was not being asked for by name.

Just as in business the same rules for the game applied as in most other walks of life. Clerking was no different. Jack drummed the rules as he knew them into all his clerks as they had been drummed into him. At the top of Jack's list: "anyone can handle the good times, but you are judged on how you handle a crisis."

The bigger the crisis the more experienced the clerk needed to be. These experiences were not in a text book or manual, could not be learnt beforehand. They were picked up day by day as they happened.

Jack's mentor Ralph had embedded several such phrases into Jack's sub-conscious. Sometimes he did not get the meaning for a while, and this certainly applied to the expression: "managing barristers is like herding cats" which was Ralph's favourite.

"It's an impossible task!" Jack had thought to himself many times as a junior clerk. He only appreciated what Ralph had taught him after he had been in post as senior clerk for some months. Until then the penny hadn't dropped.

One characteristic of counsel which most clerks picked up very quickly was that the opinion of all barristers was always 100% correct, whatever topic they were talking about. They would not accept a challenge to their opinion, unless overruled by a judge in open court, and then they would advise an appeal. So as Ralph put it: "If the cat with its nine lives is always right, what hope do other mere mortals have?"

By the mid-1990's many chambers in the Temple and surrounding area had lost their external Dickensian look as the whole area had been gradually improved. But internally not much had happened for decades.

Most of the buildings had been built centuries ago. Often they contained small poky rooms alongside lavish entertaining suites. Sympathetic interior designs were slowly improving the working environment but many lacked items regarded by other walks of life as mandatory. Air conditioning was a good example. In the summer months when Jack walked down Middle Temple Lane he would often see a large white plastic tube which looked like an extended elephant's trunk sticking out of a window carrying away the hot air generated by a mobile air conditioning unit. Some would joke that it had nothing to do with the weather or the season, it was all the hot air produced by the waffling barristers and their clerks.

Provided the clerks got a couple of weeks off, the Long Vacation holiday period was a good time to be in chambers especially for the junior clerks. Potential recruits got some work experience and the rest of the clerks could assess their prospects in a less pressurised environment.

Chambers was only used by members wanting to work on papers between 10.30 and 1.00pm in the morning, and 2.15 and 4.30pm in the afternoon. These were the main court hearing times during which the clerks could hear a pin drop around the rooms in chambers.

Such silence was not the norm in the clerks' room. The air was filled with the sound of telephones ringing, the photocopier wasting tree after tree, and voices mixed with laughter and general banter. It was not uncommon for a verbal blue haze to filter through into reception when the going got tough.

The high pressure time for the clerks was between 4.00 and 6.00pm each afternoon. It was like air traffic control on a bank holiday weekend, but every day. The clerks had to sort the diary so everyone had court work the next day, and make sure the corresponding bundles of paper were neatly tied with pink ribbon and either placed in counsels' pigeonhole or sent to their home by hand and / or via taxi.

For each case, a clerk had to contact the court to find out which court room the hearing was in, the name of the judge, and the time the case was listed to start. A good clerk would also find out what other cases were in the same list and what they were listed for to help counsel work out if their case was likely to start on time. A busy list might let counsel have time to sneak another case in elsewhere rather than sit twiddling their thumbs waiting for the judge to get to their case.

Once done and counsel had everything they needed for the following day, the clerks could go home, or to the pub.

This crunch time might get extended beyond 6.00pm into the evening and overnight in exceptionally difficult situations, but that was when Jack stepped in, usually, to save the day. Well, most of the time. This involved the delicate negotiating bit he relished.

Picture the scenario. Counsel was supposed to finish a case in the afternoon at the latest so becoming available for the case they were booked to do the next day. They may have already had conferences and / or preliminary hearings so were well into the case.

For whatever reason their previous case the day before did not finish that afternoon, and would therefore continue into the next day. As the barrister could not be in two places at once, the brief for the case listed for the following day had to be returned by counsel to another barrister, usually in the same chambers.

That meant letting down tomorrow's solicitor and their client, and if no suitable replacement was available to take the return within chambers, it had to go to a barrister in another chambers. That scenario was an absolute last resort, and unacceptable to everyone especially Jack. He lived on a percentage of the brief fee, so he was watching his money walk out of chambers. Then the air got really blue and nobody spoke in the clerks' room, especially to Jack. "It's a fucking disaster!"! Screamed Jack. "That's what is it, a fucking disaster!"

From the solicitor's point of view, he did not want the brief to be returned to another barrister at short notice. Why should he look stupid and incompetent to his lay client for a problem he did not create?

Then there was the counsel asked to take the return. Jack usually tried to pick someone more senior which looked better. But that counsel would take an instant dislike to the solicitor because he or she did not send the brief to them in the first place. They believed the quality of the work was beneath them and helping out was always inconvenient especially if it involved travel.

So Jack was left talking to a reluctant counsel who gave the stock reply. "Jack, you know I am always willing to help chambers out, but I really should not be seen doing such menial work. Isn't there anyone else who can help?" They discussed the issues for several minutes, going round in circles, with no apparent give on either side.

Jack's trump card which was only played as a last resort was to say "well, if you cannot help me out, there is no alternative but the brief will have to go out of chambers." Counsel knew they would get stick from every quarter in chambers if they allowed that to happen, and more relevant would not earn any brownie points with Jack. One day the boot might be on the other foot and counsel needs a favour or to be dug out of a hole.

So gradually work got sorted, and at the end of the day Jack could close the door on his clerks' room with a sense of satisfaction knowing it was all to be done again tomorrow.

2 THE RED LION TAP ROOM

When it came to the allocation of work, clerks would go the extra mile to avoid fuelling the jealous imagination of their barristers. Sometimes this was too difficult to achieve.

Take the relationship between Sarah Ryman and Nathan Blake. Jack knew that for attracting new work, Sarah would always be a successful hunter living by the principle of what you kill you eat. However, being good she would always attract more work more than she could ever service herself.

On the other hand, Nathan Blake was a born farmer, living off the spare meat or returns of others but still believing he was a hunter at heart. In his eyes, the failure to attract new business was not his fault, more that of his clerks.

As a result, Jack and the other clerks, usually the more senior ones, had to spend many hours with counsel analysing their practice, or lack of it. For very senior members of chambers it was about introducing the idea that they might be past their sell-by date but without using such words, and that there may be too many younger, quicker and cheaper models for solicitors to pick. For the younger barrister who was offered work for a new solicitor, it was about addressing why there was no repeat business going forward. The reasons offered never fully satisfied counsel because they were rarely the full truth.

On the other hand, Solicitors would tell Jack the truth. This included counsel "did not return their call", "did not deliver on time", "did not go down well with the lay client" or "did not feel there was any rapport". Jack and his team would pass on such comments, but it was always the clerk's fault.

The subtle and yet fundamental difference between the likes of Sarah Ryman and Nathan Blake was part of their respective genetic makeup. It did not stop Nathan feeling he was owed a living just because he was Nathan Blake. As he saw the work pouring into Sarah's pigeon hole, he could not accept that she was a more saleable product. This fuelled his jealousy and long term desire to get her out of chambers should the opportunity arise.

The condition and layout of most chambers followed few guidelines and were dictated by the London West End rental price per square foot which by any national standard was astronomically high. So it was not uncommon for chambers to lack any free space with everyone cramped into small rooms, a tiny waiting room that would double up as the library, no kitchen, no shower room and just a single unisex toilet.

So it came as no surprise for visitors to Barcourt chambers to hear that their only one toilet was in the basement with hardly room for a WC and tiny wash hand basin. Indeed if anyone needed a little "extra privacy" they were better going down to the Wiltshire Inn a short walk away. Members of chambers would leave saying they were going to "dump on the WI!"

Sarah Ryman was a regular user of the limited facilities for extended periods of time, much to the annoyance of colleagues. She needed to save time as she was always late and in a hurry, so she would get changed after court into her sports kit and jog down to the gym, or from her kit into evening attire. Her ability to pack more into the day than the average member of chambers did get her into trouble from time to time, but she would not change her habits.

Sarah was always smartly dressed, usually in a black court skirt and white shirt open just enough to tantalise the men. The lads felt the stakes were raised when she entered the clerks' room in her sports gear of black skin-tight leggings and a matching tight cropped top to go to the gym in. Her hair would be pulled back and held by a classy clip creating a stunning look which she milked in front of her equally stunned audience. The gym attire was a regular for Sarah but the lads never tired of the sight. As Dillon put it, "She makes for very sore eyes!"

That day after court and after gym, Sarah was locked in the single occupancy WC changing from her training gear to a cocktail dress that was more suitable for an evening at the Ritz than a few glasses of bubbling Shampoo in Chez Lamps. She had managed what she described as a "top and tail" wash before applying a very modest layer of makeup that she felt camouflaged the fact that she was now in her mid-thirties not twenties.

All of this took her for what seemed an eternity to poor Nathan Blake standing in the corridor outside the toilet. He was desperate to go after one cup of coffee too many during his boring conference that afternoon. Eventually he snapped and demanded she vacate or else he would not be responsible for the consequences. "For God's sake Sarah, what the hell are you doing?"

A few moments later Sarah emerged in a flurry clutching her bag of kit and toiletries, commenting as she passed her chambers colleague: "We wouldn't want Nathan to have an accident now would we?" She did not wait for a reply and Nathan was not about to give her one either. He was focused on the job about to be in hand.

Nathan barely managed to crack his face into a smile as he barged past. "Quite so" he said to himself closing the door and locking it in one movement. Once inside he expected to have to lift the toilet seat as this was common practice for the men when occupying after the ladies. This was consistent with the ladies always having to lower the seat before using the lavatory, something the men were incapable of doing.

Responsibility for starting this sorry state of affairs depended on whether you haled from Venus or Mars, and despite limitless amounts of valuable time being allocated, chambers' management meetings had never been able to reach a satisfactory solution. The answer was more toilets.

So as one of Nathan's hands started to unzip his trousers the other moved towards the seat lid that was closed. At this moment he froze as his eyes could barely believe what they saw on the lid of the seat. He had one of those double take moments as his alert mind registered what he had seen and made numerous calculations.

"Got you!" he said as he took out his new Nokia 7650 mobile phone and took a close up photograph of the toilet lid and the two small lines of white powder clearly visible on the lid. Nathan mumbled to himself. "Let's see you get out of this hole, Miss Ryman."

Once he had lifted the toilet lid and seat, and thereby scattered the white powder all over the toilet floor, Nathan proceeded to relieve himself whilst deciding that his next stop would be to the tap room of the Red Lion pub. He saw this as the obvious correct move.

On his way to the pub Nathan was already plotting in his mind the downfall of his female colleague. At last he had the opportunity to get a serious slice of the lucrative personal injury work which had accumulated in chambers over the seven years since they were both elected as members of chambers. In his eyes, Sarah had taken much of that work from under his nose.

It was only with the benefit of hindsight that he knew he should not have taken a holiday during that first summer as a tenant of Barcourt chambers.

When most of chambers were having a well-earned rest during that Long Vacation, Sarah had taken the opportunity to pick up the new work that still had to be serviced and with it, so far as she was concerned, new instructing solicitors. She understood what it meant to provide a good and swift service once she got her foot in the door, and accepted Jack's advice.

"Yes your work has to be good, but the way to repeat business is to deliver on time. After a year or so, take a look at the list of firms sending you the work. Once you have more than half a dozen sets of papers from one solicitor, the chances are that, if you keep delivering, over the years you will have hundreds of sets of papers from that loyal firm." Jack gave the same advice to all the new tenants. Some listened.

On the other hand, Nathan had never understood how Sarah got her tenancy in the first place. He had thought the chambers vote was going to go against her. He was still a pupil himself so had no right to attend the chambers meeting, but the young members who did attend and voted had told Nathan that he would be elected and they were only going to take one new tenant that year. That was normal so as not to put too much pressure on the limited amount of work available for the new members of chambers taken in the previous two years.

Apparently a few days before the crucial meeting and vote, the head of chambers Charles Wadsworth QC had been spoken to by the senior barrister James Campbell. He had been Sarah's pupil master and was keen to have her on board. Wadsworth had heard it all before.

"James, every pupil master holds a candle for their star pupil, and I can quite see the attractions of Miss Ryman." Campbell took that sexist remark for what it was and replied. "That is not an acceptable comment, and not worthy of a modern head of chambers."

Wadsworth was then on the back foot so added. "His Honour Judge Duckworth has put in a good word for her as well. He liked her style of cross examination. I'll see what I can do. Taking two pupils on as tenants will put extra pressure on the clerks to find more work."

James Campbell thought he was winning, but still added: "Nothing wrong with that. We could do with more solicitors, and Sarah will attract the right sort of work."

So the next thing Nathan Blake learnt that both he and Sarah were elected as tenants. Having decided he could live with that news, along came another bombshell.

Shortly after the meeting Sarah's name appeared on the chamber's board above the name Nathan Blake. This was the board at the entrance to chambers with all the barristers in order of seniority and it really infuriated Nathan to see his name at the bottom, only above that of Jack Temple as senior clerk. It was rubbing salt into the wound caused by Sarah's election. Apparently he was called to the bar a few weeks after Sarah, so she got the nod on the order of seniority. Nathan was expecting the additions to the chambers' board to go alphabetically, which would have placed him above Sarah. He was seething.

The rest of Nathan's cronies were already on their second drinks by the time Nathan joined them in the pub tap room. The Red Lion was a good ten minutes' walk away from chambers and the tap room at the rear had an open fire surrounded on three sides by high wooden panelling. It was just the sort of place Nathan had imagined Guy Fawkes and his fellow co-conspirators used.

The assembled huddle of junior counsel were all tenants at Barcourt chambers and all specialised in personal injury work. They included their ringleader Nathan Blake, but he was not the most senior. That honour fell to Monty Evans, called fifteen years ago and still struggling to believe he had never been in the Court of Appeal. It was beginning to be a bit of a joke amongst his peers, and Monty took it to heart.

Then there was Stephen Savage. He was loud and rough around the edges but a hard worker. He regarded himself as the last real eligible bachelor in Barcourt chambers. He became a tenant twelve years before and had the unfortunate nickname of "the SS", always storming into rooms unannounced. His comments were often in poor taste, and when he was told so by colleagues, his stock reply was: "Savage by name and savage by nature." Stephen could make instant enemies, but some solicitors liked his abrasive approach. It was what the lay client wanted in court.

Last of the quartet was Tim Shaw, qualified for 6 years and described by the group as the "silent but deadly thinker". He would sit and listen, taking in every word and analysing every possible angle on a point of law. The problem was that he would attach undue importance to the wrong points. So whilst everything he said was relevant, he lacked the depth of analysis to weed out the less important points to get to the crux of a problem. For a barrister, this was a recipe for disaster.

This gang of four were a small group of sycophants well versed in telling their seniors and betters they were brilliant, whatever the occasion, in order to curry favour. They collectively wound each other up with the end result that they were capable of taking up positions that were not in their best interests.

And so Nathan embarked on his crusade of revenge. Having bought another round of drinks so everyone was sitting comfortably, he began.

"Well, I'll bet none of you can't guess what I've just witnessed in Barcourt chambers?" he started in a light-hearted fashion. Nobody tried to guess, except Savage who suggested: "I know, you've caught Christine Denton in the head of chambers' room giving him head!"

They all thought that funny to begin with, but then turned to revulsion. Christine had a reputation for getting what she wanted by giving out favours, and the most likely beneficiaries would be at least QCs, but that suggestion horrified them.

"Well not exactly." Nathan lowered his voice for dramatic effect.

"After my conference this afternoon had finished, I paid a customary visit to the toilet facilities in the basement. As usual someone was in there. They took an absolute age even though I let them know I was in desperate need of a slash." He paused for a little more dramatic effect as by now he had the attention of all at the table.

"So who was locked in the toilet then?" asked Savage

"Well. Of course, it was Sarah Ryman" replied Nathan. Everyone had expected it to be Sarah so were a little deflated as the news. "Ah, but that's not it" continued Blake to raise the atmosphere once more.

"Eventually the toilet door unlocks and out comes a very flustered Miss Sarah Jane Ryman. She rushes past me carrying an assortment of bags and runs upstairs."

To begin with nobody was interested. The story was uneventful, as common an occurrence as Savage boasting about his sex life. Tim Shaw lighted the mood with a little banter. "Oh yes, flushed cheeks eh! What brought them on I wonder?"

Nathan was determined to give full details. "Well, I entered la toilette. It was a little steamy shall we say. The toilet seat and lid were fully lowered, so I prepared myself for a slash. I leant forward to lift the seat. It was then I saw something on the seat lid I was not expecting. I just froze."

The thoughts of the other three cronies went into overdrive. The disgusting possibilities seemed endless. "Oh my God! What had she left behind for you, Nathan?" butted in Monty. This was the question they all had thought to ask whilst in their minds expanded the long list of possibilities, some being seriously outrageous.

Nathan put them out of their misery and continued. "There in the centre of the seat lid were two thin lines of white powder." "What?!" cried Stephen Savage. "White powder" repeated Nathan.

"What do you mean white powder?" Asked Tim Shaw who now was getting into his cross examination mode. "I mean, what did it look like?"

Nathan replied. "It looked like white powder." Tim carried on his line of questioning.

"What was it?"

Nathan replied starting with his favourite word to begin any sentence. "Well," pausing for effect, "I sniffed it, gently of course so as not to inhale any. It definitely wasn't perfumed. It had an odd chemical smell I did not recognise. I am sure it wasn't talcum powder. So what else could it be?"

Nathan was mindful of his early training not to ask a question he didn't know the answer to. He already knew the answer to his own question, but Tim Shaw obliged him in the form of another question.

"So Nathan, how did you know it was coke? Did you taste it?"

Nathan was in full flow now. "Of course not. But I did smell it. I wouldn't know what cocaine smells like anyway, would I? Obviously I couldn't get too close." Several muttered their approval to Nathan's conclusion and the course of action he had taken whilst trying to think what else it could be.

"So what does cocaine smell of?" enquired Monty. "How should I know?" replied Tim. Stephen Savage nodded, but did not offer any advice for fear of incriminating himself.

"Well" replied Nathan taking his new Nokia mobile phone out of his pocket. He started up the camera and scrolled down the images he had taken. At last he paused on the photo he had taken of the toilet seat. "See for yourself. The image is not very good, but you can make out the two lines of white powder. What other white powder do you line up on a toilet seat? It has to be cocaine. Unless anyone's got any other ideas?"

The silence was deafening as they sat trying to take in what they had just been told and were seeing with their own eyes on Nathan's mobile phone. Immediately their thoughts rushed to the consequences, for Sarah in the first instance, but then rapidly to their own careers. The removal of such a competitor from chambers was a big plus.

Monty started. "Oh my God. This could cost Sarah her career. There is a zero tolerance policy towards drugs in chambers, never mind what the Bar Standards Board will say. How stupid can she be? Professional suicide."

Tim continued. "That explains why she was flushed and rushed past you Nathan."

Savage wanted Nathan to take it further. He asked: "What are you going to do? You can't ignore it."

As he too started to consider what to do next with this earth-shattering news, Nathan agreed he could not ignore what he had seen and had evidence to prove in the form of the image on his mobile phone.

Somehow the group's appetite for alcohol had disappeared to be replaced by their hunger for more information on the news they had been given. This story temporarily replaced their desire for salacious gossip, but as there was no more to tell, they left the Red Lion, concluding to reconvene at 5.00pm the following day. In the meantime, they were all sworn to secrecy.

Despite all attending universities and schools where drug abuse was rife, and knowing of a few stupid colleagues who struggled to kick their respective habits once entering the legal profession, the three members of the gang of four could not collectively or individually take on board Nathan's story. They had all struggled in pupillage and fought so hard to get their tenancies in chambers that none would risk it all for a habit that could cost them everything.

Walking home from the Red Lion, Nathan Blake started to work out in his mind what should be the next step. His first thoughts were to meet with the head of chambers Charles Wadsworth QC and go straight to the top. Even if he went to Jack, or any of the senior members of chambers, they were all going to point him in the direction of Charles Wadsworth QC. He had the responsibility to sort the problem, and get the outcome Nathan so desperately wanted.

3 THE THREE "R"S

The next day Nathan wanted to see the head of chambers. On his way out to court, he stuck his head round the door of the clerks' room and as if by sign language, got Jack's attention. Jack knew this meant he wanted a quiet word in confidence in a conference room. All the barristers did this when they did not want the rest of the clerks to know their business. They failed to appreciate that it was the business of all the clerks to know everything about their practice, and very often Jack would return from a trip to one of the empty conference rooms only to spill the beans to the clerking team.

Jack followed Nathan into an empty conference room. "Jack, nothing to do for now, but if the head of chambers wanted to call a meeting, an Extra-ordinary Chambers Meeting, an ECM say, how long would it take to organise? What sort of notice does he have to give to the members of chambers?"

Jack was intrigued so enquired. "What sort of meeting do you mean? Is this a management committee matter?"

Nathan replied. "No. The agenda is not important for now, I just need to know when it could take place if Charles asks you to set one up." Jack realised he was not going to get a full answer, so proceeded to reply.

"A weeks' notice is required under the constitution, but I would advise on a date suitable for as many members of chambers as possible to attend. What's it about?" Jack thought it was worth one more prod at the reason, but to no avail.

"Thanks Jack, that's all I need for now. No doubt Charles will get you to organise a meeting if he deems it necessary. Cheers. I'd better get over to court."

Nathan scurried off and Jack went back into the clerks' room. Jason was first to ask.

"So what did Nathan want?" Jack looked blank and replied "I haven't a clue!"

Nobody in the clerks' room had any time to consider Nathan's strange request, following the commandment "Thou shall not presume" and decided to deal only with the fact of an ECM if it happened. However it did not stop Jack running through a few possible issues in his mind. No one calls an ECM without good reason. The jungle drums around the Temple were not suggesting any imminent danger for Jack or his chambers, but he had learnt that the most dangerous times can be preceded by unusual quietness.

Jack checked the diary for his head of chambers who was working in chambers all week on a big personal injury case, so if the shit was going to hit the fan, it could be anytime. Nathan Blake's diary was free as usual after today, so whatever he as up to, it would probably kick off that week.

Whilst the diary was on his screen, Jack observed that most of the civil team, and especially Nathan Blake and his cronies, were involved in short trials and paperwork, so any skulduggery in the corner of the Red Lion would be the place to witness treason. He turned to his deputy senior clerk Jason Middleton.

"Jason, do you fancy an early swift one in the Red Lion tonight?" Jason knew Jack would have a reason for asking him such a question, and that it was likely to have been prompted by Nathan's mini-meeting with Jack before court. He waited until a coffee break to ask more.

"Jason, I don't know what that snake Nathan Blake is up to, but my guess is that it will involve plotting with his cronies at the Red Lion after close of play tonight. If I go in it will look too obvious. Could you call in? Perhaps take a couple of solicitors with you from around there – meet them in the pub so it looks like you got invited there. See what you can find out."

Jason was up for some detective work. "Sure Jack. Leave it to me."

Jason was at the bar of the Red Lion ordering beer for himself and the three solicitors who were seated in the opposite corner of the pub away from the tap room frequented by Nathan and his cronies.

Jason addressed them collectively. "Sorry gentlemen. I'm networking tonight. Can't buy you a drink" pointing to the pints of beer he was carrying for his solicitor clients.

Nathan and the cronies took that as an apology for Jason being in their pub, and as they settled into the tap room, accepted that Jason could not hear what they were saying.

On his way home in the taxi a couple of hours later, Jason rang Jack on his mobile.

"Not much to report I am afraid. You were right about the gang of four. They all turned up and were huddled around the tap room fire deep in plotting mode. They passed round Nathan's mobile phone and spent a lot of the time looking closely at something he was showing them on it. I think it was a photograph."

"Thanks Jason" replied Jack. "Blake is definitely up to something. I expect we will get to know more in the next couple of days. See you in the morning."

Jack had been married for 8 years to Barbara, already described by Jack's colleagues as the longest suffering member of the clerking team. As Jason said to her when they met for the first time shortly after Jack's appointment as senior clerk: "Babs, you're a star. Jack is a very lucky man."

Jack took very seriously his role as the provider for his family. That was why he spent long hours every working day focused on chambers. He knew that if he took his eye off the ball for a moment someone else would take his place. His watch was round the clock. Barbara knew it and accepted that she and their son Charlie would have to make sacrifices as well. She knew Jack was not likely to find a job with his lack of qualifications in any other walk of life that paid so well, and also what he was like with women before they married. She was the one he went home to, the only one he loved. For now, that was enough.

Barbara also understood that if Jack was entertaining solicitor clients until late at night he would stay over in the West End. What was the point in commuting home late in the evening after Charlie and she had gone to bed, getting a few hours' sleep, waking up at the crack of dawn and then commuting again? He would be better off getting a good night's sleep at the Wiltshire Inn round the corner from chambers.

Jack liked to think he was prepared for anything. Often he had to be. He kept in chambers his overnight bag that included a couple of sets of underwear, a toothbrush and shaving kit. These items complimented his small chambers' wardrobe of suits, shirts with matching ties and shoes for every occasion.

Jack never challenged himself over his relationship with other women. He was a married man, but a man first. As a single lad, Jack relied on his instincts. As a married man, he never went looking for sex, but if the opportunity involved getting work for chambers, he would tell himself the ends justified the means. At least that was what he told himself.

He had discussed infidelity with Jason shortly after Jason had found out Jack's affair with Elizabeth Richardson. Jack told him: "Ok, yes there are from time to time fringe benefits, but I know they mean nothing compared to Barbara and my son Charlie."

Jason responded. "Ah, but even if sex with a client helps get the work in short term, and I'm not convinced it does, aren't you risking losing the work when the relationship goes sour, and losing Barbara?"

"If I was playing around generally, just for the fun of it, yes I would be risking more than I want to. But I'm not, and I hope Babs would understand that. We both agreed some time ago that I was doing the best job I am capable of. Let's face it Jason, who else is going to pay a shed load of salary to someone like me with no qualifications? Whether I like it or not, I have to succeed."

Jack regularly stayed at the Wiltshire Inn. It was cheap, and he had a good working relationship with the landlord Michael. Jack would send him business, usually solicitors who needed a sleep over near to the courts just across the road from the Royal Courts of Justice known as the RCJ.

Michael always had a good breakfast available at short notice to set Jack and the solicitors up for their battles of the day. Michael was also in the loop regarding Jack's wife Barbara. He was very discreet and offered a good alibi when called upon. He would also keep his eyes and ears on alert when members of chambers were huddled in dark corners plotting mischief. Michael was not the only snitch behind the bar in the Temple pubs and wine bars around the legal quarter. Indeed, most landlords and staff knew Jack was a good tipper and always rewarded well for good information.

Some barristers not wholly committed to any cause beyond their own benefit would sneak off after court. They would not let the clerks know they had finished and so were available for more work. It was a chance to get a breather for a few hours. Many at that time did not have mobile phones, or if they did, would switch them off and proclaim a dead battery.

Jack was alive to most tricks counsel employed to avoid taking an extra brief last minute, especially since the day he watched his mentor Ralph go a particular extra mile.

Ralph had taken a return brief from another chambers at 11 o'clock for a hearing at 2.15pm the same day. At the time he took the brief he did not have a spare barrister to cover it, but was confident one or two would come free by lunchtime. If it worked then he would have a good opportunity to pinch some repeat business from another set.

Ralph described Counsel Peter Livingstone as a "lazy little bugger with a silver spoon in his mouth", a little harsh but true description in Jack's eyes. Ralph knew Peter was capable of using several tricks to avoid extra work. On the day in question, Peter had claimed he needed a papers day to deal with his non-existent backlog. Ralph had let him have his way.

Peter Livingstone had sauntered into chambers at 10.45 am and stayed for about 15 minutes, just long enough to empty his pigeonhole of post, check his diary with the clerks, and disappear for coffee followed by red wine in the Red Lion. He was not dressed for court which meant he had a suit on but was not wearing a collarless shirt. This would be his excuse for not going to court if any of the clerks approached him with a brief.

At lunchtime Jack accompanied Ralph when he entered the Red Lion with the returned brief tucked under his arm as well as Peter Livingstone's wig box with shirt studs, his gown and a brand new collarless shirt in the correct size which Ralph had bought on route to the pub.

Ralph passed everything including the brief across the big table in the tap room to counsel saying "You're in Croydon county court at 2.30 so you had better get changed. You can read this lot on the train."

Ralph would save the bollocking for the barrister until after he got back into chambers that evening, just adding as he was leaving "I'll put the new shirt down on your chambers' expenses."

The real art of being a senior clerk lay in having the ability to dish out a serious bollocking in language that did not sound at all like a bollocking but left the recipient in no doubt that he had been so chastised. Jack had watched his mentor Ralph do this on so many occasions he could not wait to have a go, for it was a job for senior clerks only. Any lesser member of the clerking team would not get away with it, and might lose their job. After six months as senior clerk, it was like shelling peas for Jack.

The junior clerk Dillon had asked Jason how Jack did it, and what words he used. "Dillon, out of context, it is difficult to describe" explained Jason. "You just have to listen to how Jack does it. I know that's hard if he has gone into a conference room, but you need to ask him quickly when he comes out, otherwise the moment has passed."

Jack added later. "It is about consequences. I have to make sure counsel understands what the consequences will be if he goes down a certain path, and get him to realise that to do so may not be in their best interests. Once he or she sees the light, you have won."

First junior clerk Christian Bennett was also seated round their clerks' room table at the time. "Well I'm none the wiser."

Jack's deputy senior clerk Jason Middleton was first to comment. "And that, Gordon, is why you are a first junior clerk and Jack is senior clerk!" They all laughed at Christian, otherwise known by his nickname Gordon Bennett. The team had thought the name was most appropriate to Christian who did not initially see it, but that was nothing new. He often missed the point in a conversation, hence drawing from others the comment "Oh, Gordon Bennett!"

Seniority was no defence to a bollocking. Charles Wadsworth QC head of chambers once asked Jack towards the end of such a meeting. "Jack, have I just had a bollocking?" "You may think that sir but I couldn't possibly comment!"

As 5.00 o'clock on that Friday afternoon approached, Jack and his team sensed it was all going too well. A little weekend banter had started too early as the late briefs arrived by hand and were processed. Some were for Monday which was a bonus, a rare chance to be ahead of the game for the following week. Most papers were left in counsels' pigeonhole, a small section of shelving big enough to take several sets of A4 sized papers, and would be collected over the weekend.

The phone rang. Junior clerk Dillon Hart answered and was silent for a few seconds listening to counsel on the other end. As he put the phone down he reported to the assembled clerks who continued processing the briefs and listening at the same time.

"Mr Livingstone has gone part heard into Monday. He hopes to be free for his case on Wednesday."

"Silly bugger!" replied Jack. "I bet he knew at lunchtime. He just could not be bothered to let us know. So instead of being able to return his brief for Monday well before the solicitor goes home for the weekend, I have now got to deliver the bad news just at the eleventh hour. Bad PR. Does he not realise the damage he is doing?"

Without pausing Jack continued. "Dillon, go and get the brief for Monday out of Livingstone's pigeonhole. Let's see how much prep is involved. Who took the case? What are the fees agreed at?" Jack wanted to see if there was going to be a problem with the solicitor or not.

Dillon came briskly back into the clerks' room holding a lever arch file full of papers. "You're not going to like this Jack." "I'll be the judge of that, young man. Who is it?" barked Jack. "It's Christopher Mainwaring from Baker Fenton in Sevenoaks!" "Bollocks" was Jack's reply, and nobody else said a word.

A pause followed during which the clerking team knew Jack was working out what needed to be done. When he was ready, he would tell the team and they would all listen. They were watching the master at work and would learn from his actions, especially those who one day wanted his chair at the clerking table.

Jack thought ahead and then spoke so his team could follow his logic.

"That's why Livingstone kept shtum. He knows Mainwaring favours Carey Street chambers with his best work, so if he only sends Livingstone scraps to play with, he isn't fussed if he cannot do the case. Stupid bugger doesn't realise that he is opening the door to let Mainwaring pull the brief out of chambers to send to Carey Street. Well we're not having it."

Jack turned to his number two Jason Middleton. "Who have we got?" "Not much Jack. It would mean offering someone Mainwaring has never used before." Jack interrupted Jason and picked up the phone.

"Mr Livingstone, I have your news. Perhaps we can discuss a post mortem on today next time you are in chambers." He paused to listen for a few moments. "In the meantime, what are the prospects of settling this on Monday morning? Who is your opponent?" Jack listens again and then put the phone down and immediately turned to his next clerk in order, 1st junior Christian Bennett.

"Christian, ring Sarah Ryman and tell her I have got her an opening with Mainwaring at Baker Fenton. Tell her to collect the brief tonight and drop off her Monday case at the same time. Then ring those solicitors and tell them she cannot do the case. They will be ok with anyone you have left. It is only an infant settlement rubber stamp job. They won't mind. Margaret, get me Chris Mainwaring on the phone."

The receptionist Margaret Smith was used to Jack barking orders from the clerks' room. She did not reply and put Jack straight through to Christopher Mainwaring as soon as he answered his telephone.

"Chris, how are you keeping? Looking forward to a family weekend in the lovely Kent countryside?" By the look on Jack's face the clerks could tell he had got a frosty response. Well, thought Jason, why else would Jack be ringing a solicitor after 5.00pm on a Friday afternoon other than to let him down with a late change of counsel?

"Chris, you know I hate letting you down, and I don't do it very often. However, I am hoping to turn this to your advantage. Hear me out."

Jack proceeded to offer as replacement Miss Sarah Jane Ryman, known in chambers and amongst the clerks as "SJ". She had done her pupillage in chambers, and was gaining a good reputation for personal injury work. Jack also knew that Chris Mainwaring thought of himself as a ladies' man, and would relish the opportunity to work with Sarah Ryman. If he chose to flirt and got shot down in flames, that was his lookout.

After a few sentences promoting Sarah he ended with: "I gather there is an outside chance it will settle at court. If so, I will suggest to Sarah that lunch would be a good opportunity for her to widen your knowledge of her work." Before he could say more, Mainwaring interrupted. "Splendid idea Jack"

So now all Jack had to do was persuade Miss Ryman to not only take this case, but also have lunch with a guy she had never met. He rang her.

"Miss Ryman, we know Mainwaring sends most of his work to Carey Street. This would be your chance to change his mind. He has some good work at Baker Fenton, and his partners do quite a bit of Union work."

Sarah did not hesitate. "Jack, to help you out of a pickle, I'll do it. But you will owe me." "Of course!" Jack replied with a smile and put the phone down, announcing to his team "Sorted!"

Sarah arrived in chambers about 20 minutes later to swop the briefs over. Jack approached her with the intention of explaining the opportunity he was offering to gain the work from Baker Fenton. Before he could speak, she smiled. "Jack, it never ceases to amaze me how you turn disaster into victory, but I guess it's why we pay you so much. But remember, you owe me!"

Jack replied also with a smile. "And if you win the case, there will be your reward. Try to settle and make lunch or even a drink after the hearing. Mainwaring is sure to turn up himself now he knows you have the brief. Your charm can win the day!" They both knew what he meant as Sarah turned to leave chambers already considering her wardrobe for Monday.

There was no time for Jack to bask in his success. Another problem that would take the weekend to sort presented itself via Jason.

Jason Middleton was Jack's right hand man in the role of deputy senior clerk. He kept Jack on his toes and in the natural order of life in chambers he would one day succeed him. If not, then he would be head-hunted to fulfil his dream of being a senior clerk. In his late 20s Jason was the real deal. He portrayed the smart clean cut look of a man determined to get the job done. "Well suited and booted" was how he thought of himself. The ruthless streak was well masked by his apparent willingness to do anything to help anyone, counsel or clerks. That made him an ideal role model for the younger members of the clerking team. He, like Jack, was conscious of his responsibility to train the junior clerks by example.

Jason played football on a Sunday morning although in a higher league than Jack. He had watched Jack's stomach grow over the last few years as the weight went on, and was determined not to allow the same to happen around his middle. He worked out every weekend and two evenings during the week.

Just occasionally Jason was reminded of his current station in life. There were problems he could not solve, either because he did not have the experience, or more likely they needed the weight and authority of the senior clerk. The issue with Nathan Blake fell into the latter category. Jason turned to Jack as he came off the phone. "Jack, we have a problem." Jack immediately focused on Jason.

"Nathan Blake was supposed to deliver three sets of papers back to Mr Finch at Bridgemans solicitors by close of play today. One set has a potential issue with the limitation period that expires next week. Nathan has already missed two deadlines for the return of these papers. Today was his last chance, and I think he has gone away for the weekend."

Now Jack was furious. Bridgemans were personal injury lawyers going places. He had spent a lot of time and whiskey nurturing Mr Finch, and he was "not about to let Nathan bloody Blake cock it up."

He barked out instructions to his team. "Find Nathan Blake and get him on the phone for me. Jason, ring the solicitor and tell him the papers will be hand-delivered to his office by 9.00am on Monday morning. Someone check the pigeonhole and go to Nathan's room. See if the papers are in chambers and bring them to me."

Dillon rose from his chair and said "I'm on the case" as he hot-footed out of the clerks' room. Margaret shouted from reception. "Found him. He's at home with a plane to catch. I'll put him on."

As Jack picked up the phone to speak to Nathan, his calm aura took control as he reminded himself of one of the golden rules he and his team lived by. There are two ways you can ask for something, one is nicely and the other is nastily. If you ask nicely first you can always ask nastily later. But if you ask nastily first, you can never ask nicely. So the conversation with Nathan started.

"Nathan, I gather you are on your way for the weekend somewhere. Have you dealt with the papers Jason needed for today?" "Not yet. I ran out of time today, and we've got this flight to catch to Paris in a couple of hours. I'll do them next week."

Jack drew in more oxygen than a normal breath to help retain his calm. "Is Paris a special trip? A birthday perhaps?" The line of questioning put Nathan at ease, so he replied. "Not really, it was a last minute thing. There are four of us going."

"I see" replied Jack. "What time is your flight back on Sunday?"

"Not until early evening. Why do you ask?" Nathan thought Jack was leading up to a new brief for him for Monday which would need some preparation on Sunday evening. He was wrong.

"I have told Jason to tell Mr Finch at Bridgemans that the three sets of outstanding papers will be hand-delivered to his office by 9.00am on Monday. He has reluctantly accepted that because it is when he would deal with issuing proceedings anyway, but he is very annoyed. So if you cannot deliver, I will have to get someone else to help out. Where are the papers?"

"They are in chambers. They should not take me long to do. I'll do them when I get back on Sunday evening."

Jack replied. "Fine, but if you have not collected and started them by 7.00pm, I will have to reallocate to give someone else a chance to meet the deadline. Nobody is going to be pleased at such short notice."

At last the penny dropped with Nathan. It would be very embarrassing for him if a colleague was told they were having their Sunday evening ruined because Nathan was playing away in Paris. Jack ended the conversation with: "Jason will ring you at 7.00pm on Sunday."

Jason and the other clerks had listened to Jack handle the situation. "Thanks Jack" said Jason. "The senior clerk touch wins the day!" "Not yet" replied Jack. "Set your mobile alarm for 7.00pm on Sunday and ring Blake to make sure he complies. Any problem, ring me."

The evening calm descended more quickly on a Friday as minds focused on play rather than work. It was 6.01pm, the diary had been put to bed on time and all was well with their world. Jack was with two of his clerks, Jason and Christian, heading out of the front door as the last few stragglers left.

A female member of chambers Christine Denton was leaving at the same time. Being a family law specialist, and in particular the money side of divorce, she was used to arguing about everything from bank accounts to the pet dog. So when it came to the weekend, she liked to let her hair down in the certain knowledge she was single and intended to remain so.

As he locked the chambers front door, Jack said "Do you know what the best part of the weekend is?"

Jack answered his own question before anyone could speak. "Right now – the whole weekend is in front of us and is full of excited anticipation."

"Oh yes, I'll buy that!" replied Jason. Christian asked "What are you looking forward to Jack?"

Jack thought for a moment but did not take long as he had already asked himself the very same question. "A short walk and few cold beers with colleagues." He then looked at the rear of the female barrister now walking in front of him, exactly the view his two clerks were focused on. He continued: "Then for me it will the tube home, a good meal washed down by a bottle of red, sex and lots of sleep."

There was a short silence during which they all, including the female barrister then in front of the clerks, reflected on Jack's words. Christine Denton turned towards them as she walked and broke the silence. "Me too, but not in that order. The tube ride home may be last! A result with a certain silk first would be good." She walked off in front of her staff who continued to reflect on her answer.

"Any silk we know?" asked Christian discreetly to Jack. "Silly question" said Jason. "She doesn't know herself yet!" They all saw the funny side of that comment, but Jack had the last word on the topic. "Who knows, a QC this weekend, a Judge the next?!"

4 THE EXTRA MILE

Barcourt Chambers was located just off Middle Temple Lane, close to the car park next to several chambers forming Paper Buildings and Kings Bench Walk, or "KBW" as everyone knew it. Although Jack had the use of a parking space there as one of the perks of the job, he rarely drove into the West End. His wife usually needed the car, and Jack preferred to keep his parking space to lend to solicitors who were in the Royal Courts of Justice ["RCJ"] or other local courts, especially if they had lots of papers to carry. He would arrange for Dillon or one of the clerks to meet the solicitor in the car park, collect the lawyer's car keys on arrival in chambers and the clerk would move the papers into the appropriate court room.

This little extra service – the "extra mile" – was what Jack did to get the next brief. That was his motivation for most things. Chambers had several trollies and lots of straps to hold the boxes of lever arch files in place. The hardest part was dragging the trollies up the steps into the RCJ at the rear entrance, but it was a good spot to bump into the celebrities who had lost their case and were trying to get out of the building without being seen by the paparazzi.

Dillon Hart had been in chambers as the most junior clerk for about 6 months. He felt he had a basic grasp of what the job entailed, but knew there was still plenty to learn.

As was the custom in their clerks' room, banter mixed with innuendo and laughter was the order of the day when there were no guvnors about. The language could be a bit blue, and being an all-male environment, much of the humour was in poor taste. Chauvinism was alive and well amongst the staff at Barcourt chambers.

Every clerk picked up a nick name within the first week in chambers. Dillon Hart was no different, although he did not understand where his nick name came from. On his third morning in his new job he was greeted by Gordon, alias Christian Bennett, using a poor American accent.

"Morning Mr Dillon!" followed by a chorus of laughter from the rest of the clerks. Those who understood the joke carried it further. "Hi there Marshall!" and "Hi Dodgy!" All were a reference to Matt Dillon, former TV Marshall at Dodge City in the 1970s. Of course nobody in the clerks' room had ever heard of or even watched the show "Gunsmoke", except for one of the senior barristers who alerted Christian Bennett in the first place. And so Dillon's nickname was created, and stuck.

The clerks' room at Barcourt Chambers was just like most clerks' rooms in London and the provinces. Whilst each clerk had their own desk with a computer and telephone, the desks were all pushed together in the centre of the room. Jack sat at the head of the table with the rest of the team on the flanks in descending order of seniority. If it wasn't for the paper work and computer screens, you could imagine a friendly dinner party. The atmosphere at times of the day would support that notion.

Jack sat at the top desk facing his team. He was flanked by, to his left, his deputy Jason Middleton, and to his right the first junior clerk Christian Bennett. Beyond Jason was James Dunn, fees and admin clerk. Next to Christian was the junior clerk Dillon Hart. There were two empty desks next, in theory for expansion, but actually used to dump briefs and files on which needed sorting.

James Dunn in his early 30s was the fees clerk and admin manager. Although always smart his dress sense was somehow uninspiring. It was probably the drab ties and lack of a positive expression that did it. Anyway, he had been overlooked for the top job a couple of times by other chambers, to be fair when he was a bit too young for a senior clerk's position. He now had a couple of grey hairs. Whilst solid and reliable on the straight forward stuff, on the outside he looked cool even if inside he had no idea what to do in a crisis. This flaw in his character would ultimately prove he was not top job material.

As fees clerk or even a second in command when Jason was away, he worked well with a more flamboyant senior clerk.

Eventually James had realised he did not want the pressure of the top job and moved over to fees and admin to get away from the stress of diary management. He had had a few near misses when the boss was not there to make the decisions, and now he was much happier.

So that was the Barcourt Chambers clerking team. Jack Temple, Jason Middleton, Christian Bennett, James Dunn and Dillon Hart. They looked after 34 barristers. They all worked flat out every day, and if the truth be told, they were a man short. The ratio was generally accepted to be five counsel per clerk, so logically Jack felt there should be one more at least.

But therein lay a problem. As the list revealed, it was an all-male clerks' room. Whilst this was not uncommon, it failed to appreciate the growing numbers of female solicitors and barristers qualifying in the country, and they naturally felt it appropriate at times to deal with female clerks. Jack had realised this soon after his appointment. As he disclosed in confidence to Jason one evening over a pint, "I can't go on bedding solicitor clients to get the work. It's time we recognised the world is changing and had a female clerk they can deal with if they want to."

Jason had seen this as the thin end of the wedge. "That would change the dynamics of our clerks' room for ever. Either that, or she would have to be very thick skinned. And before you know it, there would be non-clerks applying for your job Jack. Do you want that?"

Jack could see the potential problems but knew sooner rather than later his team would have to come to terms with female company in their chauvinistic world. But to him recognising a problem was one thing, solving it was another. He thought it would be easier if the pressure for an extra pair of hands was so great, the lads would accept a girl more easily. But he didn't know if a female clerk would work, and wouldn't know until he tried.

The only other member of the team was Margaret Smith, Maggie the receptionist, who had her desk just outside the clerks' room. The door between the two was always wedged open so Jack could see who was entering or leaving chambers.

After the initial rush to solve the morning crisis or two, and get all the barristers into court on time, chambers fell quiet. All that were left in chambers were counsel with paper practices working in their rooms, and the clerks' room. So there could be a couple of hours when the banter would flow covering a range of topics, usually sport, gossip, moaning about counsel, and sex, but not always in that order. This was the time when knowledge filtered down from the more senior and experienced clerks sat at the top of the table to the clerks at the bottom. It was a subconscious passing on of the skills and experiences that formed an invaluable part of the learning process for every clerk. "Watch listen and learn Mr Dillon. Watch listen and learn". It was Jason's favourite expression every time he knew something was going to happen which they all could learn from.

There was no manual to teach clerking. Picking the job up day by day in their clerks' room and listening to how the others operated was why it took years to reach the skill set necessary to be a senior clerk. On his appointment as senior clerk Jack called a clerks' meeting to lay out the ground rules as he saw them. He wanted to make sure everyone was on the same page.

He knew that if he taught the junior clerks well, the sooner they would crave promotion and be after his job. But he was also aware that if he did not teach all he knew properly, more mistakes would be made and that would reflect on him.

"Some of what I am about to say may seem obvious to some of you, but I am going to tell you anyway. Then there is no room for misunderstanding or the chance anyone can say they did not know."

"First, don't lie to me or any of my team. Lying doesn't work. It is just more digging when you are in a hole. Don't do it. Being a little economical with the truth is the same as lying. Being a bit misleading, as you may decide an occasion may dictate, is not lying but may have the same consequences. That will be a judgement call you make at the time. If you do, then you come and tell me straight away. The same applies if you can't solve a problem or you have done anything you only think might be wrong, you immediately tell me."

Jack went on to explain. "The chances are that I have come across the problem before and will know a way out. If you don't tell me, I can't help you, and the likely way out for you is through the door never to be seen again in any chambers. Got it?" Murmurs of agreement around the table followed. Jack continued.

"Then there are the extra commandments. Number eleven." He paused to allow the chorus which came in of "Thou shall not presume!" "Quite right. We deal only in facts, in certainties, nothing else."

On Monday morning Jason reminded himself of Jack's 11th commandment "thou shall not presume" which kept going round in his head as he walked down Chancery Lane towards chambers. He had taken a risk on Peter Livingstone delivering the three sets of papers for Mr Finch at Bridgemans which could backfire on him, and Jack would have his guts if it went wrong. To plead in mitigation that he had not wanted to disturb Jack on a Sunday evening, demonstrating he could handle the situation, would not save his skin.

Jason had duly tried to ring Nathan Blake at 7.00pm on the Sunday evening, but his phone went to voicemail. He had left three messages, and in response to the last, Nathan had replied with a text message which said: "All in hand. Will bring papers into chambers tomorrow"

Jason wanted to take Nathan at his word, so took the risk and assumed that he would do as his message said.

Jack and Jason arrived in chambers at 8.15 that Monday morning. Jason could not see any papers on his desk so went straight to Nathan Blake's room. He was not in.

The alarm bell went off in Jason's head. He walked out of chambers asking Jack as he passed the clerks' room if he wanted a coffee. Jack replied. "Cappuccino, and you'd better get one for that lazy sod Blake. He's sure to need one!"

Jason had thought he could get away with the suggestion of coffee, but now he knew that Jack knew his real motive was to go to Nathan's flat ten minutes away and collect the papers himself.

It was 8.35am when he rang Nathan's door bell. After a second ring, Nathan opened the door. He looked terrible, as if he had been up all night, which turned out to be correct.

"The flight was four hours late. I've nearly finished. I just need another hour." Before Nathan could make any other comment, Jason said: "I'll wait" and promptly sat down on the sofa in Nathan's living room.

The moment 9.00am arrived on Jason's watch he dialled Bridgemans on his mobile and asked to speak to Mr Finch. He spoke to his secretary who informed him that Mr Finch would not be in until 11.00am as he had a dental appointment first thing, something about a broken tooth. She asked if there was any message. Jason said not to worry as he was sending the papers by taxi and they should arrive before Mr Finch.

He then rang chambers and asked Margaret to get a cappuccino for Jack ASAP, and sat back to reflect on why he had put himself in such a position so early in the week. There was plenty of time for a crisis later on.

As Jack finished the dregs of his cappuccino just after ten o'clock that morning, Jason walked in clutching several sets of papers. "I hope those aren't the Bridgemans' papers, Jason. Are they?" asked Jack.

Jason explained what had happened. The whole clerking team were in the room so got the full blast from Jack. "Dillon, explain to Mr Middleton, your senior and would-be better, what commandment he broke."

Dillon thought carefully about his answer as he did not want the terror to be deflected from Jason to himself. "Did he lie?" asked Dillon.

Jack barked. "I don't think so. Jason, you didn't lie to anyone did you?" Jason shook his head. "No!" continued Jack. "He presumed, and what don't we do, we don't presume, do we Jason?"

Jason shook his head again. "It was an easy presumption to make, that Blake would deliver on time especially after a final promise to do so. But he didn't, and by rights Jason should be on his way home now with his tail between his legs. The consequences could have cost chambers thousands and thousands of pounds.

Jack raised his voice so he would be heard in reception. "Margaret call a cab and Jason get these papers delivered. You had better hope Mr Finch is full of anaesthetic so he doesn't realise you are late."

As there was a temporary lull in telephone activity, Jack, feeling he had the undivided attention of his team, returned to a bit of training.

"And another commandment is answer the phone within three rings. I don't care what you are doing, we all know the batting order of seniority to answer and the rule applies to me as well. Over 99 percent of new business starts with a call to chambers, so if we don't show we are keen to get the work, why should solicitors bother to hold on and wait?"

At this point, Christian felt Dillon merited some of his knowledge, and it would do him no harm for the more senior clerks to hear him, so they knew he had learnt something.

"Dillon, every guvnor thinks their clerk is only as good as tomorrow's diary. If he or she has got work, the clerk is the greatest. But if there is no work, it is the clerk's fault. You have to understand that barristers think they are God's gift in the legal world, and because they only listen to themselves, they are always right."

"Gordon Bennett!" exclaimed James. "Gordon has been listening. Wonders will never cease!"

This encouraged Christian to go on. "Many guvnors were blessed with brains too big for their heads which left no room for even a drop of common sense."

Dillon felt he could join the debate with a little humour of his own. "You'd think they would stock it at the WI". Christian looked puzzled. "Stock what?" he asked. Dillon answered. "Common sense!"

As usual, Dillon's comment was a little off the mark. The WI as the clerks called it was not the Women's' Institute but in fact the Wiltshire Inn, Jack's favoured watering hole. So Jason took up the drinks theme. "The Bar is not a drinking establishment as such, although it might as well be. Alcohol is part of daily life in the legal profession and alcohol abuse should be part of the final examinations for all lawyers. Training should be practical exercises organised by the clerks."

Jack was always pleased when his pearls of wisdom were repeated amongst his team, as he had done himself right from starting as a junior clerk. Why stop there, he thought, and carried on his teaching.

Soon after Jack became senior clerk, he could see the potential for growth but recognised he could not do it all himself. He would need his clerks to pull their weight as well, and wanted to introduce a bonus scheme for them so they all had the right attitude. The aim was that they should each have the incentive to go the extra mile, especially when fees were involved.

Jack was one of the remaining commission-only senior clerks earning a percentage of what each barrister earned. The rate had gone down over the years as chambers expanded. It used to be 10%. Jack was on 5% of all fees earned by counsel at Barcourt chambers.

From time to time there would be rumblings of discontent amongst the members who were not earning enough, and they would add into their argument that Jack's commission should be reduced as he was spreading himself too thin. More members of chambers meant less time per barrister each day and the need for extra clerks to meet the growing demand.

Jack understood that one way to combat those arguments was to make sure the clerks were seen to be getting more work in, and also getting more fees per case.

Part of Jack's regular talks to his team centred on fees.

"And finally for now, if you are in any doubt when negotiating fees, ask someone more senior to quote. If there is no time or no one to ask, whatever figure you think is right, add 10%. You can always come down, but never go up. Make the extra when you can – adds potentially to your bonus scheme. For now, get it right, stay in the room, watch listen and learn. Any questions?"

Ambition was a strong characteristic, worthy of any clerk. Jack understood that if you put a barrow boy into a suit, you can nurture his ambition. But he would never cross over to being a barrister. He would always be the servant, never the master. He could aspire to becoming a senior clerk, a position where mutual respect between counsel and clerk works for both.

Everyone thought they wanted Jack's job, but there were no more than about 500 good senior clerks' jobs in the country. Traditionally everyone was waiting for dead men's shoes. Now there were even fewer vacancies as chambers merged and the professional youngsters, the marketing graduates and MBAs entered the race to the top as well. Even solicitors and accountants had filled the demand for CEOs and practice managers.

Jack wondered what the future held for the likes of him and his team. He confided in Jason on more than one occasion. "Once a good clerk reaches the position of senior clerk, living on his wits and experience alone are not enough. They have to want to stay at the top. Otherwise, the only way is down. Like the athlete, the gymnast or professional footballer, they get found out and knocked off their perch."

Jason understood the way things were going and did not like it either. "I'm not sure what we can do, Jack, above doing the job every day and showing we are the best."

Working the phones was an early skill for any new clerk to pick up. Everyone in the team did it. At interview the potential for a good bedside manner would have been weighed up. The bit that most found difficult to master was fee negotiating. Every brief or set of papers had to be marked on the back sheet with the agreed fee. The only exceptions were those briefs in publically funded cases covered by Legal Aid.

To arrive at the right fee for paperwork cases was easy. The clerk asked the solicitor to send the papers in and on arrival the clerk would then show the papers to counsel and ask how much they wanted to charge. Many barristers knew exactly what they wanted, so making the job even easier.

Jack would have to intervene when the figures got too high, or not high enough. If counsel hesitated, the clerk would ask how much preparation was involved, how long would it take, and if any conference was needed. All these factors would help counsel's clerk, or Jack if a big case, to come up with the right fee to ask for. The same questions were asked when deciding the right brief fee for a hearing in court. Jack referred to "the three Rs" when chasing new business or fee negotiating – "right counsel for the right matter at the right fee".

The brief fee covered the preparation for trial – reading all the papers supplied by the solicitors, researching the law, drafting counsel's opening speech plus a conference with the client before the case started, as well as the first day in court. A "Refresher" paid for each subsequent day in court that the trial lasted. It was a fraction of the Brief fee.

Jealousy and rivalry have the opportunity to kick off big time when fees were involved. The amount of the brief fee and refreshers were marked on the back sheet. The same applied to the opponent's brief.

If counsel couldn't see their opponent's fees on their back sheet, they would ask. This caused Jack and his clerking colleagues a major headache if they were going to ensure their counsel did not earn less than their opponent.

The atmosphere in the robing room at court was a heady mix of adrenalin, testosterone, nervous anticipation and blind fear. The banter appeared light hearted to an outsider, but the opposite was true. A dig at an opponent, an innuendo within earshot of an instructing solicitor, or an outright challenge could soften up the opponent ready for the kill in court.

Jack dealt with all the big case fee negotiating himself. That day he had gone to see James Campbell, senior personal injury barrister, in his room to get a feel for the work involved in a particularly difficult case. He already had in his mind what the barristers would be looking for as the brief fee – the preparation work, conferences, drafting documents and submissions, and the first day of the two week liability-only trial, plus the daily refresher rate.

"So what's involved Mr Campbell?" asked Jack.

James Campbell went through in some detail everything he and his leader Charles Wadsworth QC would have to do to get the case up and running. This included according to Campbell preparation time of about 100 hours. Jack winced a bit at this amount of time, and counsel spotted his expression.

"Jack, I know you think all we have done is talk to the defence team in the robing room, which we have, but there is more to our argument on fees than that. Remember the insurers only have one claimant solicitors and two claimant barristers to pay if they lose, not six solicitors and twelve barristers if each of the six claimants had all instructed different solicitors and barristers."

Jack took the point as well as reminding Mr Campbell that his brief would be set at 50 percent of his QC's fees.

By the time Jack picked up the phone to talk to the instructing solicitor John Goldman at Featherstones, the rest of his clerking team were each seated at their respective desks looking busy. They had already each put a pound into the empty coffee mug on Dillon's desk, plus a scrap of paper with their initials on and the deal they thought Jack would get. Nearest to the actual agreed fees would win the pot of cash in the coffee mug.

Jack knew about the bets but made no comment. He too had a bit of paper in his desk draw with the figures he thought would win the bet, just to keep his hand in.

"John, how the devil are you?" The clerks listened intensely as Jack started the negotiation over the phone with John Goldman. Jack went through all the standard points that James Campbell had fed him as well as a few more Jack deemed appropriate. These included the volume of paperwork, the attention to detail displayed by his silk and junior counsel and their respective ages and experience. Jack left no stone unturned, and paused to let Mr Goldman absorb it all.

Now was the crunch. Jack reminded himself of Ralph's words on such occasions. "Jack, if you don't' ask you don't get." Jack started.

"John, for our leading counsel I would place the brief fee, taking everything into account, in the £45 to £50k bracket, with refreshers at £2,750 per day, all plus VAT. I propose we settle for the leader's brief fee at £42,500 + VAT with refreshers at £2,500 + VAT per day, junior counsel at the usual half rate throughout. How does that seem to you?"

There was silence in the clerks' room as everyone waited for John Goldman to reply. Their thoughts ranged from too high to ridiculously high. Only Jason had a very slight smirk on his face.

Jack completed a few closing remarks, and hung up. His face looked like thunder. Christian broke the silence with a side comment under his breath to Dillon. "Oh God, he's blown it."

Jason turned to Jack. "What's up, Jack?" he asked. Jack looked up. "Bugger – should have asked for more!"

Dillon could not contain himself any longer. "What, he agreed the QC's brief fee at £42,500 + VAT with refreshers at £2,500 + VAT per day?" Jack nodded his confirmation.

It did not happen very often, but Jack got really upset when his first offer was accepted. He expected to be knocked down. It's what solicitors do, so he built in an amount he can knock off to get at the figure he wanted. What stuck in the throat for Jack was he would never know if there was more in the deal than he had asked for, and he could not go back. Ralph's words rang in Jack's ear: "You can never increase a negotiated fee, only reduce it."

James Dunn referred to his bit of paper with his prediction on. "Wow, that's too good for my bet. Anyone anywhere near it?" he asked. A broader smile came to Jason's face. "I think the pot is mine with £38,000 on the brief and £2,000 refreshers a day. Well done Jack."

Jack pulled out his bit of paper from his desk draw. It showed £40,000 brief fee and £2,250 refreshers. He added. "Those were the figures I would have settled at. Anything lower and I would have gone back to counsel. Drinks on you tonight Jason!"

Later that day, in the quiet period after lunch but before counsel returned from court, Dillon was in an inquisitive mood. He spoke to nobody in particular as the full team were seated at their respective desks in Barcourt clerks' room and asked: "In our area of the Temple are all the postcodes WC1R? And why is the last part 4FS? Is it personal to us?"

Jason responded. "Why do you ask?" "Well, I've seen the initials "4FS" written on several sets of papers on the top corner and wondered why only the second half of the post code is used."

Jason lent forward and whispered in a terrible French accent. "Listen carefully, for I will say this only once." Apart from Dillon, everyone knew exactly what was coming, and switched off. Jason continued.

"There are phrases you might want to use, almost under your breath, or write down to make your colleagues in this room more aware of a situation, a delicate situation, something that needs careful handling. Should such a situation arise, put on the top corner of the relevant papers the letters "4FS". Do you understand?"

Dillon looked a little perplexed. "4FS?" he repeated.

Jason lent even further forward and spoke forcefully "For Fucks' Sake!" and wrote 4FS on Dillon's note pad. Before he could ask why, Jason added: "Because we will know someone, probably a Guvnor, is being a pillock, and it is our way of passing on that potentially invaluable information in confidence.

The clerks could see the cogs going round in Dillon's head. Eventually the penny dropped. Jason explained to make sure. "Well "Ignorant pillock" or "stupid bugger" are phrases you might like to use but can't. So you mutter "4FS" to yourself. It helps take the stress out of the job for a few seconds, until the next time."

After the next cup of coffee, Christian asked Jack if he could help him out with a choice of counsel. "We need someone to go to Birmingham next Wednesday and there is nobody available from the solicitors' usual approved suspects. What do you suggest?"

Jack looked at the diary on his screen for next week, and it did look pretty full. There was no obvious candidate. The best of those available was Tom Wallace, a very senior civil counsel who could turn his hand to most work. The expression "Jack of all trades, master of none" was applicable, but after 25 years at the Bar, Jack and the other clerks regarded him as a safe pair of hands, living for most of his career on the returns of others.

Jack had realised a long time ago that the way to handle barristers was to appeal to their wallets. It was no good targeting any sense of natural justice, fair play and certainly not common sense. So when Jack wanted something from counsel he knew what to say. He picked up the phone as Christian walked round to stand behind Jack. He could then hear what counsel would say in response to Jack.

"Mr Wallace, how would you like to go to Birmingham for the day next Wednesday?" Out of town was never popular and Wallace was less than impressed. "Oh, Jack. It will mean an early start, a train to hell and back, considerable inconvenience. Have I got anything else on then?"

Jack had heard all the excuses before but he let Wallace have his say. "Wednesday is bridge night. I can't let the good lady down."

Jack fired his first round of arguments. "How does a brief fee of £1,000 + VAT sound? It is a personal injury infant approval case listed at 12.00 noon for 2 hours so no early start, and you should be done by lunch time. That would put you back in chambers in time for your 4.30 pm conference. They want someone a bit more senior as there is a lot of money for the infant claimant, and the insurers are paying anyway. Just a single lever arch file you can read on the train up to Birmingham. You can prep your conference on the return journey. What do you say?"

Mr Wallace was what Jack thought of as a farmer, as opposed to a hunter. He did not get a lot of work in his own name, spent less time in court than he wanted, and many of his cases settled. This was part of his problem as he was seen as a settler rather than a fighter. Most instructing solicitors wanted their client to see someone willing to fight their corner all the way. After all, counsel were just doing for the lay client exactly what they would do for themselves if they had the inclination and knowledge to represent themselves.

Tom Wallace was more than happy taking this case. It required for a man of his calibre minimal effort for a good reward. Jack knew he would take the brief only because he was lucky to get £500 a day for a minor hearing, so even after the train fare, he was a happy bunny. And Jack was too because if he had refused, which was unthinkable, the brief might have gone out of chambers. And that would have hurt Jack the most.

Wallace occasionally reflected on the wisdom in agreeing to Jack for the job as senior clerk. He still had reservations, particularly about his style, but did not let Jack know.

"Yes of course Jack. Always willing to help out as you know. Which judge is it?" That last question sealed the deal. If counsel wanted to know who the judge was, they had in their mind committed to the case. "His Honour Judge Alastair Duckworth."

"Oh well, I know Duckers, we'll be done in 40 minutes. He likes to get to the judges' dining room early. Thanks Jack."

Jack put the phone down and turned to Christian Bennett who had heard it all. "You could have done that yourself, Gordon."

"I know, but he might have refused Birmingham." Christian's reply was not accepted by Jack. "Ring the solicitor and tell him you have a senior 25 year call man on the case, and next time, you bite the bullet and sort it yourself." Christian smiled. "Yes Boss!"

That evening the clerks were in the Wiltshire Inn having a couple of beers and reflecting on the day. They were in the company of clerks from several chambers so were mindful of not letting too much gossip be started at their expense. The intense rivalry at the bar is equally reflected in the competition between clerks in different chambers, as well as within a set. Yet somehow it always came across as friendly rivalry. Nobody was taken in.

As between barristers, both within their chambers and outside, they appeared friendly whilst underneath nobody trusted anyone. Counsel would shaft a colleague from another set just as easily as from their own chambers. It was as easy as buying them a pint.

They all had to get on, clerks and counsel, to oil the wheels, so often on a mid-week early evening the lads from several chambers would share gossip.

The current topic of conversation rounded on a chancery set which had appointed a new man to run chambers who was not a traditional senior clerk. He was described as a "Chambers Director".

"That's a posh name for someone who knows nothing about clerking" suggested Jason. It turned out the guy had been a solicitor in private practice and apart from briefing a few sets in London and Birmingham, he had rarely set foot in any chambers.

The assembled clerks soon drew the erroneous conclusion that he would not be a success and would be gone within six months. The general consensus was to ignore him and he would go away. All agreed that sending him to Coventry was the right way to handle him.

Whilst discussing this potential threat to traditional clerking, they started trying to define what clerking was and what it took to become a senior clerk.

"You've got no chance Dillon" said Benjamin Church, junior clerk at Carey Street chambers, who went by the nickname of Big Ben on account of him being six foot three.

"Wow, that's rich coming from you Big Ben" interrupted Jason. "You never take your hands out of your pockets to buy a round. You know, to become a senior clerk you have to speculate to accumulate." Benjamin, who was clearly too young to understand the phrase just looked blankly at Jason who carried on. "Jack and the other senior clerks always spend a lot of dosh oiling the wheels."

"So how would you describe a senior clerk?" asked another junior clerk from Carey Street chambers trying to draw the spotlight away from his colleague, Ben asked: "OK. Sum up the role of a senior clerk to an outsider. What do you think?"

This was an interesting debate which got lively over the next three rounds with chasers. They focused on the unique skill set needed to master the job.

Dillon, remembering the expression used by Jack to describe his role, concluded: "So based on what you are all saying, he or she has to be a cross between a theatrical agent, a nanny and a pimp!"

After the laughter died down, a reflective silence fell over the assembled crew. Everyone agreed each title was partly right, and they had got about as close as they could.

Undeterred by the silence, Dillon asked "So who is going to ask Jack if he likes being a pimp?"

There followed a lot of finger-pointing around the bar, but nobody volunteered. Dillon mumbled to Christian under his breath "Pimp eh? I always fancied taking money for sex."

5 SPECULATION

Early the next afternoon the clerking team were busy ringing round to collect in the briefs for the following day, checking with the courts' listing officers which court rooms were listed for their cases, and which judges were sitting. This was the information which had to be given to every barrister before anyone could go home, so the sooner everything was in order the better for all concerned.

Christine Denton had turned hiding from the clerks into an art form. She liked to finish court by lunchtime so that she was free for the afternoon's sport. However, her sport did not involve putting on sportswear, more getting her kit off. Although she was not averse to a bit of role play in the right context.

Obviously it did not work every day, and she did have a busy paperwork practice to service as well. Part of the excitement for her was escaping with her current man for a passionate afternoon, and the more risky the better. Booking a room in a pub or small hotel was almost par for the course.

Being a five foot nine inches tall blonde with strikingly well-proportioned features, especially in traditional court uniform of black skirt and white blouse, it was difficult for Christine to be inconspicuous in public. So the clerks noticed her out of chambers more than most members. That made the game more fun.

Christine was good at reporting in to her diary clerk Christian Bennett. She only ever referred to him now as Gordon who thought it was because she fancied him. Well, he did wear trousers, so he at least ticked one box according to Dillon who felt he was the clerking team guru when it came to the female of the species.

"Let's face it Gordon, you've got a pulse so you are in with a chance!" Christian inwardly smiled which he disguised with a frown at Dillon. "And what do you know young lad?" replied Christian.

"You're too young to have man talk." The implication that Dillon was still a virgin hurt him still. He snapped back. "Just because I am a little shorter than you and have boyishly good looks does not mean I am not fully experienced in that department."

The phone rang. "Saved by the bell" thought Dillon. It was Christine Denton wanting to speak to Christian who took her call.

"Hi Gordon. I've finished in Winchester so I am going to do some research in the Law Library on my way back. See you later." She hung up quickly so Christian could not suggest more work. She had other plans as she dialled her boyfriend of the day. "I've finished. Usual place in an hour?" After a short pause to hear his confirmation, she hung up and left Winchester County Court.

Researching in the library for the other members of chambers usually implied they were meeting for a small select drinks party in one of the Fleet Street pubs. If any of the clerks tried to contact them, counsel would claim their mobile phone was switched off or they had poor reception.

"Poor reception my arse." Jack shouted almost on a daily basis. "Mornings in coffee houses, lunch times in wine bars, and afternoons in the pub. Hard life!" But nobody complained that Christine Denton had called in.

James Dunn, very much the straight laced fees and admin clerk, piped up. "She's still swinging the lead like the rest of them. It is wrong."

"A different sort of lead James" instructed Jason. The clerks collectively produced a boyish laugh, save for Dunn. "Oh that's disgusting" he replied.

Should the need arise to get counsel to cover a case at short notice, it could take an ingenious clerk to track down the worst offenders. Dillon asked Jack "I'll bet you've got North American blood in your family Jack. The old Tracker instinct eh? "

Jason piped up. "That would go with the eyes in the back of his head. Take care Dillon, you never know when Jack's watching you!"

A couple of the phones in their Clerks' room started to ring. It was just after two o'clock. "Oh no. Who is going part heard?" asked Jason. This was the dangerous time of the day when counsel would ring in to warn their diary clerk of the likelihood they would not finish their case that day and so go part heard into tomorrow. That meant disappointment for whoever was instructing them on tomorrow's case.

Dillon took the first call. "Right sir, I'll tell the senior clerk immediately." Dillon put the phone down as Jack barked out: "Who is it?"

Dillon answered. "Mr Livingstone is stuck in court two and his other case has been called on into court four now. Can you get him some more time?" replied the junior clerk.

The judge in court four was His Honour Judge Cooper, a former member of chambers before Jack's time but knew exactly how clerks took risks and in particular how senior clerks operated.

Jack picked up a brief from the pile on the table near the door as he left the clerks' room to go to court. He took a taxi so he got there in a few minutes and took the lift to the first floor. On his way to court number four, Jack saw along the corridor several groups of lawyers and their clients huddled outside the entrances to each court room. Some included members of Barcourt chambers who each spotted Jack as he walked along.

As each one saw Jack had a brief in his hand, they all turned to face their respective group and made out they were deep in learned conversation, rather than passing the time of day waiting for their case to be called into court. No barrister wanted extra work just as they were about to do battle.

Jack knew this, and he did not want to be diverted from his current mission of sorting out Livingstone. That was the reason he was carrying a brief, any brief. It was his right to free passage along the corridor allowing counsel to think he had a brief which needed taking on.

The spare brief in hand also made him look busy. There were a few people milling around outside court number four, but Jack ignored them all and went first through the outer door leading to the court room.

Having made sure the court was not in session, Jack then quickly but quietly pulled open the inner door. The court room was empty except for the counsel instructed on the other side who was chatting to the court usher, the court clerk, and His Honour Judge Cooper seated on his throne reading case papers. He looked up as Jack walked forward towards the clerk sitting below the judge.

They were clearly just waiting for Mr Peter Livingstone to appear. Before Jack could speak to the court clerk, the judge spoke. "To what do we owe the presence of a senior clerk in this court?"

Jack turned to face the Bench. "Your Honour, Mr Livingstone has been unexpectedly delayed in Court two. He has asked me to apologise and crave a few minutes …."

The Judge interrupted Jack mid-sentence: "You know my views Mr Temple – Habeas Corpus". Jack thought to himself: "God, the number of times he was rescued by his senior clerk in worse scrapes than this." Habeas Corpus was the judge's little joke – produce the body i.e. get Mr Livingstone into court now!

"Your Honour, Mr Livingstone has prepared this case, and to change counsel at this stage would prejudice the client and waste more court time whilst alternative counsel got up to speed. With your permission

I will go to Court two immediately."

"10 minutes Mr Temple or find someone else." Jack bowed his head towards the judge and left the courtroom.

In the corridor he met Peter Livingstone walking as quickly as his little legs would carry him towards court four. "Ah Mr Livingstone. Just the man. Court four ASAP. I told Judge Cooper you had prepared so he expects to start straight away"

Mr Livingstone replied: "But I have not prepared it!" Jack looked at his watch and replied "You now have 8 minutes to read the papers and get there!" Livingstone hurried back to the robing room to read what he could in the remaining minutes before his expected bollocking in front of His Honour Judge Cooper.

Jack headed back into chambers as soon as he could to find out what Nathan Blake was up to following his earlier question about how long it would take to organise an ECM.

His first question for his team as he entered their clerk's room was directed to all the clerks seated at their desks. "Where is the head of chambers?"

"He's in his room on the telephone" replied Christian. Jack asked his next question. "And Nathan Blake?"

"On his way in after losing another case against Carey Street" came the reply from Jason. "Typical!" replied Jack.

Jason continued. "We've got another problem for tomorrow Jack."

"Shit" said Jack. "Who is it this time?"

Jason had taken the second call. It was from James Campbell, one of their best earners, to say that he was going part heard for at least Monday and Tuesday of the following week as they were the only days the judge in his present case could continue, otherwise it would be a month. Jack looked at the diary to confirm his worst fears. Campbell was due to be in court on the Tuesday for an inquest in a personal injury case worth millions.

The Inquest date could not be moved for counsel's convenience, and the solicitors would be really upset. He looked at the diary with Jason to see what could be done.

"Ok. If we get someone to cover Denton's infant approval case on Tuesday morning that would free her up to cover the inquest. It will mean she stays out of court on the Monday to prepare for the inquest. There are boxes of papers, but Campbell could direct her to the liability issues." A plan was evolving.

Jack turned to Dillon. "Right, get me Denton's brief for Tuesday out of her pigeonhole. I need to make sure she can return it." Dillon came back into the clerks' room empty handed. "It's not there, and I have checked her room. No sign of it there either."

"Typical" replied Jack. "Ok, where is she?" Jason answered. "She rang in an hour ago from Winchester to say she had finished. So she has gone AWOL."

"Right then, let's find her and get her to bring that brief into chambers now." Jason and Dillon both looked sceptical at the prospects of success. If Christina Denton did not want to be found then she would not be found.

Jack tried approaching the problem from a different angle. He sent a text message to Christina which read: "Brief for Tuesday to chambers by cab NOW please, otherwise I need to find you. Diary changed."

An hour later a taxi pulled up outside Barcourt chambers and the driver came into reception to drop a small parcel off. Margaret called to Jack. "Taxi driver says you will pay him. He wants £15." Jack was on the phone so Jason replied.

"Fine Margaret. Pay him out of petty cash and book it to Christine Denton. I'll have the parcel".

It was Christine's Tuesday's brief. Jason smiled as he handed it to Jack and added: "So she didn't want to be found, yet again."

Jack was happy that the brief could be returned by Christine, so picked up the phone and rang James Campbell's solicitor in the Inquest case. This was a call the clerks listened to as it was a good opportunity to hear the "master of returns" at work.

Jack outlined the problem to the solicitor on the other end who listened without any interruption. Jack summed up. "This is not a scenario anyone could have predicted. James Campbell made representations to his judge at lunchtime today who was sympathetic to the problem he was creating, but still went ahead with Tuesday. I am sure Mr Campbell will ring you when he gets back."

Jack listened to his solicitor who was furious but resigned to being let down. Jack continued. "I will, with your approval, keep Christine Denton out of court on Monday to get up to speed for the inquest, and ask Mr Campbell to fill her in over the weekend on the essential points. She will do a detailed note of evidence at the Inquest, and bring Mr Campbell up to speed on the outcome so he can continue with the case."

Silence followed as Jack listened and made a couple of notes. "Very good sir, and I appreciate your understanding of the situation." Jack put the phone down and raised his head to speak to his team. "Honesty pays. Remember that."

Jason asked Jack the question that had been on his mind for several minutes. "Jack, how did you know where Christine was?"

He replied "I didn't know. I just sent her a text threatening to go looking for her." Jason thought through what Jack had said and realised the benefit of technology. "You could not have done that ten years ago." Jack agreed. He was always pleased with himself when he had thought outside the box, or gone the extra mile to explain a problem to a solicitor. They lived in the big world too, and as he had often announced to his team: "Shit happens!"

Whilst all this was going on, nobody except Jack noticed Nathan Blake slide past reception and upstairs to the head of chambers who was quietly contemplating forty winks in the comfort of his armchair. The bold knocking on his door broke his trance.

Nathan responded to the forlorn invitation to enter the lion's den. "Oh, it's you Blake." "Sorry to disturb you Charles, have you got a minute?"

Nathan retold the story of Sarah Jane and the toilet incident he had unfolded to his cronies in the tap room of the Red Lion. He did not embellish the story as he knew he would be cross-examined by the head of chambers, and indeed by other senior members as well in due course. Wadsworth sat there in disbelief. "Do you still have the photographic evidence?" he asked.

Nathan took out his mobile phone and showed the picture to Charles. "I have tried to come up with an alternative explanation, a plausible innocent version."

Charles studied the image closely. "Yes indeed. I mean, I am no expert in identifying a line of cocaine, not even a novice in such matters. But it does look like the stuff. You say you smelt it?"

"I did indeed, sir." Nathan felt a formal attitude was called for, more respectful and appropriate. "The aroma was distinctly not perfumed, not at all."

After what seemed an age to Nathan, Charles sat back." This girl has some questions to answer. And if she gets it wrong, she will be committing professional suicide. Can you keep the photo, Nathan? And thank you for bringing this sad affair to my attention. I must consider my next step, and quickly. We don't want anyone finding out about it until we have decided what action to take. You haven't told anyone, have you Nathan?"

"Of course not, sir. I came straight to you. I have only asked Jack where you are today, but no more." It did not seem appropriate to advise the head of chambers at this stage that his three cronies were in the loop. They were all sworn to secrecy, so no harm in a little white lie, thought Nathan.

He felt mixed emotions as he walked back to his room. He did not think for one moment that the head of chambers would sweep the issue under the carpet. On the contrary, he was a pillar of honesty if lacking in long term foresight. He could not focus on the end game, just living his career day by day. Some wondered how on earth he had got silk. His advocacy was regarded as pedestrian, and only got the role of head of chambers as the most senior barrister who was also a QC in chambers.

Jack's phone rang and he could see from the display that it was an internal call from the head of chambers. He thought immediately of Nathan's question, and as Wadsworth only rang down for him in a crisis, he was going to get some answers, even if they were not what he wanted to hear.

Charles was seated behind his desk as Jack entered the room. "Jack, do sit down. We have a problem" and proceeded to pass on to Jack the full story as told to him by Nathan only ten minutes before.

"Jack, we have to be very careful here. Obviously total discretion is vital." Jack nodded in agreement.

"I could hear her version of events and then dismiss her immediately if I am satisfied the complaint is upheld. She would have 24 hours to appeal or be gone. I don't want that responsibility over counsel's career."

"So I have decided to call an Extraordinary Chambers Meeting under the constitution and offer Miss Ryman the opportunity to explain herself, but she is not to be given any advance warning. Otherwise she will just concoct her defence carefully and we won't get at the truth. Do I make myself clear, Jack?"

Jack nodded again, although this time he was uncomfortable at the thought of Sarah not knowing what the charges were which could change if not destroy her career.

The minimum notice period for an ECM under the constitution when expulsion of a member was on the agenda was seven days. "Can you organise it, Jack?" asked Charles. "Issue the notice to everyone. We will need a venue at a secret location away from the Temple. There isn't a room big enough in chambers as I expect the whole membership will attend."

"Leave it with me, sir. I will consult the diary and draw up a plan. Would you like me to run it past you before implementing any aspect?" Charles did not hesitate in his reply. "No, Jack. That won't be necessary. Just get on with it. Shocking business."

As Jack left the room, Charles looked up from his papers. "Jack, no mention on the notice of the reason for calling the ECM. Nobody must know otherwise it will be all round the Temple before you can blink. And I leave it to you to ensure that Sarah Ryman attends. You can tell her on the morning that she is on the agenda, not before. She is not to know the full allegation beforehand either. Do you understand, Jack?" Jack nodded in response.

Jack called his team together in the clerks' room and explained there would be an ECM in about seven days' time, once he had checked the diary to maximise attendance. He added: "and before you ask, I will not be telling anyone the reason the head of chambers has called the meeting. Nobody is to know, and it is best none of you know so no one can point the finger at you if it gets out. Just tell the members that Charles Wadsworth has issued instructions for an ECM, and that is all you know."

Once the notice went out, there was much speculation both within chambers and around the Temple. Rumours of the resignation of the head of chambers, a split in the members with a batch leaving, financial corruption, fraud, as well as merger talks all featured in the gossip. Jack and the head of chambers stuck to their word and did not divulge anything to anyone. Only Nathan Blake and his three cronies knew what was going on, and Nathan made them well aware that with so few in the loop, to break silence could easily be traced. They were putting their own tenancy at risk, reminding them also that so far as the head of chambers was concerned, only Nathan knew. So Stephen Savage, Monty Evans and Tim Shaw all knew they had to be silent too.

Jack had picked the Russell Hotel on Russell Square as a suitable venue, far enough away from the regular haunts of the Bar, and easy to get to. He picked six o'clock so everyone would be back from court, and conferences would have ended. So a good turnout was assured.

To simply show Sarah the door was not in Jack's eyes an acceptable solution. Whilst it could at worst be the end of a very promising career, at best it would consign her to a chambers move which could have a destabilising effect on its existing members, and might even encourage solicitors to show their dislike of what had happened by moving their work.

Lawyers often exercise such a right by using their feet to brief elsewhere. Jack reminded himself that they don't tell you what is wrong, you just don't hear from them again, and won't speak to you when you try follow up calls.

So the solution, as Jack saw it, was to get Sarah a tenancy somewhere else without anyone knowing what had happened. Which chambers would take Sarah on? The answer would be none if they knew the full story, thought Jack. Even half the tale would be enough to slam the door of most sets firmly in her face.

Jack concluded that he needed to call in a few favours from his fellow senior clerks and had to sell Sarah very hard. Anyone would question why such a talented junior counsel wanted to jump ship just as she was gaining a good reputation.

Jack thought carefully about how much to disclose. If Sarah did not appear before the ECM then the "case" against her brought by Nathan Blake was not "proved" and it would remain just a nasty rumour within chambers. Jack could contain that by warning the tenants that it was not in their interests to spread any gossip. He felt sure the head of chambers would back that up.

Jack had several meetings over the week leading up to the ECM with Sarah. She had no idea what the problem was with Nathan, and had no inkling of the trouble she was in. Nathan could not tell her enough for her to work it out, and nor could anyone else.

"Listen Jack, if you can't tell me what this is all about, I don't know how to react." She pleaded for his help. "You're telling me I should leave chambers when I have worked so hard to get my tenancy, but you don't say why. This is crazy! How am I supposed to know what I have done wrong?"

Jack agreed it was a ridiculous situation. ""Ok, strictly between us, a matter has come to the attention of the head of chambers regarding your conduct which if proven would lead to your immediate expulsion from chambers. More than that I am not at liberty to divulge indeed that is more than I was instructed to say until the day of the Extraordinary Chambers Meeting."

Jack could tell that Sarah was searching her mind for a clue in her past conduct, but without success. "Help me Jack, what am I supposed to do?"

Jack outlined how he would get her into another chambers if that was what she wanted, and what he would do about the current situation. He told her it was important they both appeared to be on the same page, especially if she were to get an interview at another chambers.

"I think we have to put this whole issue down to a clash of personalities. Sarah, Who do you think hates you more than most in chambers?" Jack asked. "Right now, all of them!" Sarah replied. "But I guess Nathan Blake would be top of the list. He has never forgiven me for getting my tenancy at the same time as him, and hates my name being above his on the chambers' board. In the last week, since the ECM notice went public, he and his cronies have been really odd. Their behaviour, which has never been good at the best of times, is as if they would rather ignore me."

Jack responded. "Nathan has always been jealous of your success. He has a chip on his shoulder that you have got work he should have had."

Jack knew he only had a few days to plot to avoid Sarah's departure so decided he had to confide some of what he knew to her. He could not tell her everything, just that she was the reason for the ECM, and the only item on the agenda. At a further meeting they went over the same ground again.

"Sarah, all I can say is you must be prepared to defend yourself as if your career depends on it. I am going against my specific instructions from the head of chambers. He told me not to tell you until the morning of the ECM, but I felt, you and I together, needed more time than that to plan an escape route."

"Jack, I appreciate you telling me, although I am at a loss to understand what is going on. How about I just go and confront Charles now?" Jack stopped her before she could add anything.

"You do that, Sarah, and we will both be out of a job. I cannot put it any other way. You have to hear what he has to say at the ECM."

Sarah had no intention of allowing herself to be subjected to such humiliation. Jack, for his part, sensed Sarah was looking for a solution that avoided the ECM. "The only alternative I can suggest, and we are not there yet, would be for you to resign from chambers."

Sarah erupted. "Jack, you more than most know how hard I have fought to get my tenancy here, the sacrifices I have made."

They talked on into the early hours. The more Sarah contemplated her situation, the more depressed she became. The best Jack could do was to get Sarah to agree to allow him to sound out a possible move to another civil set where not too many questions would be asked. Jack translated that into being economical with the truth. That would only work, as he saw it, if the evidence against Sarah was never heard, certainly not every detail.

The answer was becoming clearer to Jack. He could not stop the ECM, but he could stop Sarah attending if she already had a new chambers to go to. There would be no need for his chambers to air their dirty laundry in public, so he could promote Sarah's departure under the cover of a team mutiny.

Jack went back in his mind to what Jason had reported to him from the taxi as he left Nathan Blake, Monty Evans, Stephen Savage and Tim Shaw in the tap room of the Red Lion. They had all been huddled round the fire plotting something. Jack concluded it was no coincidence that Nathan Blake went to the head of chambers the following day, so it was highly likely that all four of them knew exactly what the allegations were. So it made perfect sense to Jack to offer a new home for four counsel at the same time. One would be Sarah plus the three cronies Savage, Evans and Shaw who would be used as camouflage to get Sarah in without interrogation. Carey Street Chambers would regard this as not just good business, it would be seen as a major coup with Sarah as the pick of the bunch.

Nathan Blake would not leave Barcourt chambers. There was no advantage to him unless and until Sarah left. Once she had gone, Nathan felt he would pick up her work.

If the cronies were plotting to leave, they would have to keep quiet, and probably would, in order to get their move to a new chambers. They might even get a crack at some of Sarah's work in their new chambers.

Jack decided it was better the cronies did not know about Sarah's move as part of the four leaving Barcourt chambers until their departure was a certainty. He did not want any last minute slip-up.

The next morning, Jack had coffee with the other senior clerks to discuss the problems posed by a new Listing Officer at the RCJ. Several Appeal Court cases had been listed at short notice, and as a result several briefs in more than one chambers had been returned late in the day. Solicitors were very unhappy at the new broom in the Listing Office trying to make his mark by increasing the number of cases heard in the Court of Appeal. Something needed to be done, and all the affected senior clerks felt a united approach was the best step forward.

After coffee, Richard Murray sidled up to Jack who had taken a second chocolate biscuit. "Think of the waist-line Jack. Those shorts are already under a lot of pressure on Sunday morning!" "Richard" replied Jack. "Looking as skinny as ever I see. I'm surprised you are here. I didn't think any of your guvnors go up to the dizzy heights of the Court of Appeal." Jack smiled, happy with his repost.

Richard ignored the cheap jibe, preferring to go for the jugular. "So what's on the agenda for the ECM next week? Your replacement?!"

Jack did not reply immediately as he tried to disguise his shock at Richard even being aware of the existence of the ECM. "And what little birdie has been feeding you porkies, Richard?"

Richard was not about to be deflected. "Well, I am reliably informed you are having an ECM at which serious allegations are to be made. Expulsion is on the agenda. What do you say? Can I have a quote?"

Richard was enjoying the moment. Jack did not want any of the other clerks picking up their conversation, so responded, looking Richard straight in the eyes: "I don't know what you are talking about."

Jack walked off towards the main exit believing then was not the right moment to offer Richard the four members of chambers, Sarah Ryman and the three cronies.

Back in his clerks' room, Jason could tell Jack was unhappy at something. He had a pre-occupied look on his face. He said: "Penny for them Jack?"

Jack thought about not saying anything, but then decided that a problem shared was a problem halved. "Jason, if you had to point the finger at a member of chambers who would leak a piece of confidential information, who would it be?"

Jason resolved to just answer the question as it was put to him, rather than try to get for himself answers to more questions. "Ok, well you're not talking about idle pub gossip, so it has to be someone with more opportunity than most to be indiscreet. I guess the one who commits more indiscretions than anyone would be Christine Denton, but we may not be talking about sexual indiscretions."

Jack laughed as he replied: "I like your deductions, Doctor Watson!" He said no more and looked up the diary to see where Denton was that afternoon.

Later that day, Jack asked Christine Denton for a quiet word in one of the empty conference rooms. "Christine, I have a slightly delicate question for you, and I would ask you to consider very carefully your answer. Not for my sake, but for the sake of others, you understand."

Christine knew by Jack's tone that the question was loaded with something serious. He went on: "I am asking you first as one with their finger on the pulse of what goes on at Barcourt." She was flattered but also apprehensive by Jack's comment.

"Are you aware of anyone mentioning our proposed ECM to anyone out of chambers, to any other barrister in the city?" Christine thought carefully before replying. "I don't think so, no. Why do you ask?"

"What about to any clerk?" Christine's face dropped so significantly that it was obvious to Jack that he had hit a nerve, and she knew Jack had seen her response. She was speechless so Jack continued.

"You see, Richard Murray at Carey Street chambers spoke to me this afternoon and he clearly knew all about the ECM, not just its existence but what was on the agenda. That information has to have come from a very limited number of members of chambers. It could not be any of the clerks because I have not told them."

"Jack, I am so sorry. I'm afraid a little post-sex pillow talk may have been to blame." He asked: "Would that be Clive Marshall?" Christine looked surprised. "How did you know?"

"He is an attractive guy and is the only part-time clerk in the Temple you know who works mornings only, and you like your afternoon recreation. What exactly does he know?"

"Well, only what we members know, which is that it must be a disciplinary matter which may lead to the expulsion of one or more members of chambers." Jack needed to be sure that was all Murray knew, and that he had been on a fishing expedition for more information. He probed further: "Are you quite sure there is nothing more?" Christine sighed: "yes, absolutely."

6 AN EXTRAORDINARY MEETING

The day after the notice of the ECM had been issued, after his conference in chambers which had finished sooner than he expected, Nathan Blake was sitting with is feet up on his desk, basking in his imagined impending glory. He considered his future which looked pretty rosy from where he was viewing matters.

He would get his hands on the better work Sarah Ryman had taken from him and it didn't involve him having to leave chambers. She would be the one to go, and that would be within days, if not hours. When members of chambers were minded to move sets, they often went the same day. This was designed to have the least impact on the careers of those leaving as well as those still in chambers.

Nathan would get the clerks to ring round Sarah's main solicitor clients and secure their business. The icing on the cake would be her removal from the chambers' board next to the front door. "At last, justice!" or so he thought.

Jack too reflected, not on Sarah's actions but more on Nathan's behaviour before the head of chambers when he had told the story for the first time. He was unaware at the time that Nathan had told the full story to the cronies in the Red Lion the evening before that meeting with Charles Wadsworth QC. In any event he was sure Nathan would want to stay. He had worked hard to get Sarah out and would want the rewards for his efforts. Jack knew there was no love lost between them.

He needed to work out a clear plan for sorting this mess out. His priority was Sarah Ryman. To keep the lid on a scandalous story, she had to be found a new home. There were not many civil personal injury sets which fitted the bill, although without the gossip, Sarah was undoubtedly a good professional catch.

Following the notice of the ECM, Stephen Savage, Monty Evans and

Tim Shaw too reflected on the knowledge they had known the whole sordid affair, and far more importantly, the likely effect on their individual careers. They all had reasonable volumes of work but knew they did rely on returns to fill their court diaries, although they would never admit as much. They always looked after number one first, and in that spirit convened a special meeting of just the three of them in the tap room at the Red Lion. It was arranged without Nathan's knowledge, indeed specifically set for a day he was in court in Birmingham.

Stephen Savage took the chair in the absence of Nathan, although he did let Tim Shaw buy the first round. He regarded himself as a schemer, a plotter from the same mould as Nathan, so started the meeting.

"Gentlemen, we find ourselves in a very tricky situation. We all know the end result for Sarah Jane Ryman. There is nothing we can do for her. She is the author of her own misfortune. We must protect our own positions as we find ourselves in the unenviable position of being the only members of chambers to know the full facts, except for the head of chambers and Nathan." Monty and Tim agree with his analysis so Stephen continued. "I conclude this puts us in a dangerous position should knowledge of what we know ever become public."

Further agreement by the other two was followed by Tim Shaw. "Indeed. I don't think we can attend the ECM. What if we are asked a leading question by the head of chambers?" "Or anyone else, for that matter?" added Monty. "I would find it an impossible situation."

Further private reflections followed. It was thirsty work, so Tim ordered another round from the bar. Savage decided now was a good moment. "I have had an approach from another set." This came like a bolt out of the blue to both Monty and Tim, but being good advocates, they took it in their stride. Monty asked "Who from Stephen?"

"Carey Street chambers." Tim followed up Monty with a supplemental question: "Oh yes. How did that come about?"

Savage continued his tale. "I had a call out of the blue from their senior clerk, Richard Murray. He said he wanted to discuss an important matter and could we meet ASAP. I saw him yesterday in a pub up west. What he said was very interesting. I told him I would meet you guys and consider what he had to say."

Monty was puzzled. "Why would you want to discuss his offer with us?" Before he could elaborate, Savage cut in. "Because the offer to go to Carey Street chambers is for all three of us." "What!" exclaimed Tim "You're kidding? What about Nathan?"

Savage replied. "Nathan is not included. Richard and I concluded he would want to stay in chambers now he has got Sarah's thorn out of his side, and if he didn't, he would be welcome anytime. What do you think?"

The grass looked decidedly greener on the Carey Street side of the hill as all three talked themselves up to a position of absolute delight at the prospect of moving. They would definitely not attend the ECM. Monty summed it up. "Just wouldn't be right." Then added: "How did their senior clerk know now was a good time to approach you Stephen? The secrecy surrounding the ECM has been pretty water tight."

Savage was not sure if he should divulge the reason, but in the end felt full disclosure was needed. "Well, I have been seeing one of the family members at Carey Street for the last few weeks, and I let her know that I would appreciate a call from her man Richard Murray. He rang and we agreed to meet."

"You crafty old fox. Does she, the girl friend I mean, know anything more?" enquired Monty.

"Absolutely not, and I finished with her the day after so as not to cause us or her any problem." Tim piped up. "Is that why you went out with her in the first place, Stephen?" He answered "You may think that, Tim, but I could not possibly comment!"

Stephen Savage, Monty Evans and Tim Shaw concluded their meeting in the tap room with unanimous agreement to accept the offer of moving to Carey Street chambers. Savage agreed to speak further to Richard Murray and suggest they move forty eight hours after the ECM. That would give them all time to see the head of chambers and depart on amicable terms.

Stephen Savage did not disclose to either Monty Evans or Tim Shaw the full reason he had been approached by Richard Murray, or his white lie to them. It would have been catastrophic for him to have explained that he had told the now former girlfriend in Carey Street Chambers the "full story" of Sarah's cocaine misdemeanour. This had been a bad case of talking too much after sex, but if he could keep a lid on it and get them all moved to Carey Street chambers, then the means were justified.

The next day, Richard Murray could barely contain himself as he put his mobile phone down on his desk. He had just spoken to Stephen Savage and confirmed his conversation with his head of chambers. Carey Street now had three more members of their civil team, and all being well they should be moving in over the weekend. He would definitely pop into the WI for a beer that evening, and with any luck he would rub salt into Jack's wound at losing three barristers.

By the time he got to the Wiltshire Inn, Jack was already deep into the Evening Standard. There were usually two or three copies of the latest edition lying around the bar. Richard crept up behind Jack and whispered in his ear. "You reading chambers news, eh Jack?"

Jack did not rise to the bait as he had his own agenda for speaking to Murray.

"Chambers hasn't got any news, Richard. What are you up to?" Richard went on unimpressed with Jack's response.

"Have you heard you are going to be short on numbers by the weekend?"

Just for once Jack did not know what he was on about. "Go on" he said. So Murray did.

"Well, probably as we speak, three of your civil team, correction ex-civil team, are packing their bags ready to move up market to Carey Street."

"Oh really, and who might they be?" asked Jack without lifting his eyes from the Evening Standard.

"Messrs Stephen Savage, Monty Evans and Tim Shaw no less. No hard feelings Jack, all is fair in love and chambers, eh?!"

Jack lowered the newspaper, and looked at Richard straight between the eyes. "Congratulations Richard. How would you like one more?"

Richard was in full flow and enjoying every second of his triumph. "Why not, who else wants to jump ship?"

Now came Jack's test to find out just how much Richard knew. "How about Sarah Jane Ryman?"

Richard paused to pull up a chair. "Really? Seen the light with the others has she? I'm not surprised. Of course I will have to put it to my head of chambers, but I would think we can find extra room for her."

"Fine" replied Jack. "Leave it with me and I will get her to give you a call on your mobile in the morning. Must dash. Train to catch."

Jack had not expected Richard to first approach him about Stephen Savage, Monty Evans and Tim Shaw leaving Barcourt chambers.

That came as a real surprise, although perhaps to be expected as they had all been seen in "plotters corner" in the Red Lion. His plan to get Carey Street to take Sarah was working easier than he thought. Richard did not appear to have a clue why Sarah wanted to leave, thinking it was more to do with the other three he had got. He wondered if all this would mean Nathan Blake would leave as well, but then dismissed the idea as Nathan would be too engrossed in his own newly enhanced importance to join them.

So Sarah had a new chambers, Carey Street, to go to. All that was now needed by Jack was to persuade her it was the right move. In reality it was the only option she had, and he made that quite clear when they met for breakfast the next morning in the Crown café bar on the Strand. "You're right Jack, I know. One side of me says let's see how the ECM goes before I make the final decision. The other says go now so there is nothing in the public domain to prevent my move or damage my career."

The appointed time of 5.00pm for the Extraordinary Chambers Meeting arrived. Most of the members of chambers were assembled in fairly solemn mood, expecting the worst. Notable by their absence were Savage, Evans and Shaw, but Jack did not expect to see them. They would be in hiding somewhere, probably with a pint in hand.

Charles Wadsworth QC was pacing up and down the rather limited area behind the table and chairs reserved for himself and Jack, and the rest of the members were in rows of chairs facing him.

Sarah had not been seen in chambers that day by anyone. Charles Wadsworth had half expected her to contact him to ask for a reference and to resign but she had not.

Jack was expecting a call from her during the afternoon, but was not concerned that she had not rung him. He had wanted to ring the senior clerk Richard Murray at Carey Street but knew that would be a mistake, so he sat patiently waiting for the drama to unfold.

Jack looked at his watch again. It was 5.05pm and there was still no sign at the ECM of Sarah Ryman or the three cronies. He put his mobile phone on silent.

At 5.10pm, Charles sat down and announced: "Well, we are short of a few members. We'll give them another five minutes and then we'll start."

Jack's mobile phone buzzed to advise him he had a new text message. It read: "Sorry Jack. Can't do ECM. I'm sorted. Thanks. Sarah."

The head of chambers looked at Jack who turned towards him and whispered: "She isn't coming. She has gone."

Charles had to think what to do now. There was no time to adjourn for further instructions which was what he usually did when he was stuck or lost for words. So at 5.15pm he called the meeting to order.

"Colleagues, thank you all for coming, and apologies for the apparent secrecy surrounding this event. I can now advise that you were called to discuss a matter of grave importance for a member and for chambers. However, the need to do so has passed. The member of chambers has resigned and is no longer a member of our set. So that only leaves me to thank you all for attending, and to formally close the meeting."

"Charles, that's most unsatisfactory" opened James Campbell. "Who has left?"

Charles got up to leave. "Sarah Ryman. I declare the meeting closed."

The members were flabbergasted by the way the meeting was concluded. There followed amongst them a general discussion about Sarah Ryman, mixed with outrage at having an early evening wasted, and inquisitive banter about the reason Sarah had gone. Nobody had seen her that day, and nobody except Jack knew where she had gone.

Back in chambers, the serious dissatisfaction expressed about the way the head of chambers had handled the event continued for several days and many of the more senior members made their feelings known to the members of the management committee. James Campbell, whose opinion carried more weight than most as he earned more than most, was particularly vociferous. He told Charles Wadsworth to his face: "This is no way to run a chambers. The members have a right to know what is going on and to have a proper vote on any important issues."

Several members let Jack know they were not happy. He had to agree with them all. The best he could offer publicly was to suggest they air their views at the next management committee meeting, or at the AGM. The latter was not a real option as it was several months away, and all would be forgotten by then.

The next evening Jack was in chambers. Just before 6.00pm when the diary had been put to bed for the next working day, he told the receptionist Margaret to go home and then shut the clerks' room door behind him. The clerks knew something was up as their door was never shut. Jack started by telling the clerks what had happened at the ECM, and followed by saying that they were losing four members of the civil team.

"Oh my God" was the general response from the clerks seated around the central table in their room. They had never experienced four members all leaving at the same time and realised it could be a disaster for chambers and their jobs.

Jack continued. "Guys, for our part we are going to do two things. One, we carry on as normal, but with more effort to win new business for those who remain. It is time to go the extra mile, and then a marathon on top." Everyone nodded in approval.

"Two, we print out a list of all the solicitors who instruct Sarah Ryman, Stephen Savage, Monty Evans and Tim Shaw. Break the list down between the five of us, making sure we each pick the ones we know the best, and we ring every single one. Tell them counsel is moving at the weekend, and whilst we would very much like to keep their valued instructions in chambers, we will respect any decision they make." Jack took silence to mean further agreement.

"So no one can point the figure at Barcourt Chambers to allege we have tried to steal clients. Then we keep the list, and in a few weeks' time, we hit them all again to try to get them back. By then, with any luck Richard and his gang of incompetents will have pissed them off to the point we can get them all back, and more. Got it?"

More silence so Jack concluded. "Right, now let's shut up shop and get down to the WI. I'm buying and if Murray or any of his cronies start bragging, don't react. Just take it on the chin. Richard's mine. OK?"

The team felt better but even though they knew they had no right to do so. At least Jack had given them a plan, and they all agreed it was the right thing to do in the circumstances. There were lots of unanswered questions, and they knew that in due course, when the time was right, Jack would answer them all. Right now, it was a needs to know basis only. They trusted Jack.

Jack confided in Jason at the Wiltshire Inn that evening after the lads had gone home with a few beers inside them, plus a couple of chasers to help them over the day. Jason stayed as he knew Jack would tell him what he could.

Jack gave him the full story about Sarah Ryman, as well as his conversation with Richard Murray at Carey Street, and the behaviour of Savage, Evans and Shaw.

Jack also went into detail about the fiasco at the ECM, and the complaints about how Charles Wadsworth had handled the event.

As soon as Jack had finished and sensing the mood of chambers could turn against Charles Wadsworth, Jason asked the most relevant question first. "So how do you get rid of a head of chambers, Jack?"

"Good question Jason. The members can do it via a vote of no confidence in him, but that is not likely to happen. We are more likely to see members either individually or in groups excise their rights with their feet. And that in turn could result in chambers imploding. Not a happy prospect for any of us."

Jason struggled to sip his beer as he listened further to Jack. "There is one way we could try without it potentially back firing on us, or more likely me." "Go on, how?" asked Jason. Jack replied "Get him a judicial appointment".

Jack and Jason both knew that persuading a good QC to take a pay cut of at least fifty percent and become a Circuit judge was never easy. Only those who were struggling in private practice, usually well past their sell-by date, were interested in applying, and they were not the type of candidates the Lord Chancellor would favour.

"Jason, I am not about to let Charles Wadsworth QC ruin all our hard work and stand by waiting for members to leave. He have to be proactive about getting a new head of chambers."

Jason replied. "I agree, but that won't be easy on either count. What if Charles Wadsworth doesn't want to go, and even if he does, who would take his place? We just don't have a charismatic silk to galvanise chambers and lead the members forward."

The two clerks sat in the WI for a couple of hours, and in that time did not encounter any of the clerks from Carey Street. Both did not find this odd. Jason remarked: "I suppose Murray has told his lads to keep away from us to minimise the risk of anything going wrong before the weekend."

Jack agreed. "I'd do the same. They want to get all their existing briefs for the four moving in and their aged debt over to their system before they start bragging. I don't have a problem with that, but heaven help any one of them who starts crowing in my presence."

Jason reflected. "I feel very sorry for Sarah tonight. She is a good barrister, and she did not deserve to be treated that way. Mind you, she brought it on herself, and she is going to have to sort her drugs problem sooner rather than later. If she gets caught again, all this could come out, and her career at the Bar will then be over, once and for all.

"I agree. She needs help. But does she recognise she does?"

As Jason finished his drink, Jack looked at his watch. "I think I am going to stay in Town tonight. Barbara is not expecting me. I warned her the after effects of the ECM might take a while to sort out, and I would need to be around for any post mortem. Do you want another?"

Jason declined and left while Jack was making sure with the landlord Michael that he could have a room for the night. "Sure Jack. Your usual is available."

Jack regularly used a room at the back of the Wiltshire Inn to avoid the traffic noise from the Strand, and it was one of only three rooms which were en-suite with a full sized bath. He loved a good soak at the end of the day. It helped melt away the blues and allowed him thinking time. He had heard about a solicitor charging a client for thinking time in the bath, and the court had upheld the fee. Jack was not in the same position but he would make someone pay for his thoughts and the cost of the room.

Jack decided he deserved a Cointreau on ice, his favourite night cap. He called over to the bar: "Michael, oranges please!"

Michael placed a double Cointreau on ice on the bar, knowing Jack liked a proper measure. He then placed a second identical drink alongside the first on the bar. "Are you joining me Michael? Have you had a hard day too?" Michael looked up. "No thanks, Jack. You will have company in a few minutes, and I don't play gooseberry."

Jack's eyes lit up. He did not need to ask any more questions to which he already knew the answers. "Thank you, Michael."

As Jack sat down at his table with both glasses, Elizabeth Richardson walked into the bar and approached him. "Well fancy meeting you. Do you come here often?" she asked.

"I come as often as I can!" he replied. Jack gave her a warm kiss on the cheek as they were in the public bar. "Beth, this is a lovely surprise. How did you know I was here?"

Jack's internal male instincts acted like a body alarm clock which warned him when his body was going to indulge in sexual activity. It knew when the line had been crossed and intercourse was going to happen, as if he was turning from male think to animal instinct. In that respect, he was like most other red-blooded males, only more alert to the possibility of sex.

Whenever Beth came into the room, Jack's instincts kicked in big time. The couple had gone past the verbal foreplay stage in their relationship months ago so they could talk freely without serious flirting, although Beth liked to play with Jack's emotions some of the time. Jack did not take Beth for granted, but knew her arrival signalled her intentions for the rest of the evening.

Beth answered. "I've been covering a case for Geoffrey Ashdown across the road in the RCJ, and when it finished this afternoon I rang your chambers. The word on the street is that Sarah Ryman has left your chambers to join Carey Street, and she is taking three more with her. Apparently the gossip is that you had an ECM yesterday to sort it out. How did it go?"

"News travels fast! It was fine, just given me and the clerks a load more work to sort out, but next week we should be back to normal.

It is a shame to lose Sarah, but it could not be helped."

"Has she gone for pastures greener?" asked Beth. Jack replied: "For now, but watch this space." Jack wanted to change the subject as he did not want to be forced into lying to Beth. There was always the risk he would be found out. She had a knack of uncovering the truth.

"Enough of me. How did your case go?"

Beth launched into a moan about Geoffrey Ashdown, and more particularly his choice of counsel. "Why he didn't come to you with this high value case only he knows. It was perfect for your James Campbell. A messy case on liability that needed a good thinker on his feet, and we would have got home one hundred percent. Instead he went for a senior guy at Carey Street who, rather than fight in court, recommended at the lunch break to our client that they take a 25 percent cut for contributory negligence which was on offer. You know, Jack, there's always a litigation risk, but he would not let the client have their day in court."

Jack smiled to calm Beth down. "There's no accounting for taste. I mean, you're here aren't you!" It worked so he changed the subject. "Enough of work. Fancy another Cointreau? Actually, let's take one with us upstairs. I was going to have a lovely long soak in the bath. You are welcome to join me. You could scrub some of the parts other scrubbers can't reach!"

"Careful Jack, flattery can get you into trouble!"

Jack carried their fresh glasses as he let Beth lead the way. Once inside the bedroom, Jack stood in front of Beth and admired her long dark hair. "Looks like the day will have a happy ending after all." Beth kissed him firmly with her open mouth and replied. "Oh I do hope so! Now you run the bath and I will be in for a good scrubbing!"

The next morning, after an English breakfast, the full Monty courtesy of Michael at the Wiltshire Inn, Jack had said his good byes to Beth for now, and was in chambers by 7.45am. He was going to lead by example and get on with the daily tasks, some of which were his to do, but most were for his clerks to do. Opening the post and DX, the lawyers private mail service, would speed up the morning for everyone. This meant the lads would have time to set about making the calls to solicitors about the four members departing that day.

As the clerks drifted in around 8.30am, the head of chambers poked his head round the corner of the door. "Jack, a word please."

Jack followed Charles Wadsworth into his room. "Close the door, Jack."

Wadsworth let off steam. "Recent events, or non-events, were a fiasco. I don't know what Miss Ryman thought she was playing at, but failing to turn up to answer the allegations against her was not acceptable. Losing Savage and the other two is bad enough, and I know she had to go, but the manner of her departure was just not good enough. In any other circumstances and if it were not for the bad publicity Jack, I would be going straight to the head of chambers at Carey Street."

Jack was about to suggest that would not be a good idea when Charles continued. "I know that would not be wise in the circumstances, but she has made me look a fool."

Jack had to bite his lip. He thought: "No, you did that all by yourself!" Instead Jack nodded in agreement and tried to change the subject, or at least in part. "I have spoken to the clerks and we are implementing a plan today to speak to all the affected solicitors. We will retain as many as we can."

Charles was pleased but Jack's comments did not wholly deflect his thoughts. "I am the one left placating disgruntled members of chambers. It really is not good enough."

The two further discussed how Jack and the clerks would put a brave face on the situation, and Charles expressed his gratitude for their coming efforts. As Jack got up to leave, Charles added: "Jack, I am not sure I am cut out for this head of chambers stuff. I'd hand it over tomorrow if there were someone who could do a better job."

Jack felt a little pep talk was needed. "You'll be fine, sir. Your former senior clerk used to remind us we are judged on how we handle a crisis. It will all work out, mark my words."

As Jack walked back into the clerks' room, he thought he just might have the opening he was looking for to get rid of Charles Wadsworth QC. Over a coffee with Jason later that morning, he confided in him. "Jason, you remember in the WI last night we talked about getting rid of the head of chambers?" Jason nodded. "Well, he may just have given me an idea!"

7 THE BODYGUARD

The specially convened ECM had been an Extra-ordinary Chambers Meeting in every sense of the words and an unsettling event for the whole of chambers. Indeed some of the senior members could not recall a meeting ever being called before to vote on the expulsion of one of their colleagues. Normally they expected on the very few occasions it was necessary for them to consider a member's conduct that the head of chambers would have quietly got the problem sorted behind closed doors.

Then there was the chambers management committee. They were furious that they had not been consulted by the head of chambers and that he had taken matters into his own hands. As James Campbell put it at their meeting a few weeks later, "What is the point of having a constitution and an elected management committee if the old style dictatorship is going to prevail?"

Jack attended that meeting and felt he should come to the aid of his head of chambers. "His decision was based on the evidence as he saw it, sir."

James Campbell was not impressed. "Jack, to this day none of us have seen the evidence. Have you?" Jack replied "No, I haven't seen it either." Ouch, thought Jack, hoping that little white lie didn't come back to bite him. It was true he had never seen the picture on Nathan Blake's mobile phone, but he did have the rest of the story.

Campbell went on. "If we had been consulted, I for one would have tried to convince Sarah Ryman to leave chambers quietly without the need to air our dirty laundry at an ECM. Nobody wants the reputation of chambers to be damaged by this woman's actions, but if she had not gone then chambers would have to act. Calling an ECM was unnecessary, a knee-jerk reaction that made the affair public whilst the members remained in the dark."

At the one end of the scale of dissatisfaction some of the committee members expressed surprise at the failure to be consulted by the head of chambers. At the other end including James Campbell, some wanted Charles Wadsworth to resign.

Totally unaware of the trail of wreckage they had left behind them, life carried on for Stephen Savage, Monty Evans and Tim Shaw who all still regularly huddled into the corner by the fire in the tap room at the Red Lion. Old habits die hard.

They had been in just the same place and position on the evening they waited for the outcome of the ECM at Barcourt chambers, the meeting they had collectively decided not to attend.

They had chosen not to attend as they already knew what the meeting was for and the outcome. On this occasion they were not following the unspoken rule that said if you did not attend a meeting you could later criticise any decisions taken. They preferred not to be asked any difficult questions which might have led to a problem for them personally. So it was best to stay away.

However, that course of action meant that none were aware of Sarah Ryman failing to attend, and had no idea that she too was going to join Carey Street that weekend along with them.

Richard Murray knew where he would find his three new male members of his chambers. He popped his head round the tap room door and asked: "Can I get anyone a drink?" Everyone declined but invited Richard to join them, which he did with a glass of red wine.

They discussed various administrative issues regarding the move for the three into Carey Street, and Murray promised help from his team to get everyone settled in as soon as possible. He mentioned that they had already started to work through the firms of solicitors by ringing to protect as much of their work as possible. He preferred to focus on the opportunities for new business which was the theme of his marketing to get them on board in the first place.

Murray then chose his moment to mention the bit of news he did not think had reached Stephen Savage, Monty Evans or Tim Shaw.

"I have a bit of extra good news which you may not be aware of. Barcourt has lost one more civil counsel who will be joining us over the weekend as well as your good selves." He paused to see if the three faces gave away any clues.

Monty Evans broke the silence. "And who would that be?" he asked in a matter of fact way. The three showed no signs of knowing what was coming, so Murray continued.

"Well, I think you are the first to know that Sarah Ryman is joining Carey Street chambers." Monty Evans continued in the same vein. "Oh really, that will be nice."

Tim Shaw thought he should say something too. "Yes, indeed. Do you know why she is leaving Barcourt?" Murray had already prepared his stock response to this question. He was expecting to be quizzed by members who had heard about the ECM, but not the reason for it.

"Yes. I understand she wants a fresh start and saw an opportunity when she learnt you guys were coming to Carey Street. I spoke to Jack Temple and he was instrumental in her jumping ship."

The gang of three felt they could all breathe a little easier now, overlooking the fact that Jack Temple would not give up anyone or anything he did not want to, at least without a fight. Stephen joined in. "Ah, very good. I am pleased Sarah will be joining us" he said, spoken like a man who had been at Carey Street for years rather than hours. He added "No doubt we will all get on like a house on fire."

Richard left soon after as there were plenty more he wanted to tell his breaking news to. The gang of three looked blankly into the fire that was beginning to die down. Tim Shaw broke the silence.

"He doesn't know, does he? He hasn't a clue" Monty was next. "I don't think so. Unless he is under orders to say nothing. But I don't see Jack telling him any more than he needed to. No, I am sure he doesn't have a clue. Jack has played him to a tee."

The most relieved of all was Stephen Savage, following his blunder by telling all to his then ex-girlfriend and member at Carey Street chambers. He could not say anything to the other two, and he would have to live in his new chambers now with not only her presence, but also Sarah Ryman, the cause of the whole incident in the first place. Savage realised he was going to have to be very careful in the future. Finally he commented in general terms.

"Well gentlemen" he said raising his glass. "Here's to a good few days' work, a satisfactory outcome and to the tap room. Long may we enjoy good company, good ale, and the warm friendship of our beloved inn?" he raised his glass and proclaimed: "To the Red Lion!"

The other two responded in kind with "Here here!"

The departure of one female in chambers brought forward the arrival of another. Whilst mulling over these recent events, Jack concluded that it was high time they had a female in the clerks' room. He was well aware of the demand for a female clerk to sit between the female barristers in chambers and their female instructing solicitors, and it would be just the right time to generate a buzz in the clerks' room and chambers generally.

For the socialising side of the clerks' room they needed someone who would join in the fun but at the same time be a steadying influence. Margaret in reception did not want a clerking job. She was happy meeting and greeting solicitors and their clients, and preferred to be at home once chambers front door was closed each day. Jack decided she did not want to handle the pressure.

Having a female in the clerks' room just might help the lads grow up a bit and mature. Jack could not make too much of that point as he had been a bit of a lad himself, indeed still liked a night out to feel he was still one of the team.

One of the stories circulating the Temple at the time focused on a young female clerk Jenny James. She was no relation to the barrister Christopher James, and had come to Jack's attention following an assault incident she had been involved in. He decided to watch her in clerking action at a civil listing meeting. These were regular clerks' meetings with the court listing officer to get cases listed for trial hopefully for counsel's convenience and to avoid double booking.

Jenny was a little out of her comfort zone, having learnt handling criminal cases in her early clerking years. So this was a good opportunity to watch Jenny James battling with her male counterparts. He could witness first hand for himself how she coped under a bit of pressure, and whether she would stand up for her guvnors.

Jack was good at protecting his own guvnors at such meetings. Without seeing the other barrister's diary, he could see through their clerk's prevarications and get the dates he wanted. And he was up for a bit of prevaricating himself, especially if he gained a few points on a competing clerk. Since he became senior clerk, he got Christian Bennett to attend the listing meetings unless he had good reason to attend himself.

On the day Jack went along, Jenny James had a rough time with Richard Murray. Each had a senior barrister on opposite sides of a big case. Richard was throwing his considerable weight about. It was completely unnecessary as his counsel would have more gaps in his diary than anyone could fill. He just didn't like female clerks, and thought they should be banned from attending such meetings. Her presence meant the male banter had to be restricted. He felt women were encroaching on male preserves, and regarded relaxation of male-only membership as the thin end of the wedge.

"What next? Knitting patterns and darning classes at listing meetings?" Richard proclaimed. He resorted to gender attacks when he was losing, and Jenny realised this as she dug her heels in. She stuck to the point on her case.

She argued "My counsel has only one slot for the next two months. It is not in the interests of the parties to delay. I submit the dates I have offered are reasonable." The court listing officer listened carefully and took her side which to any half sensible clerk was for the particular case the right thing to do.

Murray lost and stormed out of the meeting. Jenny took praise from the listing officer, and Jack thought she would be a safe pair of hands to send along in the future.

A couple of days later, Jack suggested a lunchtime meeting with Jason. A favourite of Jack's for a quiet off the record meeting was the Old Bank of England pub off the Strand. It was an evening venue for counsel so lunchtimes were quiet. The pub had enclosed seating areas on the first floor where in times past major financial deals were brokered in relative secrecy.

Jack bought lunch. Jason knew there was no such thing as a free lunch so was waiting for the inevitable request. He did not have to wait long.

Jack casually asked him: "So what is the story about a female clerk rescuing a male barrister in distress?" Jason smiled as he loved to tell this story.

"Oh, it's a good one. Apparently one of the guvnors at Old Bailey chambers was walking down Kingsway early one evening when he was approached by a couple of hoodies. There was a scuffle and one took out a blade. Jenny James, so the tale goes, was on the other side of the dual carriageway and saw what was going down. She leapt over the central barriers and laid into the lad with the knife. According to counsel, she took him out with some kind of high kick that knocked him out cold. The other lad took one look and fled. Pretty cool don't you think?"

Jack was not impressed. "I see. And just how much of that is fact, and how much is an embellished story line?" Jason would have none of Jack's remarks. "It is all true. One of the clerks at Old Bailey apparently took a photocopy of their counsel's statement he did for the police, and it is all gospel. Why do you ask?"

Jack thought for a couple of moments. He had made up his mind he wanted Jenny to become their first female clerk. He knew the rest of his team would not be happy to begin with as the dynamics of their clerks' room would change. They could debate it all day but Jack knew it was the right thing.

He asked Jason "What do you think about her joining Barcourt as a first junior clerk?"

"Well, she is female, in case you hadn't noticed!" exclaimed Jason. His tone implied that he felt Jack was wrong to consider a female clerk. Jack was serious. "It's about time the lads grew up a bit, and showed a bit of respect. I think she would be good for everyone, guvnors as well as clerks."

Jason was taken aback. "That's a bit rich coming from you, don't you think? Anyway, just because she is a kick boxer doesn't mean she is any good as a clerk."

Jack was waiting for that point to be raised and replied. "I watched her at the last civil listing meeting. She stood up to Richard Murray and won the listing officers praise. She is good, Jason, and she can look after herself."

Jason had heard enough to realise Jack's mind was made up. He accepted Jack was right to introduce an additional clerk into their team. He was well aware they were short staffed, and now would be good to try a female in the clerks' room.

"Jason, I want you to get a message to Jenny James and set up a meeting for me this week. Suggest somewhere she is comfortable with and make it after hours." Jason conceded and replied: "Will do."

Jenny James, aged 25, had a slim but not petite build with hidden strong muscles and carried no spare flesh. She worked out in the gym several times a week, but focusing on her core strengths rather than muscle show. At five feet eight inches tall with jet black hair down over her shoulders, she was a real head turner around the Temple in her tight white blouse and black skirt. Jack considered her to be a real asset if he could get her on board.

Jenny was known amongst her own clerks and around the Temple as "JJ". That was until news of her bravery became common knowledge. Thereafter she picked up the nickname "The Bodyguard" and was flattered to be associated with Kevin Costner, but preferred JJ. She had come to clerking via her uncle, himself a senior clerk in the Temple, who had arranged with a colleague a work experience job in chambers as a school leaver. She loved it, telling her uncle afterwards that is was all "just common sense and attention to detail." He thought she would have a good career in chambers, with every prospect of becoming a senior clerk.

She was a quick learner and made friends easily, both male and female. In her spare time, her main hobby was as a Taekwondo instructor. She could handle herself, and was not intimidated by male bullies. Her sport gave her the confidence to sort out any situation. When she had seen the two lads approaching her counsel on Kingsway, she just took control. The Taekwondo gave the clerks something to tease her about but the story of her bravery gave her respect. Nobody was willing to test her skills which meant she did not have to put up with some of the male banter.

Jack met Jenny in a café off Holborn at the end of a busy week. She seemed genuinely flattered by his interest in her career, and did not take any persuading. She had spoken to her now retired uncle who gave her the thumbs up on joining Barcourt. He told her to "Watch and listen. Jack will teach you what you don't already know."

Jack sat down having brought over two coffees. He asked Jenny "So, how much notice do you have to give at Old Bailey?" "Wow, that was a bit quick!" she replied. He explained "We wouldn't be seated here if you didn't want the job, would we?"

Jenny smiled in recognition that Jack was right. Why else would he have asked to see her? He continued. "You do realise you will be the first female clerk ever at Barcourt chambers and we have some outdated chauvinists. Some will say that includes me!"

"That is the way all around the Temple and the chambers in Lincoln's Inn. I want to be known as a good clerk. The rest I can handle." Jack liked her attitude. "You'll go far. Let me guide you up the ladder."

The terms of her future employment were easy to agree, and Jenny was happy as she walked off to start her weekend, knowing that in another four weeks' time she would be joining Barcourt chambers.

Jack's next project was to organise a bonding weekend away for his team, and he wanted Jenny to be included. He appreciated it would take some organising, and the funding would not be easy. He would have to persuade the management committee it was in everyone's' best interests. In the meantime, he needed to integrate Jenny into the clerks' room.

Late on the Friday afternoon before Jenny was due to start the following Monday and when the diary had been put to bed, Jack addressed the clerks in their clerks' room.

"Mr Dillon, you are going to have to be on your best behaviour next week." Dillon responded: "I'm always on my best behaviour, Jack" he said. "That's what worries me, Dillon. And the same goes for everyone. Over the weekend you are going to have to rethink your attitude towards ladies, show more respect, and change your ways."

Christian could see a problem. "I'm not sure a weekend is enough time for Mr Dillon. And I'll struggle to change the habits of a lifetime. Besides, there is nothing wrong with how I deal with the fairer sex."

Jason pipped up "I did warn you Jack. These lads are pretty set in their ways." Jack was not giving up, and laid into Dillon.

"Christian, as of Monday morning the empty desk next to you will be occupied by the first female clerk to join Barcourt Chambers. Dillon, you will be responsible for making her feel at home, showing her the ropes and the way we do things, and it will be on your head if she does not feel welcome. Do you understand?"

The mood changed as the lads could envisage their cozy way of life disappearing out of the window. Jack continued.

"This will be a culture shock for some members of chambers, and they need to see that we as a team embrace this change." Jason added "You all know the female members of chambers at times want to deal with a female clerk, as do the growing numbers of female solicitors. The world is changing. It's time we changed with it."

Jack was tempted to ask Jason what had changed his tune, but there was no need. He appreciated the support from his number two.

Come the Monday morning, everyone was in by eight o'clock, including Jenny James. The clerks' room had a buzz of excitement as all the lads were in newly pressed suits, cleaned shoes, ironed shirts and bright ties. Jenny looked as smart as usual, thought Jack.

Dillon did the introductions although most had met Jenny around the

Temple at some point before. Members of chambers popped in to say hello, the men briefly whilst the ladies took their time to let Jenny know they were available to help if she needed any.

As the atmosphere calmed down, and the daily routines got under way, the lads' inquisitive nature got the better of one or two them. Dillon was first to crack.

"So Jenny "he asked. "What do you like to be called? Jenny, Jen or JJ?"

Jenny replied: "Any of those. At home if I get Jennifer, I know I am in trouble. Nobody calls me Jen. The most common is JJ."

Christian joined in. "I suppose since your heroics, the name "the Bodyguard" springs to mind?" Jenny smiled as she was just waiting for someone to bring that story up.

"If that's what you prefer, then it's fine with me, although I would rather not brag about it. It's over now, and unlikely to be repeated."

Dillon turned his attention to Jack. "So Jack, is that why you employed JJ. You felt you needed a Bodyguard!"

Jack realised he was going to get loads of stick for breaking the male dominance of the clerks' room. He would be teased about having to get himself protection. Jokes would be made up at his expense. He was not bothered.

At the end of the day, Jack knew he had won over the rest of his team. The female members of chambers treated Jenny like a younger sister and thought they were protecting her from the worse aspects of the male banter in chambers which they had all suffered from time to time. In reality, Jenny was perfectly capable of looking after herself, but she was pleased they showed interest in her.

The events of those past few weeks surrounding the departure of Sarah Ryman and the three cronies had put a huge burden on the clerks at Barcourt Chambers. They all realised that if they were not careful, chambers would implode putting them all potentially out of a job. It was true most of the clerks would pick up work in another set, but there was a stigma about being part of a failed chambers that none wanted to experience. It was all too easy for barristers to blame their clerks when things did not go well, never contemplating the cause may lie closer to home.

As a result of the newfound excitement around the clerks' room, the following month witnessed the clerks attracting new business and lots of extra cases for just about every member of chambers. The diary was as full as Jack had known it ever to be. All the male clerks wanted to impress Jenny, and she played her part in promoting the benefits of having a female team player, particularly for clients where a female contact was right.

Jack had driven them hard and so decided a reward was in order, and he persuaded Charles Wadsworth QC and the Management committee that a bonding weekend was needed for his team. It was a thank you as well as a chance for the team to socialise and not talk about cases for a few hours, and most important to give the lads a good opportunity to get to know Jenny out of the clerks' room.

The head of chambers saw this first adventure as forward thinking and progressive for his chambers, and would show the doubters he was up to speed with modern staffing techniques. He told Jack when confirming approval by the management committee that chambers would pay for their flights and hotel accommodation, but the staff would have to pay for their own food and drinks: "Jack, the committee think this is an excellent idea. Your team have had a difficult few months and come through it well. We don't want to encourage excess, but you can take £500 out of petty cash to buy them all a couple of drinks."

Jack broke the news to the team on a Friday evening and asked them to all turn up on Monday morning with dates for a weekend they could do, and one suggestion each of a suitable venue. He did say there were only a couple of rules.

"First off, we will go from chambers bang on six but not before, and must be back home by nine on the Sunday evening. Secondly, the venue must not be focused on a sporting venue or event. I don't want to spend the weekend glued to a TV either. Lastly, it will be outside the main football season. Got it?"

Jason was the one who did not support a premier league team, so he approved the rules without hesitation. Dillon was not so sure. "Jack, does that mean I will have to go for a walk?" Christian took the opportunity to put Dillon down.

"Don't panic, Mr Dillon. You'll have the Bodyguard with you!"

Next Monday, Jason asked if everyone had a slip of paper with their respective dates, and their suggested venue. They handed him their slip, and he opened them in a conference room with Jack.

"Most have put several dates, so I don't see any problem if you want to pick a weekend towards the end of May. The bank holiday weekend works as people can recover at home on the Monday. It depends on whether you want to be at home then."

Jack looked at his private diary. "That would work. I will stay on for a few days after and get Barbara to join me with the lad. She deserves a break, and I only have to pay for their flights. So where does everyone want to go?"

Jason looked again at all the entries and concluded: "It looks like Spain, Jack. There are likely to be plenty of flights, a short travel time. If we leave at 6.00pm, we can be in a bar somewhere by 11.00pm, no problem." Jack looked at the choices of venue and thought Spain was a good option.

"Ok, how about the Beach Palace at La Manga in Spain? We can fly to Murcia, the theme for the weekend can be sangria. What goes on tour definitely stays on tour. Saturday we can have a break from drinking. Jason can organise in advance a trip to a vineyard!" Jason laughed as he had picked that venue.

Jack continued with more ideas as they occurred to him. "The lads can share twin rooms to keep the cost down which will please chambers. Just you, me and Jenny will have single rooms. We'll make sure the room rate includes a full English breakfast, so apart from a snack during the day, which can be liquid, we only need to pay for an evening meal and drinks."

Jason was excited at the prospect of his own room, mainly because it recognised his growing seniority and concluded: "Sounds like a good plan to me!"

Jason was tasked with sorting out the flights and rooms, and downloaded some brochures with all the facilities on offer.

Jack called the clerks' room to order and laid out the plan. Christian was the first to respond whilst everyone else was buried in the glossy brochures. "Looks like it could be nice and hot. Jenny, will you take your bikini with you for a bit of sun worship?" he asked, addressing his question to the whole team.

Jenny replied "Only if you promise to take yours!" Everyone winced at the thought, except Jack who thought to himself how well Jenny coped with the lads. "Gordon," he said, "You'll have to do better than that."

James Dunn was busy making a few calculations. "So if we arrive late on the Friday evening, we'll be too late for a meal. A sandwich at the airport will do."

Dillon suggested the rule "eating is cheating" should apply to the whole weekend, but Christian thought that was carrying the drinking just a bit too far. Jason agreed, and Jack said "I have to remember some of the trip, as I have to report back to the management committee."

Dillon reminded Jack that "What happens on tour stays on tour" but accepted that they had to talk about something when they got back, otherwise members who were paying would be suspicious."

So in the spirit of good camaraderie and team spirit, Jack was able to report to the next management committee meeting after their return from La Manga that "the whole experience was a resounding success. Everyone behaved themselves as you would expect when representing Barcourt chambers abroad."

"Well done Jack" said the head of chambers. "Everyone certainly seemed on good form when you got back. Would you repeat the exercise again?" Jack reflected on some of the stories which would remain on tour, and replied "Oh, I think so."

8 "HAIL CAESAR!"

Chambers had settled down a bit since the departure of Sarah Ryman and the three cronies, Stephen Savage, Monty Evans and Tim Shaw, but Jack had learnt to never rest on his laurels. He knew that a problem could come up and bite him without warning at any time. He was expecting the next issue before it had arrived.

The departure of Sarah Ryman in particular annoyed Jack. He felt she had been poorly treated. Although he knew that if there was any truth in the allegations, then it was inevitable that she would leave. Some of her solicitor clients had gone with her to Carey Street, and he was content that he had not tried to damage her reputation with those solicitors who had followed her. He rose above such low tactics and it made him feel good as well as leaving the door open for the solicitors to return. His reputation was more important.

That was more than could be said for Richard Murray who had taken every opportunity to steal work from Barcourt, and then some. To say Jack did not like Murray was a major understatement. He hated everything he stood for.

Opportunities to get one up on Murray personally were limited, so Jack had to rely on vicarious and cunning tactics through his clerks to get at Richard's team.

There were a few occasions when Jack and Richard would attend the same pubs or professional events, and whilst Jack and his lads would mingle in pairs to work the room, Murray would stay routed to the spot flanked by at least two of his clerks. Jack had instructed his team to publicly refer to them as the "Lavender Hill Mob", a description which annoyed them in particular Richard.

It had reached the point that when the Carey Street clerks saw anyone from Barcourt clerks' room approaching, they would disperse as if they had caught the whiff of something unpleasant approaching them. Consequently Jack knew he had won that little battle.

One of the main social events of the year was always the annual The Legal Charities Garden Party. This was the chance to check out who had invited whom, or even who had not invited whom, and who was available to be courted for work.

Such an occasion, from a clerking as well as counsels' point of view, brought to the surface elements of jealousy and snobbery. It was the ideal opportunity to remind those considered to be of a lower rank of their unfortunate station in the legal world.

Such an imaginary divide between the elite and the rest existed between clerks as well as barristers. There was an apparent "North South" divide along an equator otherwise known as the Strand. In the clerking world the boundary divided the elite Chancery sets to the North and the common law sets to the South.

The Strand ran for just over three quarters of a mile from Trafalgar Square to Temple Bar outside the RCJ where the Temple Bar Memorial stood. It was a great dragon statue atop statues of Queen Victoria and the Prince of Wales. At this point the road became Fleet Street passing Chancery Lane, the home of the Law Society.

Those clerks in chambers on the South of the Strand and Fleet Street aspired to work in Chancery chambers to the North of the Strand in places like Old Square and New Square. None of the clerks located in chambers to the North would take a step down the clerking ladder of success by accepting a post in the South such as Paper Buildings or King's Bench Walk [abbreviated by all to "KBW"].

The exception to the unwritten rule was Carey Street chambers. Their premises were located on the road behind the Royal Courts of Justice leading to New Square and Lincoln's Inn, the home for several of the chancery chambers. That put them on the Northern side of the Strand and so with the elite. At least that is how they viewed their importance, a view not shared by any of the other chambers on either side of the Strand, and especially not by Jack.

As far as Jack was concerned, Carey Street chambers was a common law set and as they did not undertake any Chancery work so could not class themselves as amongst the elite on the Northern side of the Strand. Needless to say, Richard Murray took the opposite view.

Such snobbery amongst clerks was displayed best at the annual Legal Charities Garden Party, usually held in June. There was nothing like a warm summer evening and alcohol to bring out the best in dresses, and the worst in drunken behaviour. Three charities usually benefited, one being the Institute of Barristers' Clerks' Benevolent Fund. The event was billed as "Networking and catching up with old friends and perhaps meeting new ones!"

All it took was a few glasses of bubbly on an empty stomach, and once the main guvnors had moved on to the swanky restaurants, the clerks and younger solicitors especially would get started on the banter that inevitably would lead to the evening entertainment.

The few female clerks, mostly new to the event, were heavily outnumbered by the lads who had been around for few years and knew how to hold their drink and could banter with the best. Of course there were exceptions to the rule, the black sheep in the flock, and Jenny James was one. She came to her first garden party before she joined Barcourt chambers and had held her own.

On the morning of the garden party that year, Dillon and Christian reminded Jenny of her performance the year before. "Are you taking balloons with you this year JJ?" asked Dillon. "Yes, the bodyguard needs to be prepared for her next rescue mission!" added Christian. Jenny just smiled knowing it was better not to rise to their bait.

The lads had been referring to the balloon incident from the previous year. On that occasion, a junior clerk at Alpha Chambers, Peter

Underwood, had been asked by his senior clerk to go along with him to help serve out the drinks and nibbles. He had gone along with their first junior clerk who at that time was Jenny. She had warned Peter to keep sober, at least until the barristers from their chambers had left.

Peter was a small lad and at the age of twenty four was unlikely to grow any more. He did not hold his drink too well. To compensate, he had a wicked sense of humour which made him an easy target for practical jokers. He had the ability to laugh at his own misfortune as well as at the antics of the other clerks. Some from his own chambers thought he was more suited to being a comedian, but ribbed him by suggesting nobody would know he was a stand-up comedian as they could not see if he was stood up. This was a regular joke amongst their clerks and Peter took all of this in good humour for making people laugh was his forte.

Peter loved his job and had always wanted to be a senior clerk. He fancied his chances with the ladies in his chambers. Indeed, he fancied his chances with most women. His stock joke was "well if they've got a pulse, they're good enough for me!"

He and Jenny did the business at the garden party and took their reward back to chambers with them in the form of two bottles of red wine each. They saw that as one bottle each and two for their colleagues and went into Alpha Chambers clerks' room bearing their gifts which went down well with the other clerks.

As soon as their diary had been put to bed, Peter announced that he was still thirsty, and suggested the entire team decamp to the Red Leicester, the nearest pub to chambers. Nobody needed any encouragement as the red wine had merely served to encourage everyone's appetite for a session.

As Jenny walked into the pub, which was lively with plenty of clerks hitting the chasers hard, she realised the night could turn messy.

Within minutes she watched Peter lay his head back on the bar so the barman could pour a shot of Tequila directly into his mouth straight form the bottle. The rest of his team followed suit. The banter was mainly based on male testosterone, and whilst Jenny was not concerned for her own safety, there were one or two lads already looking to be out of control.

Peter may have been drinking more than his small frame could reasonably take in a short space of time, but he was well aware of his physical disadvantage against the big boys. It was not long before he announced that he wanted to move onto the next drinking establishment. Jenny realised too that Peter was no match for the other lads, and some fresh air and somewhere to deposit the alcohol his system was likely to reject at short notice was a good idea.

The pub had been decked out for a lunchtime birthday party with lots of streamers and balloons left over which Peter had gradually been collecting. He looked to Jenny like a kid in a sweetie shop and she knew he would not let the balloons go easily. A better tactic to get him out of the pub was to let him take the balloons with him.

"Come on, Peter" She said. "Let's tie as many balloons as we can around your trouser belt."

"Good call JJ" he replied and proceeded to collect more balloons. With both his hands full and needing to steady himself, it was down to Jenny to struggle and undo his belt enough to tie well over a dozen balloons on.

Mission accomplished, Peter thanked Jenny. "Marvellous". Jenny was pleased with her handy work and replied "Come on, Peter, let's hit the road." Getting him out of the pub door was tricky. As soon as one balloon was pushed into place in the door frame, another would stick out on the wrong side.

Outside the cool evening air hit Peter's face and temporarily freshened him up. He was balanced on Jenny's arm as they headed off down the Strand towards the Wiltshire Inn. Jenny knew there would be other clerks in the WI as well, so she could deposit Peter into the care of others when she wanted to go home.

Peter and Jenny looked a pretty picture arm in arm walking down the Strand on the opposite side of the road to the Royal Courts heading towards their next watering hole.

Peter spotted ahead of them a bunch of fifteen to twenty Japanese tourists who were coming out of the Crown Inn, the pub located right in front of the zebra crossing leading to the front door of the RCJ and seemed not to know which direction they should go in next on their brief tour of the West End. They had done the three castles in a day, being Conway, Edinburgh and Windsor, and had a bad dose of coach lag.

As Peter saw the tourists so the tourists spotted Peter. He realised he and his balloons were being observed and so went into acting mode.

Letting go of Jenny's arm he made a pathetic leap forward as if he was going to be lifted into the air and then proceeded to grab with both arms the next lamp post.

Jenny begged him "Oh, no. Come on Peter, no amateur dramatics please. It won't end well." Peter ignored her remarks and called ahead to the tourists who by now were walking towards them thoroughly intrigued by this small man surrounded by party balloons tied to his belt.

He welcomed his long lost friends with "Greetings cousins!" As they got closer Peter could feel the empathy between himself and his fellow small people whom he felt sure would willingly help him in his hour of need.

He tried to leave the security of his lamp post but felt the forces of gravity were unable to keep his feet on the ground as his toes lifted him off. "Help!" he cried, and to Jenny's surprise all the Japanese tourists answered Peter's cry for help. They rushed towards him and grabbed any available part of Peter believing they were preventing him floating off down the Strand. None of them spoke any English but still understood the mission which they had gladly accepted.

Peter and Jenny were now on the kerb next to the zebra crossing which led across the Strand to the RCJ. "Once more, dear cousins, I need your help. This time help me to cross my Rubicon. Tis but a short crossing but fraught with danger lest I float away into the night." As he spoke, Peter pointed towards the RCJ.

After some debate, the Japanese realised that the wide road in front of the courts was far too wide to expect Peter to negotiate to get from one post to another on the far side. There was only one course of action open to them.

Jenny joined in. "Thank you, thank you" she repeated. "Now we have to cross the road" and too pointed to the front of the RCJ. To help she stepped into the road bringing the taxis and busses to a halt.

And so it was, with the traffic stopped in both directions that the procession embarked on its short but mad journey across the Strand carrying Peter, now to be known as "Julius Caesar", and all his balloons wafting in the night breeze. He was carried triumphantly shoulder high as befitted a rock star at his concert. Jenny regretted not having her camera to match all the pictures being taken by the foreign entourage.

On the far side of the Strand the tourists gently returned Peter's feet to the ground making sure he had grabbed a firm hold of the nearest flashing lamp post on the pavement, bowed to him, and set off back across the Rubicon engrossed in viewing the images they had now on their cameras. "Farewell my friends!" shouted Peter who was not heard above the din of taxi and car horns by now impatient with the foreigners' disregard for safety on the English roads.

Although Jenny continued to have trouble with Peter who was now into full theatrical mode, he was willing to make progress towards their destination, the WI, as he was becoming increasingly desperate for the toilet.

Eventually they burst through the doors of the Wiltshire Inn. Their entrance was sufficiently loud to stop the banter long enough for everyone to see who had arrived, realise it was Peter, and then carry on.

The WI was full, including Jack and his team plus a few of their solicitor clients whom they had taken along from the garden party. Christian said it was his round and asked what Jenny and Peter were drinking. She replied "I'll have a glass of red, but Peter has had enough." Several clerks made fun of Peter and tried to burst his balloons as he passed through the crowded pub en route to the gents' toilet.

Jenny told a group of clerks in graphic detail their adventure down the Strand and the Japanese tourists. She played heavily on the role of Julius Caesar crossing the Rubicon which was thoroughly enjoyed by her appreciative audience.

Afterwards Jason was curious and wanted to display his own wit at the expense of Peter as portrayed in the story as a small person. He asked the assembled company "Did Dudley Moore ever play Julius Caesar?"

A debate followed with more wise cracks about the Roman Emperor and the Rubicon. The laughter had just about died down when Peter made his return. "Hail Caesar!" was the chorus. Peter had no idea what they were on about. Jenny concluded "He's forgotten already!"

Peter felt a lot better for his wash and brush-up and decided he could manage a beer, and he was hungry. The drinking motto "Eating is cheating" was not a phrase he could live by. So crisps and nuts were his starter and main course, washed down by a large glass of lager.

It had been a long day and Peter felt the need to sit on a bar stool. He could mask his lack of height from the barmaid and rest his tired body which needed to recover after his exhausting journey down the Strand to the WI.

He engaged in conversation with the barmaid whenever she was not serving. Peter had not seen her in there before and proclaimed to Jenny that the girl was in love with him. Jenny suggested he play it cool which he thought good advice.

The crisps had not yet hit his digestive system, so he moved onto the nuts which the barmaid had kindly placed in a large bowl on the bar, rightly thinking Peter needed all the help he could get to sober up.

His casual theatrical mood took control of Peter again as he decided it was time to impress the young barmaid across the bar from him, and taking the advice of Jenny to play it cool, proceeded to select a suitably large peanut and gently toss it in the air above his head.

Now the clear intention had been to catch the falling peanut in his mouth, but Peter was a bit too slow and wobbly to line himself up for the catch. Indeed that first peanut plopped into his glass of lager. The barmaid thought that was the trick and warmly applauded which was the incentive for Peter to try again.

The chances of Peter succeeding with this trick were remote. He was sitting on a bar stool but his feet did not reach the floor. He tried several times and on each occasion the peanuts landed on the floor. The debris of fallen peanuts around Peter began to accumulate.

He became more determined with every failure to catch at least one peanut in his mouth, but with each attempt Peter was throwing the nut either too high or too wide to stand any chance of success. So in desperation, Peter picked up the bowl of peanuts, emptied the entire contents into his hands and tossed them all at once into the air above him.

By now most of the other clerks were watching Peter as he leant back, shut his eyes and opened his mouth. As could have been predicted by anyone there, Peter leant back too far, lost his balance on the stool and fell backwards to the floor where he lay motionless.

"So that was the fall of Julius Caesar then!" shouted Jason. Most laughed as Jenny shook her head in disapproval and bent over Peter. "Call an ambulance, someone" she asked in a resigned tone as she witnessed a small pool of blood appear under Peter's head.

Jenny's nursing skills were not lost on Jack who was seeing her for the first time out of a clerking context. He had been impressed by her story-telling and now was impressed by her caring nature.

So when there was any mention of balloons, or crossing the Rubicon, or even the Roman Empire, Julius Caesar, Peter Underwood, came straight to mind. As he would tell anyone, he was "a legend in his own lunchtime!"

That year, Christian knew he could set the tone for the garden party day with a few extras to adorn Barcourt chambers drinks' table. So just before lunch, he disappeared for twenty minutes or so. He returned with a triumphal entry into their clerks' room holding two large bright red balloons to a chorus from his colleagues of "Hail Caesar!"

Jason was the first to comment. "Oh, here we go. It's going to be one of those days. You can just tell." He was in part referring to the festive mood kick started by the arrival of the balloons, and partly by his acceptance that he was in charge of putting the diary to bed that afternoon whilst the rest of the gang got pissed. He didn't mind playing the role of Cinderella as long, as he added, "you leave some champagne for me."

Yet again the sun shone on the afternoon of the Charity Garden

Party. Some guests would be early to put in an appearance and then escape, whilst others arrived later on knowing they were in for the duration. And then there were the clerks who arrived as soon as they could after lunch and did not leave until every last drop of alcohol had been consumed.

This would include volunteering to hoover up the left-over drinks, or "mine-sweeping", an expression used to describe wandering round the venue and downing the contents of any abandoned glasses, whatever they contained. The more drink consumed in this manner the bolder the lads got to a point when they would empty a glass immediately it appeared to be abandoned. "Waste not want not" was often used as the words of justification which meant the glasses could be put straight back in their rental trays to be machine washed back at the caterer's depot.

Jack's lads were masters at this event, seen as a game to them and mine-sweeping was the starter to the evening's entertainment. They had stiff opposition, none better than Carey Street Chambers clerks, led by Richard Murray. He in particular liked to show off his drinking prowess, although he left the mine sweeping to his minions. He knew his wines and often boasted of his trips to Bordeaux and the vineyards in the area. He was particularly proud of his visit to Chateau Margaux and the wine tasting in their cellars.

"Quality not quantity" was his motto, although he did not practise what he preached, as Jack liked to observe. "On the cooking wine again I see Richard?" was an opening wind up, followed by "I suppose you always spit, never swallow?"

Today Richard felt he had the upper hand. It was the first garden party since his chambers had acquired the four civil members from Barcourt, and he wanted to rub it in to Jack. His team were ordered to go on the offensive and "take no prisoners. It's about time we put Barcourt in their place, on the wrong side of the Strand."

Jack was expecting some low behaviour by the lads from Carey Street but never felt the need to prime his team. He knew they were always up for a verbal scrap with the opposition, and copious quantities of free booze was a recipe for some fun.

The opening gambit came from Richard. "Afternoon Jack, a wonderful day don't you think?" was a question not demanding an answer, so Jack did not reply. Silence was as good as a jibe when Jack was dealing with Richard who continued. "Must be a bit quieter in chambers with fewer members. We've never been so busy."

Jack knew he was referring to Sarah Ryman and the cronies led by Stephen Savage and taking the opportunity to wind him up. Jack remained calm so Richard pressed on.

"Boundaries can be funny things. One side of the road is lush fertile ground, but take a step across the road, and the other side is like a desert with no opportunity. A bit like crossing the Rubicon, eh Jack?"

Later on in the afternoon, most of the barristers and solicitors had left for the pubs and restaurants in the area, so the clerks could get about the business of mine-sweeping and returning the garden to how it had been that morning. Removing tables and chairs was a group activity amongst the clerks who all wanted to continue the evening as soon as possible.

Jack decided it was time for him to respond to Richard's earlier remarks. "Richard, you do realise don't you that once a common law tramp, always a common law tramp. You live on the wrong side of the Strand, and no matter what you say, or spin you try, you will always be a tramp."

Jack saw the veins in Richard's neck visibly pumping as they traded more derogatory comments. Gradually their respective clerks gathered round to watch but not interfere. A public display of animosity between two senior clerks was a rare event, and would be talked about for some time, probably until the next time it happened. So the bragging rights had to be witnessed as they would be used at listing meetings and other clerking events to help get one over on the opposition.

Christian whispered to Dillon. "Jack is really holding back. I guess it is because he lost Sarah." Dillon responded "Just watch. It is not over yet."

The more Richard gloated over taking barristers from Jack the less Jack retaliated, except to keep going at his drinking prowess. Jack called out "Fetch a bucket, someone, Richard needs to clear his throat."

Richard was starting to get angry. "Jack, we won. That's life. I cannot stop solicitors wanting to use my guys. It's business. Just accept it, you lost, just like Ralph did"

Richard had been referring to Jack's mentor who had lost a group of junior counsel to Old Square many years ago, and it nearly caused Barcourt to implode. Jack respected Ralph's efforts to hold chambers together, which is why he now had a set to manage at all.

Jack didn't like Richard's tone. "That's out of order. None of us would be here if we had not been taught our trade by the likes of Ralph. You disrespectful wino"

Richard had had enough and was about to blow. He had wanted to let Jack have it for years. "That's rich coming from a man who would walk over his own mother's body to get a brief."

Jack responded in kind. "Typical. No style no grace no upbringing."

Richard carried on:" who said you were perfect, Shirley?"

The Temple garden fell silent save for the noise of the birds singing. Waiting for Jack to reply seemed to take forever. Christian whispered again to Dillon. "Oh fuck – that's torn it!" He knew nobody called

Jack by his apparently secret nickname "Shirley Temple". It was such an obvious choice for anyone wishing to get under Jack's skin, but only the very brave or mad tried it on.

Jack looked Richard in the eye, paused and said:" Do you know what Richard, I was going to tell you to go fuck yourself, but on second thoughts, I'm going to do it for you."

Richard smiled. "Oh yes, is that a threat?" trying to take the upper hand finally. "No" replied Jack leaning forward so Richard alone could hear his words. "It's a promise."

Jack then turned to Christian and Dillon. "Come on guys, we're done here."

The silence remained long after Jack had departed the garden as those left reflected on what Jack had meant, all secretly realising Richard had gone too far and was likely to regret it.

As one put it: "I would not want to be in Richard's boots. Jack does not make threats he is not prepared to carry out."

As they arrived back in chambers, Jack pulled up Dillon. "What happened today didn't happen – got it? So there is nothing to tell anyone, and I mean anyone. Understood?"

Dillon nervously replied:" Sure Jack –see no hear no speak no." Jack smiled at him. "You got it my little wise monkey." Jack said.

Jack was content to wait for the right time to exact revenge on Richard for calling him Shirley, but resolved to make it part of his plan to get Sarah Ryman back in chambers with her work.

9 RISING STAR

Later the following week Jack met up with Jason for an early doors drink in the Wiltshire Inn. He had done a lot of thinking in the first part of that week, mostly taking an overview of where chambers was in the grand scheme of things in the Temple, and what he felt had to be done to protect and improve their situation. But he was conscious of not just listening to himself on something so important, and Jason was the only other clerk senior enough for him to confide in. Jack thought how lonely it can be at the top, and it was a good excuse to share a bottle of Chablis with a mate.

Jason was a keen angler in his spare time at the weekends. After a frantic week in chambers he liked to relax and recharge his battery during some quiet down time on the river bank. Living and working in the fast lane was having an effect, and if he could catch a fish or two whilst relaxing, then he was happy.

Jack didn't like fishing. "Too much time sitting around waiting for something to take the bait. And what's the point if you have to throw the fish back in the water?" Jason argued the subtle skills of teasing a fish to accept the bait on offer, but he knew he would not win that particular argument with Jack.

"No Jason, it's like counsel with a brief, what we catch we eat. And we only want the best, top quality. There's plenty of fish out there, it's just finding the right ones and giving them the right bait."

Jack poured another glass of Chablis for Jason and topped up his own glass. He decided now was a good time to talk about chambers. "Speaking of fishing, I think it is about time we went on a serious fishing expedition for a top personal injury silk, and use that QC as the bait to attract a team of juniors."

Jason could see the obvious problems such a strategy would pose. "Where do you start? It's a chicken and egg situation. The silk wants the good juniors with quality work, but the juniors want the status a good QC offers. Which do you get first?"

"Nobody said it would be easy, but Jason, you know we have to protect chambers. If we don't, we could oversee the demise of Barcourt and that would be a disaster for us both. The leadership has no steel, the juniors know it as well as the senior members, and it won't matter how efficient we are, once a few more get it into their heads the grass is greener elsewhere, we might as well shut up shop."

For Jason to hear Jack sound so negative was unusual. "So what do we do about it?" asked Jason.

Jack went straight into his plan. "It's time you went on a fishing expedition for top quality barristers, and you start by looking for a recognised top silk in the personal injury field. I want you to make a list of all the QCs in that area with a good reputation, and then a similar list of quality juniors. I don't care how long the list is. We can cut it down once we have all the names. Lots will fall away as they will never leave their existing chambers"

Jason was pleased to be given such an important task, especially as it showed him that Jack had confidence in him. "I can start with the personal injury bar association members list and check it against the current edition of the Bar Directory. Then what?"

"I want a top five list of the best QCs who are the most likely to jump ship to Barcourt chambers, and then a similar list of rising stars who would be attracted to a new home. Can you do that?"

"Jack, consider it done. How long have I got?" asked Jason.

Jack replied. "How about Monday morning? It will give you something to think about on the river bank!"

On their way back to chambers, Jason pondered on his busy weekend while Jack realised he had started something, without knowing where it would all end. They just knew something had to be done.

Jack had already done his lists, but he wanted Jason to produce his own without Jack's influence and to make sure he had not missed anyone out. He also thought it would be a good idea to share the problem with an outsider, someone who could give him a different perspective.

That could be achieved by bouncing his idea off a solicitor he could trust to keep quiet, and for that he could only think of one such person. So back in chambers, Jack went into an empty conference room and rang Elizabeth Richardson.

She took his call and after making sure they were both free to speak, Jack went straight in with his request. "Beth, I'd like your opinion on something." She felt immediately she had the upper hand. "Wow, there's a first! Are you feeling ok Jack?"

Jack seeking the opinion of a female did not match her view of his chauvinism but she was flattered he had ask her and curious to find out what he wanted to know. So before he could comment further, she said: "Ok, ask away."

Jack said; "If you or your firm were short-listing personal injury silks for a major case, who would be in your top five?"

"Oh, has one of your juniors got a big PI case, and they need a high profile silk to lead them? Someone special outside your own chambers? Must be big for that to happen."

Jack let her think that was the reason as he did not want to give too much away at this stage.

"Something like that Beth, yes. Who would you use?"

The personal injury bar was a fairly small group and everyone knew everyone, so it was of little surprise that Beth named all on Jack's list. She did add one female silk as well, Nicola Mortimer QC, partly because it was an all-male list but also because she came into the category of rising star with potential rather than today's hot ticket. Beth also liked the idea of Jack's junior counsel trying Nicola Mortimer out without having to risk her own client and firm on someone who might not succeed.

"Beth, as ever you are the real star. Much appreciated. Please keep it to yourself for now, and let me know when you are coming down next so we can meet up." Beth replied:" Will do, Honey!" As a parting shot, Jack could not resist a bit of marketing.

"Of course, you can bring the date forward by sending in a brief which needs a conference in chambers as a matter of urgency." Beth knew he wanted more work but refused to take the bait. She replied: "Good bye Jack!"

The following Monday morning after everyone had gone to court, Jack invited Jason into a conference room with a coffee. They compared their lists of possible QCs and juniors. They were remarkably similar, and neither had any women on them. This did not surprise Jason, and he never even challenged Jack to come up with a couple of female alternatives to add to the list. Jack raised the gender issue.

"You know, we have been successful with the recruiting of a female member in our clerks' room. It would be good to strengthen the female numbers. There are lots more female solicitors and they like the option of a woman for their clients. Leave the lists with me and I will get back to you. Thanks Jason and not a word."

Jason was pleased with Jack's response to his efforts. "No worries, Jack. Let me know if I can help any further."

The more Jack thought about who to try to head hunt as a top QC, the more he was attracted by the idea of Nicola Mortimer QC. She was part of a big chambers with several areas of expertise in Grays

Inn, and had three other personal injury QCs around her. He could promote her as the face of the future. On the principle of "if you don't ask, you don't get", Jack resolved to approach Miss Mortimer at the first opportunity.

For any barrister, the process of moving chambers could take time. There were many factors to take into consideration, but once decided the event usually happened very quickly and in some cases overnight. Jack realised that he needed to sow the seeds early with Nicola Mortimer and let her know what was potentially on offer at Barcourt chambers. It would take several meetings and neither of them could afford for anyone to find out what he was proposing. Just to be seen talking to someone was enough to start a rumour. The timing had to be right for counsel as well as chambers.

Nicola Mortimer QC had been called to the bar twenty years ago and been appointed a Queen's Counsel just five years before. At forty five she regarded herself as fully experienced in all types of personal injury work, and ready for any challenge that presented itself. She was content with her work load which gave her time for family life with her husband and two young teenage children. A regular at her local gym, she kept herself trim which allowed her to be a little more flamboyant with her court and chambers dress sense. At five foot seven with short dark brown hair, she had a strong presence in court that matched her sharp analytical mind.

Jack had not met Nicola Mortimer so engineering a chance meeting was not easy to arrange. Jack had been watching the civil lists in the RCJ to identify a case involving the QC.

Eventually he saw his opportunity and decided to meet her in the RCJ robing room. He got there just before 10.30 when most courts start the day, so the robing room was quiet. He had intended to follow her to her court room and hand her a private note, but his chance came when all the barristers left except Nicola.

As she approached the door to go to court, Jack stepped towards her so he could open the door for her. "Miss Mortimer." Before he could say anything else, Nicola interrupted. "Yes Mr Temple." Her words caught Jack as he realised she knew who he was, but he did not open the door. Nicola saw this look on his face, so continued. "I know who you are, Jack. What can I do for you? I am due in court."

"Miss Mortimer, I would welcome a private discussion with you in total confidence on a matter of potential importance. Forgive my approach but I felt I needed to be discrete."

"I'm intrigued. But now is not the time nor the place. As she spoke, Jack took his card out of his pocket and handed it to her. She put it into her pocket as Jack opened the door and said: "Thank you Mr Temple."

Two weeks passed by and towards the end Jack thought he had blown it, concluding she was not interested. There were not many other reasons for a senior clerk from another set of chambers to approach a barrister so his motive was fairly obvious. Nonetheless, Miss Mortimer was curious, but did not want to appear desperate. So she decided she would leave it for a sensible period.

Jack was walking towards Chancery lane tube station just before 7.00pm when his mobile rang. He did not recognise the number but answered anyway. It could be new business so he gave the caller his professional voice. "Jack Temple."

"Jack, its Nicola Mortimer. My dry cleaners found your card in my pocket. Nearly lost it. Too busy for my own good. What can I do for you?"

Jack stopped just before the steps down to the tube station and checked there was nobody near him he knew.

"Miss Mortimer, good of you to call. I was hoping we could meet somewhere discrete for a chat." Counsel interrupted Jack. "Call me

Nicola, my clerks do. Where do you have in mind?"

"How about the Russell Hotel on Russell Square? It should be far enough away."

"That would be good for me. Shall we say in half an hour?" "This evening?" asked Jack just to be sure. "Yes indeed. The residents lounge." Jack disconnected the call and immediately rang his wife Barbara to warn her he could be a bit late as something had come up after he had left chambers.

Jack got to the Russell Hotel ten minutes early and ordered himself a gin and tonic. He had just settled into a comfortable arm chair in the corner with a panoramic view of the room when in walked Nicola Mortimer. She spotted him straight away and walked over. Jack got up and offered his hand. "Nicola, thanks for coming. Can I get you a drink?"

Looking at Jack's glass, Nicola said "a gin and tonic would be fine, thanks."

As Jack walked back to their corner he realised he was about to embark on the biggest sales pitch of his life, but did not dwell on the consequences of failure. As Nicola took her first sip, Jack went straight in.

"Nicola, with your permission I will cut straight to the point. The way I see it, there is an opportunity for us both to achieve what we want. It is a matter of recognising the chance, and then taking it."

Nicola smiled and interrupted with "Carpe diem." Jack continued. "Rather more than just seize the day, more by seizing the day and the future will be laid out before you."

"Go on" said Nicola.

"Ok, my assessment of where your career is at present. You are a successful female silk with a growing reputation for big personal injury cases, but you are at a crossroads stuck in a bit of a traffic jam that is holding you back from your ambition to become Head of Chambers. You have two options. One is to wait for dead men's shoes which could take years. The other is to seek a new home with the right prospects."

Jack paused for comment but none came, so he went on. "OK, let's work backwards from an assumed retirement age of 70. At that point you are in the Court of Appeal or higher. Where you end up is not up to me, it is all up to you. But at that age when you retire, you need at least fifteen years judicial service under your belt to qualify for the full pension which currently stands at half your annual judicial salary for life. If you were to put aside a sum each year to achieve an annuity fund that would pay out such a large pension, you would have to be devoting a lot of your current income with no guarantee of the annuity rates."

Jack paused this time for a sip of his drink and observed Nicola was thinking about his words. "So to accrue the necessary fifteen years you would have to aim for an appointment to the High Court bench at around 55, and your CV warrants the High Court rather than the Circuit bench. The sooner you come to the attention of those involved with such appointments the better.

"Yes there is a drive to appoint more female advocates to judicial office, and you could stay put, but you may well miss out on the ambition of being a Head of Chambers with all the opportunities that could offer."

He paused again and still no comment. "So what I am offering is the chance to have five to ten years as a head of chambers, to stand out and show the profession just what a successful female silk can do."

Nicola decided she had heard enough to ask a few questions. "They said you were good. And how much of your proposal comes with your chambers backing? And what's in it for Jack?"

"I have my own ambitions for chambers. Charles Wadsworth is likely to go to the Circuit bench soon, and whilst that leaves a vacancy at the top, I would prefer to see the right outsider take the helm. There are several boxes to be ticked, and you would tick them all. You are a rising star in your field, female which is important as I will explain, and with the drive to make your mark on a set that is going in the right direction."

"Explain," said Nicola.

"Our existing senior members of chambers have good reputations, but none have that star quality to attract top lawyers and work. You do. As head of chambers, doors to that work would open for us all. I can provide you with the right clerking team."

"Yes, I gather you poached that girl who used her karate skills to fend off attackers." Jack replied. "Yes but it was Taekwondo. Her appointment has taught me that any clerking team needs the right balance of male and female clerks. There are more and more lady solicitors, as well as more female counsel. It is obvious to me at least that the all-male clerks' room has had its day."

"I want to build a strong personal injury set and attract the right counsel. I would start with getting back Sarah Ryman who was treated badly by Charles Wadsworth. Before you ask, I cannot discuss what happened until you are on board, but I am confident you would agree."

"All these steps are showing the profession that there is a new breed of counsel willing to take bold steps when necessary."

Nicola interrupted. "Enough Jack. This is all very interesting, but there is one question you have not answered. How much of what you say comes with your management committee's approval?"

"This is a preliminary off the record chat to see if there is any common way forward."

Nicola saw it differently. "You're on a fishing expedition, Jack, and you have gone out on your own. I can't take any such proposal seriously. What did you expect me to say?"

"Nicola, it may take me weeks or even months to put the package together. All I want right now is to know that you would look at a deal if I am able to offer one. I am not looking elsewhere. I just have a list with your name on it, and yes it will be a challenge for me to deliver just as it will be a challenge for your career. But I would not be here if I did not believe it was right for both you and my chambers."

There was a pause in the conversation as both took a sip of their drinks. Jack was pleased with the silence as it meant he had not been blown out of the water, at least not yet. He decided to press on.

"Bringing a female clerk on board has taught me that working with women is good for the clerking team and enables us to offer a rounded experience for counsel and clients alike. You may know members of the bar, male and female, who would welcome the opportunity to work in your chambers, especially in the knowledge you had control of a dynamic and forward thinking clerking team."

Jack had played all his cards and sat back to finish his drink. Nicola looked as far as he was concerned to be at least giving his proposal a chance, but felt she needed to see a way forward in the immediate future. So Jack concluded the discussion.

"No notes, nothing recorded, we never had this conversation. I will only contact you if I am in a position to go forward. Unless you tell me otherwise, I will send a text message to the mobile number you rang me on. I have stored the number but not under your name."

Nicola finished her drink and looked around the room, making sure she did not recognise anyone "Ok, for now I will go along with what you say, but I make no commitment whatsoever, and if anyone asks me if I have spoken to you, I will say no. Now I must go before I am missed."

Both got up to leave, and Jack offered his hand. "Thank you Nicola, that is all I can ask for now. I will only contact you again if I have something positive to tell you. I will wait on here for a few minutes to give you time to leave." Nicola started to leave adding her final words "Thank you Jack, and good luck!"

Jack took her final sentence as a positive reaction to their discussion, but realised there was still plenty of work to be done. He left after five minutes with a spring in his step as he walked towards the tube station.

Sat in the tube train going home Jack reflected on the growing influence of women in his working life and how he had got the right female candidate in the clerks' room. He was confident he had picked the right person to run his chambers, however long it took to get her on board.

10 NEGOTIATING TACTICS

Since the arrival of Jenny James into the Barcourt clerks' room, Jack had become the target of more lively banter than in the past. He realised he had changed their clerks' room dynamics forever which he saw as a good step forward. He also understood the world was changing and women were more acceptable work colleagues. The lads were just getting their own back.

Often when he was going out the clerks would ask if he was going to take his bodyguard with him, or say: "Jack, haven't you forgotten someone" or "Jack, don't you need your bodyguard?"

An alternative was to have a discussion about films they had seen which would always end up with mention of the Bodyguard and someone asking Jack if it was his favourite film. Jenny took the banter in good spirit as did Jack. He felt it served to remind the lads that they had moved on from their testosterone haven.

That day the mood was a little more serious as everyone had a lot to do getting the early morning tasks sorted. After 10.30am, all the clerks at Barcourt chambers were at their desks processing the post and DX mail which had arrived that day. Dillon was deep in thought.

"Jack, I'm confused. You and other senior clerks talk about team spirit in the clerks' room, and how it is something you have to build. That was why we had the bonding weekend in Spain to build our team spirit?"

Jack was only half listening, but not really understanding Dillon's question. "So what's your point Dillon?" he asked.

"Well I read an article which…" Christian butted in. "Steady on Mr Dillon, you'll be reading books next!" his comment raised a smile from the other clerks who just carried on. Dillon ignored it.

"The article quoted Steve Archibald who had said that team spirit was an illusion only glimpsed in victory. Is that right?"

Jason was confused so asked "Who is Steve Archibald when he's at home?" Dillon knew the answer. "Great striker, played for Spurs and Barcelona."

Jack decided he would have to get involved in the debate. "Football is a team game with each player having his own role to play. A clerks' room is the same but it is how we all work together for the same goal that enables us to win as a team. So a win is achieved by the collective individual efforts, or the spirit, of each one of us seated round this table."

Dillon and the others reflected on Jack's words, but Dillon looked as if he was still not convinced. Jack thought an example might help.

"So Dillon, when we have a counsel double-booked, and one clerk goes to find the brief to be returned , another orders a taxi to deliver it to the alternative counsel whilst I ring the solicitor to let him down, and Jason lines up the alternative counsel so the problem is sorted, that is a result. Steve Archibald would call it a victory, but it was achieved by virtue of our team spirit"

Dillon smiled. "Got it!" Christian could not resist a final swipe at Dillon. "I'd leave the reading alone if I were you, Mr Dillon. Stick to page three in the Sun, it's much better for you!"

Jack was well aware of the total secrecy needed as far as Nicola Mortimer QC was concerned. Any leak could cost him his job, but he felt confident it was within his capabilities to limit any disclosure to trusted colleagues only. That meant his deputy Jason Middleton, and only Jason.

The possibility of chambers imploding had not gone away, and in Jack's opinion, would not until Charles Wadsworth QC was removed as head of chambers. That was never going to happen by an internal coup, so he had to find a way of getting Charles to leave of his own free will. He just might step down as head of chambers, but he would still be around which meant Sarah Ryman would not apply to return. Sarah was a rising star and Jack wanted her back. If that also meant that Nathan Blake left, Jack's opinion was "Well so be it".

He decided the first step was to see if there was any possibility of Charles securing a judicial appointment. His head of chambers never took a step forward unless he felt the ground beneath him was firm to solid.

So Jack set about discretely speaking to former members of chambers who were now judges, and a few other close links he had with the judiciary, to sound out Charles' prospects of making a successful application to become a circuit judge. The general views around the Temple and the courts were that Charles Wadsworth QC was not High Court material with the prospects of the Court of Appeal and beyond. He was more cannon fodder for the criminal work of the Crown court and minor civil County Court trials. Jack thought his head of chambers would realise his station in the judicial world as well as anyone, so no need to spell it out.

To his surprise nobody was against the idea of a Circuit appointment for Charles, indeed one or two were very positive. Jack made a list of those he spoke to so he would have the ammunition at his fingertips. Charles would then see for himself and judge how firm the ground would be. Next step was to talk to Charles who was in his room as usual.

"Jack, what can I do for you?" was his standard opening remark. "I am hoping it is more about what I can do for you." This got Charles' attention imagining Jack had a tasty brief to offer him. He said "Another multi-party action with contested liability?"

"Not this time I'm afraid. But potentially even better. Can I take you back to what you said to me after the ECM and the Sarah Ryman fiasco?" Charles was not pleased to discuss those dark days as he saw them. "If you must. Not my finest hour."

"Well, no disrespect to your age, but if you fancy a judicial appointment, you might want to entertain the idea sooner rather than later. And to that end I have taken a few soundings, totally confidential of course, amongst our judicial friends and senior colleagues. The results are pretty good as you can see from my notes." Jack handed Charles the single sheet of A4 paper which contained Jack's findings.

Jack went on. "That is the only copy, and I have hand written it so it is not on the chambers system either."

There was a lull in the conversation whilst the head of chambers absorbed the information now presented to him. Jack witnessed the weight lifting from Charles' shoulders at the real prospect of him escaping chambers. Charles spoke first.

"Well Jack, you know I am not happy in my present role, and I do find the thought of a judicial appointment appealing, but where would that leave chambers? I am not convinced there are any natural successors at present."

Jack wanted to remain positive and take away any negative thoughts offered by Charles.

"I'll worry about that one. I have a few ideas, but let's take one step at a time. For now I'll leave the list with you."

No more was said on the subject until a couple of weeks later when Charles called Jack back into his room. "Jack, you will be pleased to know I have applied for a position as a circuit judge. I'll let you know how it goes. If I ask you to keep me free in the diary, don't ask what for. Is that ok?"

Jack smiled. "Understood sir!"

On his return to the clerks' room, Jack resolved to meet with Jason as soon as possible. He knew that if an appointment came it would be by letter to his head of chambers and involve a trip to the House of Lords within a few days, and from that day he would have no head of chambers until there was an election.

Jack and Jason met in the Crown Café Bar the next morning for breakfast. They ordered the full Monty. "Fernando, two of your finest fried eggs with all the trimmings please for me, and my friend will have the same. We have a busy day ahead."

They took up their usual table at the back of the café round the corner and so were out of sight. Jack told Jason what was happening and that only the two of them must know.

"Of course it is not a foregone conclusion that Wadsworth will get a post, but he has been told he stands a better than average chance. So Jason, we need to be prepared."

Jason thought on what he now knew. "You can imagine the plotting going on in the Red Lion tap room, each group wanting a different new head of chambers and everyone looking after their own practice and sod the consequences. There could be blood on the walls at Barcourt."

Jack interrupted him. "That is precisely why we need to present a prospect for the role of head of chambers that does not let that happen. We need someone who offers an acceptable solution that the vast majority can live with. And part of that candidate's attraction must be the ability to bring good counsel and good work in."

Jason picked up on Jack's logic. "The members have something to buy into, and someone to deliver what they want for their own practice." Jack nodded. "Exactly."

The next morning, Jack took his customary look through the dairy to see who was going to visit chambers that day and noticed that Stuart Brookes, an experienced junior barrister at Carey Street Chambers was due in at 4.30pm for a conference with Charles Wadsworth QC.

Stuart Brookes had been a pupil with Charles Wadsworth QC some ten years before but was not offered a tenancy for reasons never explained to Jack. He had been snapped up by Carey Street and now, as far as Jack was concerned, was a rising star so on his radar to get back into Barcourt chambers at the right time. Although he was a couple of years senior to Sarah Ryman, Jack felt she attract him if the timing was right. Together they would be a formidable force within their personal injury group, and demonstrate to Nicola Mortimer QC that they could deliver her quality silk work.

Jack had always felt he could sell Brookes to anyone. He was one of those counsel the clerks wanted to clone. He turned to Jason. "Stuart Brookes is coming in today for a conference with Wadsworth. Do you remember him in the last few months of his pupillage?"

"Oh god yes" replied Jason. "He would hover over you whilst you were opening the post and before you could log his papers in, he had taken them and was gone. He would then return an hour later with the advice or draft pleadings done."

Jack went on. "And ask for the papers to be sent back that day, by hand if possible. He'd generate a shed load of work. A true hunter."

Stuart Brookes had not seen Charles Wadsworth since he left Barcourt and was now going to negotiate his first really big deal with his old pupil master and head of chambers. He was determined to get a good result. Jack decided to try to speak to him to understand why such a promising youngster had not been offered a tenancy at Barcourt chambers.

About five minutes before the conference was due to begin Stuart Brookes walked into the clerks' room as if he was a long lost friend returning to visit. Jack got up and walked towards him. "Mr Brookes, good to see you. How are you keeping?"

"I'm very well thanks Jack. How is everyone?" The rest of the clerks exchanged pleasantries with Brookes who then turned to Jack. "I hear good things about Barcourt under your watch, Jack. You must be doing something right."

Before Jack could answer a phone rang. It was Charles Wadsworth asking for Brookes to be taken to his room. As it would just be the two of them, the head of chambers had said he would have the conference in his room so leaving a conference room free for someone else to use,

In this case Brookes was acting for a claimant who had been hit on the head by a forklift truck at work and was not likely to work again. Charles Wadsworth QC was acting for the employer's insurers and after a couple of poor results in the High Court, was equally determined to cut the settlement figure down. He needed a good result to re-establish his credibility with his instructing solicitors and their insurance company clients.

An hour before the conference Charles Wadsworth had called Jack into his room. "Jack, could you lay on some tea for Brookes at 4.30 and come and join us. It would be good to show him there are no hard feelings about his departure." Such a magnanimous gesture was almost unheard of. "What is he up to?" thought Jack.

Jack showed Brookes into the head of chambers' room. "Stuart, do come in. I have asked Jack to join us for a cup of tea. Do sit down. Jack, will you be mother?"'

Jack poured the tea. After a few more pleasantries, Charles Wadsworth started to reminisce.

"Brookes, do you remember your first visit to the Coroner's court. What a day that turned out to be!" Immediately Brookes looked unhappy at the prospect of Charles Wadsworth QC launching into the anecdote and tried to change the subject. "Jack doesn't want to hear that old story" he said in a dismissive manner. That got Jack intrigued, even though he sensed it was playing into Wadsworth's hands. "I don't think I have heard that one."

Charles Wadsworth QC was in. "Do you remember the East Coast mainline tragedy when the woman and her son were killed on the track? Gruesome pictures in the press, but the Coroner's bundle were even worse."

"Don't remind me" said Brookes resigned to what was coming next. Charles Wadsworth continued.

"Jack, the court room was packed. Brookes took one look at the bundle of photos and immediately passed out. As he hit the court room floor, his body totally relaxed as you would expect, and he relieved himself."

Jack could tell Brookes was unhappy, but Charles carried on. "The Coroner adjourned for half an hour whilst someone went looking for a mop and bucket."

"Thank you Charles" Brookes interrupted. "I'm sure Jack does not want the gory detail."

Jack had indeed heard enough. Charles Wadsworth knew that by telling the story to a third party and clearly embarrassing Brookes he had taken the high ground for his negotiations to follow. He then realised why he had been invited to tea. Jack left the room so the conference could start, thinking to himself what a cheap trick Wadsworth had played.

An hour later on his way out Brookes called Jack to one side. "Good to see you again Jack. Sorry you had to hear the Coroner's story. Typical of Charles. His timing is as clumsy as ever. I knew one day he would bring it up."

"No worries Mr Brookes. He has not improved has he?"

"No. One day it will be his downfall, just not today."

"Indeed. Take care." Jack wanted to talk more to Brookes whom he had a lot of respect for, but as usual the phones were going mad so he left it.

Ten minutes later Charles Wadsworth QC sauntered into the clerk's room carrying the bundle of papers from the conference with the air of a winner. He had endorsed the back sheet "Settled at £125,000 on basis of 25% contributory negligence." Jack muttered to himself: "You little shit. That is less than half what the insurers told you in the instructions they would have settled for."

Jack looked at the computer screen for the case and noticed the suggested fee for the conference was £750. "Make it £1,500" he said to James Dunn the fees clerk. "Then I can take Brookes out for lunch and find out why he left us."

A few days later Jack was hunting down one of the junior members of chambers for an extra brief. He was in the Robing room at the RCJ and spotted Stuart Brookes on the far side of the room putting his wig on. Jack walked over. "Morning Mr Brookes."

Brookes replied. "Good morning Jack. What brings you to the robing room this fine sunny day? Let me guess? More work to hand out."

They both smiled. Jack took the line of questioning up. "Are you available at 2.00 pm for an infant settlement? Marked at £750 for half an hour's work."

Brookes raised his eyebrows in disappointment. "Oh if only Jack."

Jack lowered his voice a little and said "I wonder, could we meet to discuss that situation some time? Off the record of course."

Stuart Brookes knew he was being touted but did not mind. "That would be good. I'd like that Jack. Are you still on the same old mobile number?" Jack nodded and left the robing room.

Stuart Brookes and Jack met up for breakfast at the Crown Café Bar at 7.30 one morning. Brookes had not been there before and none of the barristers in Carey Street chambers had mentioned it so he felt comfortable talking to Jack there.

"A little bird told me that Charles Wadsworth may be on his way out. There is a rumour to that effect in our chambers." Jack said nothing so Brookes carried on. "I have to confess it was me who started the rumour to get back at him for the coroner's court story going public. Silly really but you saw what he did over tea before our conference. He needs stopping."

Jack decided to make his play. "Strictly between us, what if I were to tell you that the rumour may be true?" Brookes put his knife and fork down and sat back. "Really? Tell me more. My lips are sealed."

"Well, let me say that the wheels are in motion for a traditional exit for a head of chambers." Brookes knew exactly what Jack meant. "He's applied for a judicial post. Is he likely to succeed?"

Jack went on. "So it would seem. Early soundings suggest he may have backing in the right quarters. I am putting in place a contingency plan for such an eventually."

Brookes interrupted. "And does that plan include me which would explain why we are having a great breakfast?"

Jack carried on. "Of course I cannot divulge closely guarded secrets at this early stage, but let me just add that if such a plan were to include you, it could only do so if I knew why you did not get offered a tenancy at the end of your pupillage. I cannot plan how to deal with that if I don't know what happened."

"Jack, there is no great mystery. After the unfortunate incident in the coroner's court, Wadsworth took me to one side shortly before the tenancy vote and said he had sounded out a few of the senior members of chambers. He said they were not happy about potential damage to chambers' reputation if they took on a possible weak link."

Before Jack could reply, Brookes went on. "I didn't buy that excuse. It was Wadsworth himself just did not like to support someone who had, as he put it, pissed on his chips, literally."

"So he probably never asked the other members?" asked Jack. "No, I don't think so. Nobody has ever mentioned what happened at the chambers' meeting which sealed my fate, but I think someone would have by now if they were going to."

Jack summed up the position. "So as I see it, if the head of chambers was no longer in Barcourt, there would be nothing to stop you applying to return."

"Nothing, except I am now settled enough at Carey Street to not want to rock my career boat unless there was very good reason."

Jack chose his words carefully. "Ok, so if I told you that the contingency plan involved attracting an external new head of chambers with a good reputation in your field of work, a rising silk, and that person in turn was attracting star juniors who would collectively draw quality work to Barcourt, would that be enough to get you on board?"

Brookes thought through the information presented to him. "Yes I think so. Indeed I would go one step further to say that if all that were true, I would be able to bring a couple of hunters with me."

Jack went on. "And if Carey Street were to lose their senior clerk over a scandal, the ground might shift in favour of a chambers split?" "Jack" exclaimed Brookes "What more do you know?"

"Oh, no. I am not starting more rumours. Everyone in the clerking world knows I do not get on with Richard Murray, so any rumour would immediately be attributed to me. So definitely no comment!"

Jack left their breakfast meeting feeling in good heart and as soon as the post and DX was dealt with, took Jason aside in a conference room to update him on his conversation with Brookes.

"So, Jack, we may have two more to add to the junior counsel list. What are you going to do about Richard Murray? You did make him a promise."

"I know" said Jack. "I have to work on that one as hitting him hard could start the ball rolling in our favour."

Making life difficult for a rival was always going to be tricky to achieve without causing Jack any grief within his own chambers. It could get him a bollocking from his head of chambers even if Charles Wadsworth did secretly approve.

Stitching up Richard Murray at a forward listing meeting was bread and butter work which Jack would leave to his clerks. It would cause friction between the clerks in both chambers, with lively banter but no serious undertones.

Jack needed something far more serious which only he could set up and know about. He realised the opportunity was not there just yet. So he turned his attentions to Sarah Ryman. He wanted at the very least to keep in touch with her, and at best to see if she might return to Barcourt chambers. He still had her mobile number so rang her out of hours to see if they could meet.

A week later, Sarah Ryman invited Jack to her flat in the evening so he could discuss further her possible return to chambers. She was not sure it would work for her and she told him.

"Jack, I don't really want to go through the drugs allegations again. It is history for me now. And who is to say they will believe me anyway. May be I was hasty in walking out, but I did not want any more from that prick." She was referring to Charles Wadsworth QC the head of chambers.

"What you don't know Jack is that I went to see Wadsworth at his home the night before I left chambers. You recall that was the night before the ECM to kick me out."

Jack nodded to confirm his recollection of the events Sarah was talking about.

"Well, we were in his study at home when he confronted me. He told me that he had heard Nathan's version of events in the toilets, and he had been shown a photograph Nathan took at the time. I have to say the evidence against me appeared compelling, and with my previous history of drug abuse, albeit minor and a long time ago, Charles would have been hard pressed not to report the whole sorry affair to the Bar Standards Board."

"I was lost for words, not knowing for once in my life where to start to defend myself. So I chose not to. The head of chambers took guilt from my silence and then said: "My dear, I think the best for everyone is for you to resign from chambers with immediate effect. Let me have a letter to that effect dated today, and take a week to find yourself new chambers.""

Jack expressed sympathy for her situation and she continued. "He then said that if he was asked for a reference by a head of chambers in respect of my application to join another set, he would put forward appropriate words to indicate a personality clash here was to blame for my departure."

Sarah paused to allow Jack to absorb what she had told him. "So you see Jack, I had no choice. If I wanted to stay practicing as a barrister in another chambers, I needed a good reference and no drugs issues in the public domain."

Jack took a sip of wine which gave him the time to consider his reply.

"You and any of the others who have left Barcourt cannot do anything about the head of chambers from the outside. But from the inside, sooner or later the opportunity will arise for others to back a move for change. The time to consider a return is when there is a new head of chambers in place and Charles Wadsworth is no longer a member. Also, right now you do not know who his successor will be. There may also be important changes under a new regime to the management committee."

"That's true" Sarah said. "But I still have to get through the first hurdle and clear my name."

"Yes" replied Jack, "At least now you know the full extent of the case against you, you can prepare your defence properly. Agreed?"

As Jack left Sarah's flat he concluded that Barcourt chambers was going nowhere fast under the current leadership. He had to encourage change at the top.

He thought his best chance to get the work back lay with the Carey Street chambers clerks. He was sure one day they would make a few cockups with her solicitors. There were rumours at listing meetings of counsel getting double booked and their clerks not handling the crisis well.

Jason reported such a story to Jack which reinforced his view. "Apparently, Carey Street left a trainee solicitor at court without counsel for a hearing and the lay client was furious."

Jack summed up the situation for Jason. "It is just a matter of time. Richard Murray will be the author of his own misfortune!"

11 THE DETECTIVES

Early one morning as the first few arrivals came into Barcourt chambers to start their working day. Dillon was curled up fast asleep on the big sofa in the chambers' waiting area which formed part of reception. Jason and Jack had passed Dillon on their way into the clerks' room and both decided he needed the sleep.

Dillon was out cold which as it was just after eight o'clock in the morning was very unusual for him. He regarded himself as an early bird.

Jack told Jason "He can have another twenty minutes which might make the world of difference if he is hung over."

A few minutes later both Jack and Jason looked up from their respective seats in the clerks' room to see a very attractive girl in a very revealing party dress come from the direction of the stairs down to the toilet and walk out of chambers, pausing for a moment to look at Dillon. She said nothing and did not look into the clerks' room.

Jack and Jason looked at each other and then at Dillon who did not show any signs of life. Jack said "Leave him there. When the rest are in they will give him so much grief he won't do it again for a while."

The look of wonder and amazement on the other clerks' faces as they passed Dillon on the sofa made Jack and Jason smile. Eventually Jack told James Dunn to "Wake the lazy git up." James got a glass of chilled water and threw it over Dillon's face.

It had the desired effect. Dillon sat bolt upright and screamed. "Bad dream, Dillon? Or was it a nightmare?" asked James. Dillon was speechless, trying very hard to work out where he was and what had happened.

As the laughter amongst the clerks subsided, Dillon felt sick and rushed downstairs to the toilet. Christian Bennet shouted after him "you're in luck, there's nobody down there. Don't make a mess!"

The rest of the team got on with the early morning routines of opening the mail, booking new work in, and sorting out diary issues that had arisen over night. About half an hour passed before Dillon made an appearance at his desk, looking very sheepish. Christian laid into him first, and before long it was a free for all bashing Mr Dillon time.

Jack appeared to have had enough and called time out so some work could be done and normal service was resumed. Dillon thought that would be it until Jack and Jason opened up another line of enquiry. Jack started it.

"So Dillon, who was the girl?" Dillon looked blank. After a pause for thought he replied. "What girl?" Jason took up the cross examination. "The very attractive girl in a very low cut party dress who left chambers shortly before you were woken up."

Dillon struggled to take on board the question. "What?" That was all he could muster, and then turned to look out to reception as if still trying to work out where he was and see the girl for himself. Jason carried on.

"Dillon, she's gone. Who was she? Come on, you know you will end up telling us all, so you might as well spill the beans now. What happened?"

"I don't know what or who you are talking about" said Dillon. "I don't remember anything about last night at all. What happened?"

Jason replied. "When Jack and I got in this morning you were out cold on the sofa in the waiting area. Are you saying you don't remember the girl?" Jack took over.

"That's a real pity because she was an absolute stunner, and before you ask, I am not winding you up. Last night you were clearly punching above your weight, and if you cannot remember her, then shame on you."

Dillon could not believe his bad fortune. "Oh no, not another night I want to remember!"

Jason added "You are lucky we don't have CCTV in the waiting area or you could be starring in your very own porn special by now!"

Video conferencing kit was relatively new to chambers, rather like fax machines when they first arrived on the scene. A lot bought the very expensive equipment to "keep up with the Jones" and impress the opposition but did not use it that often. It took a while for the penny to drop that you needed firms of solicitors on the other end of very expensive telephone lines for the system to have any benefit. As Jack pointed out to the management committee. "It takes two to tango, and some of the senior members prefer a conference day out than stay in their own chambers."

At a previous management committee meeting, Jack's words had fallen on deaf ears and the £10,000 contingency budget was spent on what was described as state of the art technology. It was also decided to let all the solicitors and chambers in the area know the video conferencing suite was available for hire. That way at least some income could be derived from the capital expenditure.

Jack gradually got used to the idea of the new toy. Jason was all in favour. "We can get conferences organised for counsel who are stuck in a long trial out of town, and save solicitors a lot of time and travel costs. Eventually it will be used for court hearings and prison visits."

Jack was not taken by that argument. "Some like a trip to London, and the chance to bill their clients for the time out of the office. But it is a service we can offer even to our competitors so we will embrace the brave new world."

He appointed James Dunn as the man to take responsibility for managing the equipment. "You're our administration guru so you are the right man for the job. Get to know all about it, go on a course if there is one, and you handle the bookings." James was pleased to take on the role. He felt good that Jack trusted him.

It took about a year for the business of hiring out the kit to take off, and it was not without teething problems. Getting the special telephone lines to work was a nightmare, so James with Jack's approval introduced a set of rules for the use of the equipment.

The most important rule was that an hour before the video conference was scheduled to begin, the two parties involved would test the telephone lines. This involved ringing from the system the dedicated telephone number of the other participant and checking the picture and sound quality.

Any other chambers or solicitors using the system were encouraged to follow this procedure to avoid wasting time once the video conference parties had assembled to start the event.

Sometimes Jack would get involved if a local chambers were hiring the kit to link to a firm of solicitors who did not instruct chambers. He would use it as a marketing tool. Otherwise he left it to James.

So it was no surprise to Jack when James asked him one day to follow him to the video conference suite as he had something to show him. Jack was in a hurry as usual, so barked at James as he entered the room.

"Ok James, what is it that needs my attention?" James replied. "I think you should see this."

As part of the equipment they had installed there was a video recorder. This meant meetings could be recorded on to DVD, a facility not always used, but it had saved some situations when there was a dispute over what was said.

James pressed the play button and suggested to Jack "You might want to sit down."

Initially Jack ignored that advice, but after a minute or so sat down in front of the screen in disbelief at what he was seeing.

Jack had seen a few porn films before but not taken much interest. He preferred as he called it "the real thing" to watching someone else doing it.

The scene was of a smart conference room in an office. Jack could see the side profile view of a woman in her late thirties seated on the edge of a large central table with her outstretched arms around the neck of a man. Her skirt was high about her waist exposing the bare flesh of her raised legs and her blouse was open exposing her full bosom. She was having sex with a much younger man. His trousers and boxer shorts were round his ankles. Jack did not recognise either person, but there faces were clear enough to identify them, and they were oblivious to the camera on the video recording equipment being on.

James broke the sound of moaning on the screen. "I have not shown you all of the recording to save time. It runs for about an hour going right up to the start of the conference. This starts after a few minutes and runs for about twenty minutes so unless you knew it was switched on you would probably not be aware of the recording at all. I fast forwarded to see if the conference had gone ok."

"Do we know who they are?" asked Jack. "When did this happen?"

James answered. "I have checked the diary and also the time code burnt into the video. It was two weeks ago when Carey Street hired the suite for a late conference at 7.00pm with a firm in Manchester. So it must have been between six and seven o'clock when the conference started. I guess they tested the link at six and left it on in readiness. Someone must have pressed the record button at the same time.

I have got the video conferencing telephone number of the other party to the conference off the system. Because it was Carey Street and an out of hours booking, I left them to it. So I don't think they know what has happened either."

James handed Jack a note with the special telephone number on it. He recognised the 0161 part of the number.

Jack started to play the detective. "So this was early evening, around 6.15 pm, in a Manchester law firm's video conferencing suite. We don't know who they are, and they don't know we have a video of two people having sex in their conference room shortly before the video conference.

Jack thought for a few moments and then spoke to James. "This is pure dynamite. Give me the original DVD. I need to do some more detective work and then decide what is to be done, if anything. Not a word to anyone, especially none of the team. If we are not careful someone will get it into the public domain. They may think it is anonymous but the police could follow the audit trail right to us. Understood?"

James nodded as he took the DVD out and handed it to Jack.

As he returned to the clerks' room, Jack wondered if Richard Murray was aware of what had been recorded. He would know who was in the video at the very least, but Jack did not want to give away what he knew. Richard would ask why Jack was interested in one of his conferences.

Back at his desk, Jack asked Jason to make an enquiry for him. "Jason, can you ring your opposite number at Carey Street, Barry Nicholson, and ask if anyone left some gloves in our conference suite a couple of weeks ago at their late video call. I would like to know which firm they linked with in Manchester. It may be worth a feedback call to them, but don't let Barry know your real reason for the call."

Jason thought Jack was on a marketing expedition, so thought nothing more of his request. Later that day he spoke to Jack to relay the information he wanted.

"It seems the firm was Porterhouse & Mayfield. They are a medium sized commercial outfit with a good reputation for commercial property."

"Thanks Jason. I wonder what they were doing using a second rate common law set when they could have the pick of the chancery bar." Nothing further was said on the matter.

Jack still felt he did not have all the facts to take the porn video further. He had looked up Porterhouse & Mayfield in the Law Society Directory, but was none the wiser on who was having sex on the DVD. He realised it could be anyone, a paralegal and a boyfriend having a quickie after work, or a solicitor and a lay client. He accepted that the lad was a bit of a stud, and he reminded Jack of his own stature in his early twenties.

A few weeks later Jack was attending the listing meeting with Jenny. He wanted her to stitch Carey Street up on dates for a major personal injury trial due to take place in the autumn. After the meeting, Jack asked Jenny if she wanted a coffee at the Crown Café Bar. Jenny was not sure why Jack was being so friendly, but could not think of anything she had done wrong.

"Jenny, you seem to have settled into our team pretty well. Any issues from your point of view?"

"No" replied Jenny. "All good thanks. The lads are great, and I really don't mind being called "the bodyguard". It is quite sweet really."

"Good. They are learning to respect a female in their midst. It has been a good learning curve for them. I thought you handled the Carey Street clerk well this morning. Who was he?"

"A new lad down from Manchester. I have only seen him once before. Apparently he is related to Richard Murray. He seemed a nice guy."

The moment Jenny mentioned Manchester Jack remembered where he had seen him before. It was in the porn video. At last a breakthrough in the mystery of the porn stars.

Jack decided it was time to bring Jason on board the investigation. The following day over breakfast at the Crown Café Bar he brought Jason up to speed on the whole matter.

"So Jack, why is Richard Murray giving a job to a relative of his who features in a porn video?"

"I have no idea, and that is where you come in." Jason was ahead of Jack for once.

"Would you like me to have a word with one or two junior clerks in Manchester to see what I can find out about our porn star?"

Jack replied. "I thought you'd never ask!"

Jason knew most of the Manchester clerking world. Being a fraction of the size of the London Bar, most Manchester clerks knew everything there was to know about their work colleagues.

Jack and Jason reconvened their meeting a few days later in an empty conference room. Jason started.

"It turns out that this lad left Manchester under a bit of a cloud. Apparently he had been having an affair with an older woman, a solicitor at Porterhouse & Mayfield and a good client of chambers, and it had gone pear-shaped. It cost their chambers a valuable client with a lot of work. His then senior clerk nearly lost his job over the scandal which was hushed up, but it meant the lad had to leave clerking, or leave town."

"Interesting" said Jack. Jason went on.

"There's more. It turns out Richard Murray is his uncle, and he agreed to take him on as a junior clerk to get him out of Manchester. Nobody at Carey Street knows his background. I'm not even sure if they know Richard is his uncle."

Jack had heard enough. "Well, Richard Murray, how very generous of you. Thanks Jason for some thorough detective work."

"What are you going to do with this information Jack? It's hot stuff!"

"For now, Jason, just sleep on it!" Jack had more pressing matters to attend to.

Major public enquiries were a source of quality work and often for more than one member of chambers. All the interested parties would get legal representation so each legal team would have the same preparation to do and attend every day. These events could last for weeks or months, sometimes more than a year. Some counsel would have to work hard throughout whilst some with clients with small parts to play would get away lightly, in the role of "tail end Charlie" as Jack called them.

To get involved with such an enquiry meant watching the media to spot when one was going to be appointed, and then follow up possible leads with the firms of solicitors or government departments likely to be instructed. That meant all the clerking team keeping their ears very close to the ground at the right time.

The appointment of two or three members of chambers to such an enquiry was good publicity for chambers and a feather in the clerking cap, but it was not without issues that Jack had to address.

The trick from Jack's point of view was to get a senior counsel who was past their sell-by date or nearing retirement, or a "farmer" as Jack called them, to be briefed as opposed to a "hunter" who would be too busy anyway. A good hunter could not afford to take months out of their practice which might not recover.

Jack wanted the business as there were lots of fees involved and it would keep a farmer out of his hair for months if not longer. He would sell the idea to such a farmer by suggesting it was good money for their pension pot and good publicity for any future application for higher office. The same argument fell on stony ground with a good hunter.

The six o'clock news that evening reported on the appointment of a retired High Court judge to head an inquiry into the biggest local authority failure to carry out housing repairs in rented accommodation involving hundreds of cases in multiple districts.

First thing the next day, Jack and his team were on to their contacts at several local authorities making sure they could help if called upon. For the hard-pressed and under-paid local authority lawyers such an enquiry was the worst news they could get, so an early offer of help was welcomed.

The phones in the clerks' room were too busy for Jack and Jason to speak on which counsel to put forward so they adjourned to an empty conference room. Jason started.

"Who are you thinking of Jack?"

"I want to target those who are the biggest moaners, the ones with poor repeat business to get them out of our hair for as long as possible. That will give us more time to focus on getting new fresh blood into chambers."

"How about those on the management committee who are always complaining their practices are being ruined by the clerks." After some discussion when various names were mentioned, Jack called a halt.

"I am thinking Peter Livingstone and Tom Wallace for starters, especially Livingstone. Let's try them with the main local authority and go from there. Once we get a couple on board some of the others will come to us to ask why they are not instructed. We can review each on merit at the time." Jason agreed.

Tying up three or four counsel in one enquiry would have a calming and stabilising effect on the other members of the civil team. They would have extra work to cover for those in the enquiry.

Jack knew he would need to tempt some potential enquiry counsel with the possible fees to be earned. Some had massive tax bills to pay and such a cash injection would solve a lot of problems. Others would use the money for school fees, or for the older ones a large tax free payment into their pension fund.

So Jack had to find out what work was involved and the volume of paperwork to make a stab at the fees to ask for. The inquiry was due to begin in the autumn and scheduled to sit for two hundred days, hearing evidence directly from some 450 witnesses,

Jason offered some figures to Jack. "There could be over one hundred lever arch files per brief and allowing for preparation time, the whole matter could take counsel out of action for about a year. That's worth a shed load of money to any counsel. What are you thinking of Jack?"

Jack did not reply but went deep into thought. If he could get three members of chambers briefed he would be adding about one million pounds to the chambers turnover for the year. Obviously that would boost his income nicely, but as he later told Jason at the Crown Café Bar over breakfast "it shows counsel that we want to join chambers that we can attract top public high-profile work as well as quality private work. That is all good for the long term plan."

12 FIRST DATE

"Crisis, what bloody crisis?" shouted Charles Wadsworth. He was addressing the suggestion made by a senior colleague at the chambers management committee meeting a few months later that there was a crisis in chambers.

"There is no crisis because it does not exist. A bunch of junior counsel huddled in the tap room at the Red Lion dreaming of greener pastures elsewhere does not constitute a crisis. Do I make myself clear?"

The committee members remained silent as it was apparent they were not going to get anywhere with the current head of chambers in such a belligerent mood. Jack, who always went to these meetings but did not have a vote as he was not a barrister, sensed that Charles had lost the plot, probably because he was relying on getting word of his appointment to the Bench soon so they would have their new head of chambers which they all clearly wanted.

Jack stayed behind after the meeting as usual to get his instructions from the head of chambers based on the decisions taken. This time he got a further tirade of abuse on behalf of the other committee members.

In the end Charles concluded his monologue. "And you can bet they will all turn up at my celebration party, drink my alcohol and very expensive canopies, and like all good sycophants wish me every success on the Bench in the hope that one day when it is my turn to give feedback on their judicial applications I remember how well they supported me. Well, this particular elephant will have a very long memory!"

Jack returned to the relative calm of the clerks' room which was now empty. It was around 7.00pm, and the team had retired to the WI expecting Jack to join them later. He looked at the diary for the junior members of chambers, the ones who were allegedly plotting the downfall of the head of chambers. Of the five juniors mentioned, three of them were not in court the following day, and two of them had not put their wigs on all week. That was unacceptable to Jack who resolved to provide a short term fix.

Jack walked into the Wiltshire Inn and was greeted by Dillon. "Jack, let me buy you a drink? What will you have?" Jack knew as did all the team that when he was on licenced premises he always bought all the drinks for his team. That was the accepted protocol as they all knew that Jack earned several times more than any of them. Indeed on one occasion Christian Bennet worked out that Jack probably earned more than the rest of them put together.

The way that Dillon had put the offer to Jack was his way of thanking Jack for turning up as Dillon had started a tab behind the bar. If Jack had not gone in that night, Dillon would have had to pay as the landlord's rule was that all bar bills had to be settled on the day or face a banning order. Christian Bennet picked up on this. "Lucky boy Dillon. Could have been another banning order for you without Jack's arrival!" The rest of the team saw the funny side as they had taken drinks off Dillon as well.

Jack raised his glass, a pint of Guinness, to his team and took his first sip. "Before anyone is incapable of remembering, there will be a clerks' meeting in chambers tomorrow morning at 8.00am sharp. Don't be late Dillon!"

Everyone looked at Jack for some clue on the importance of the meeting in the morning, but he gave no indication, save to say "Now enjoy the evening as we will have work to do tomorrow." They all took that to be a positive message which was what Jack intended.

At 7.59am the following morning everyone was seated at their respective desks in the clerks' room at Barcourt chambers, except

Dillon. As the local church clock chimed eight o'clock, James Dunn opened the conversation. "Breakfast on Dillon again. I hope he remembers the brown sauce this time!"

As predicted by Jack at the WI, Dillon was ten minutes late. He arrived with several paper bags, one for each member of the clerking team with their names on. He proceeded to distribute them to everyone.

"James, bacon on brown with brown sauce, Gordon Bennett sausage and bacon on brown, Jason bacon on white with red sauce, and a banana and apple for the bodyguard! Everyone happy?"

Jason interrupted as Jack had his mouth full. "Bringing the breakfast in does not excuse being late. And you forgot the coffees." At this point Margaret the receptionist came in with a tray of take-away coffees and said "Sorry to be so long. I did not want to spill any."

Jack decided not to chastise Dillon any more, but would have a word with him later when he needed bringing down a peg or two. He launched into his reason for calling the meeting.

"Some of the juniors have been spotted in the tap room at the Red Lion in plotting mode, so after the management meeting last night I took a look at their diaries for the last few weeks. The simple truth is they are not in court enough, and that breeds discontent."

He went on. "So, over the next few weeks you are going to make sure that any spare briefs go to them. You will flood them with more work than they can handle. Any extra late returns go to them, and make them travel all over the place. We will show them the grass is plenty green enough at Barcourt chambers. Got it?"

There was unanimous agreement round the clerking table. Jason understood that Jack could not tell them about the head of chambers' application to become a judge, nor any of the planning he was up to. For now Jason would encourage the rest of the team to deliver what

Jack was asking for.

That morning a senior and well respected member of the management committee James Campbell asked Jack to walk with him over to the RCJ shortly after 10.00am. His case was not due to start until 11.00, but Campbell wanted to talk to Jack about the outburst by the head of chambers the night before.

They made their way through security to the interview room next to court 31 which was not in use so they would not be disturbed.

"Jack, we need to discuss the so called crisis referred to at the management committee last night. I am getting vibes to suggest that although in the early stages, a rebellion is on the way. We may have a vote of no confidence in the head of chambers if we are not very careful. I am sure you understand what is going on. I for one would struggle to support Charles Wadsworth, especially after the way he handled the Sarah Ryman affair."

Jack wanted to tell James Campbell about his plans and what he knew, but realised he could not divulge anything. So he stuck to what he could say.

"I had a meeting with the clerks at eight o'clock this morning and outlined what we will do in the short term to quieten any unrest. That will help for the coming weeks. As for the long term, I will need your help to work out a plan for the future. I have the beginnings of such a plan, but I cannot disclose any information at this stage."

Campbell sensed something was up but knew Jack had to be discreet. "I take it by your words that it involves other counsel not in chambers." Jack nodded.

"Then if your plans are to have any chance of success, you must tell me what you can as soon as you can. Otherwise you cannot rely on my support. Do I make myself clear Jack? "Jack nodded again so Campbell went on.

"I have never seen Charles lose it as he did last night in chambers. He must realise his outburst was unacceptable." Jack decided to speak. "I am sure he does, and for what it is worth, I think he knows that his position as head of chambers cannot be sustained long term."

"Jack, I know you get on well with him, as you should as the senior clerk. Make him aware that the clock is ticking on his position. You look after the juniors and I will placate the senior members of chambers without telling them anything. That should not be too difficult to do. Most of them are too engrossed in their work to put their heads above the parapet!"

Jack responded. "Ok, and I will get each one of the juniors on their own for a quiet word to say that senior members of chambers are working together to resolve the issue, and they need a little patience."

"Jack, as you well know, patience is a commodity in short supply at the bar, and you and your clerks are only as good as tomorrow's diary. So make haste."

Jack understood what needed to be done in the coming weeks, and he trusted his team to deliver.

Unfortunately the same trust to deliver was not there when it came to counsel, as Jack found out yet again the hard way when he returned to chambers and the clerks' room.

He was greeted by Jason who had reported a complaint by a solicitor client. Apparently John Goldman, a partner at Featherstones in Manchester, wanted to speak to Jack urgently about a conference in chambers the previous day with Christine Denton. Mr Goldman had sent along to the conference his bright young junior partner who had not been impressed with Miss Denton's performance. He would not say more as he told Jason to get Jack to ring him as soon as he got back into chambers.

Jack opened the telephone conversation.

"Mr Goldman, you asked me to ring you. How can I help?" Mr Goldman did not waste time on pleasantries. "Jack, apparently Christine Denton was not prepared for her conference in chambers yesterday afternoon. My partner who attended was less than impressed with her attitude and even less with her handling of the client. It sounds to me like a classic case of counsel not reading the papers and winging it on the day. That is not acceptable for my firm as you well know."

Jack was contrite. "Indeed not Mr Goldman. May I make some enquiries and yet back to you?"

John Goldman accepted Jack's request and hung up. Jack was fuming. "Silly cow. What was she thinking? Featherstones are a good firm with lots of quality work. Look after a young partner well and you get work for years. She should know better. Where is she now?"

Christian looked her up in the diary on his screen. "She is due in chambers this evening to collect her brief for tomorrow." Jack had a plan. "Tell her I need to see her before close of play today. Tell her it's on an important matter. That way she won't know what hits her."

Hearing excuses from counsel was part of everyday life for Jack and his clerks. The list of excuses was as long as Jack's arm. Not returning calls was a regular complaint, as well as arriving late at court. Top of the list was not delivering papers on time which had a string of reasons, all of which added up to being lazy but in Jack's book it was a lack of client care. It was all about repeat business. He was often telling his clerks his main philosophy. "You have to want the next brief. If you think you are entitled to it as of right, someone else will get the work."

Christine Denton collected her brief for the following day from her pigeon hole and called into the clerks' room. "Jack, you wanted a word?"

Jack took her to the empty conference room rather than talk amongst the clerks. Christine knew it was not good news. "Jack, what's the problem?"

"I have had a complaint about the conference you held in chambers yesterday afternoon for Featherstones. The complaint comes from their senior partner."

Christine Denton immediately went on the offensive by attacking the solicitor who attended the conference. "What's that young brat been saying about me? I didn't like his attitude from the start. He kept interrupting me, trying to lead the client."

"That was because he did not think you had read the papers. Had you?"

Not reading the papers before a conference with the lay client was not a complaint often levelled at Christine Denton. "I saw the solicitor before we met the lay client and told him I wanted to see how he would stand up to cross examination. You know the score Jack. If he cannot do it in conference, what will he be like in court? He could get torn to shreds."

Jack interrupted. "That young brat happens to be a junior partner at Featherstones, and a bright guy. He was put on notice that you may not have been fully prepared by that introduction. Go on."

Christine continued. "Well, I don't accept that, but anyway. I said to the client "I've read the papers but why don't you tell me in your own words what happened?" He then went on to run through the accident. The solicitor was agitated throughout, interrupting his own client and leading him. He was not experienced in cross examination and made the interview much harder than it needed to be. What is he saying?"

"That you had not read the papers before the conference and were not properly prepared."

Christine continued on the front foot. "That's ridiculous. Of course I had read the papers. I always read the papers, you know that Jack."

Jack paused as if to question her words. "I just wonder, Christine, if you were tied up on other matters during the afternoon which may have limited your preparation time, if you get my drift."

Miss Denton knew exactly what Jack meant as she recalled her afternoon of passion in a hotel room with her clerking lover. "I may have been detained a little longer than usual, but for good reason."

"I'm sure" replied Jack. "But did you have enough time to properly prepare the conference?"

There was a short but significant pause in the conversation whilst Christine considered her response. "I did have enough time, as it happens, I just prepared for the wrong conference. I had taken the wrong set of papers with me yesterday morning, so I had to wing it. I had no other choice, except to cancel the conference which was too late. And I was not going to do that. One factory machine failure accident is like another. Just my luck they send a young whipper snapper who thinks he knows how to cross examine."

Christine was now firmly on the back foot. "What do we do Jack?"

"Well for a start you cannot charge a fee for the wrong conference. So tonight read the correct papers and draft an opinion on liability referring in passing to the conference and the lay client's credibility as a witness, prospects of success and on quantum as well if the papers have sufficient information to do so, and let me have it first thing in the morning. There will be no fee for the advice either. Call it an apology if you like. Otherwise you do nothing. Leave the rest to me."

Jack could tell from the look of reluctance on Christine's face that she did not want to do the advice so Jack continued. "Featherstones are a major player in your field. Do you want me to have to explain to your colleagues in chambers that you are the one who blew the work away?"

Christine thought for a moment and then replied. "I'll drop the advice into chambers first thing." "Thank you Miss Denton."

The next morning the opinion on liability and quantum was faxed to Mr Goldman at Featherstones just after 9.00am. At 9.30am Jack put a call through to Him.

"Good morning Mr Goldman. I sent a fax through first thing." Mr Goldman cut in. "Yes Jack, I have it before me now thank you, and I have read it. One of Miss Denton's better pieces of work. Very thorough and clear."

"There will be no fee for the conference or the advice. Miss Denton has accepted that her preparation was not as thorough as she expects of herself, and asks you to accept her sincere apologies."

Mr Goldman replied in a calmer tone than he had the night before. "Jack, your speed and quality of response to my complaint shows you care for the service you provide, and it would be unfair to punish you for another's failings. So on this occasion apology accepted, but let there be no more slipping of standards. Are we agreed?"

"Yes indeed, and let me know the next time you are in London. Lunch is on me?"

"Jack, I think you mean lunch is on Miss Denton!" Jack concluded the call. "Absolutely Mr Goldman. Absolutely!"

The rest of the clerks at Barcourt heard Jack's conversation with Mr Goldman and learnt from the way he handled the apology. So Jack took a moment to reflect with them. "So what have we seem in action here?" he asked. Dillon piped up first. "Anyone can handle the good times, you are judged on how you handle a crisis."

"Not bad" said Jack. "But not the one I was thinking of." Jason knew the answer. "Actions speak louder than words."

"Exactly." Said Jack. "Getting the advice done and delivered before the phone call took the heat out of the crisis, plus allowing for a good night's sleep to calm Mr Goldman down."

The clerks returned to their daily tasks feeling a little wiser but also pleased it was Jack handling the crisis rather than them. Jack and Jason reflected on the day that evening in the WI. Jason opened.

"The diary has been filling better for the juniors in the last couple of weeks, and some of them seem to be a bit happier. It is a bit like snakes and ladders. We make steady progress a rung at a time, and counsel cock up big time and we all slide down the snake. Typical!"

"Jason, that's what we do, and who we deal with. They are not going to change. The world won't change just because we want it to. Our job is to provide the best possible back-up so these guys can realise their potential. Individuals do the work but that reflects on us all collectively. So get me another pint of Guinness before I die of thirst!"

Dillon had been talking to some of the clerks from other chambers on the other side of the pub, but had decided he had to go. So he approached Jack and Jason just as they were getting another drink in at the bar.

"Trust you, Mr Dillon" said Jason. "You can smell a free drink at a hundred yards!"

"No for me, thanks Jason. I've got to go" replied Dillon. Jason looked interested. "Oh yes, on a promise are we? Do we know the unfortunate girl?" Dillon did not respond to Jason's enquiries, but instead turned towards Jack: "Good night Jack, see you in the morning." Jack smiled. "Good night Dillon, and behave yourself."

That week had got off to a solid start for Dillon. Work had gone well for him and he felt his confidence growing with the knowledge he was picking up on a daily basis from the clerks around him. He was getting a traditional upbringing in clerking.

His private life had also taken a turn in the right direction. He was leaving the pub to meet up on a first date with another clerk Charlotte from chambers in the Temple.

Charlotte was a first junior clerk who knew how to look after herself. Dillon thought of her as street wise. She was being taught the clerking skills in the same way he was.

He had picked up on a rumour about Charlotte at a listing meeting that suggested she was being groomed to look after some silks at her chambers who specialised in personal injury work, and had a close working relationship with one in particular, a Nicola Mortimer QC. Everyone thought the silk was a rising star at the bar, so her clerk would be well trained.

Dillon had met Charlotte at a listing meeting a few weeks before and taken an instant liking to her. To Dillon she had a classic hour glass figure, short brown hair to match her brown eyes. She had a sense of humour and acted more like one of the lads than the other female clerks he knew, not that there were many. Her nickname was "Charlie" which Dillon thought was a great compliment to her style and appearance. He felt drawn to her but not in the way he usually selected girls to chat up. For once he thought it could be more serious than usual.

Dillon arrived ten minutes early at the Chinese restaurant in Red Lion Street, just off Holborn. It was a favourite of Dillon's and not somewhere he had taken girlfriends to before. For some reason, he did not want to go somewhere too classy as he was not after a one night stand. He wanted to impress Charlotte that he was a normal guy who treated his girlfriends with respect, that he was capable of showing her a good time without going over the top.

The Chinese waiter spoke good English and he could tell by the body language that the couple were on a first date. He was a little more attentive to help the situation, constantly smiling at them both. He had made up his own mind about Dillon's motives for the night.

At the end of the evening Dillon went to the toilet. While he was away, Charlotte asked the waiter for the bill and made him understand she wanted to settle it before Dillon returned to their table. "I want it to be a surprise."

The waiter replied:" Of course madam, but I think he would prefer a ..." She cut him short to pay the bill but they both knew what he meant. Dillon was both surprised and impressed that Charlotte had paid, especially as he had intended to pay the whole bill himself.

As Dillon and Charlotte went to leave the restaurant the waiter held the door open and smiled knowingly at Charlotte. Outside, as they got into a taxi, Dillon asked "So what was the waiter smiling about?" She replied: "You don't want to know." Taxi driver asked: "Where to my lovelies?" Charlotte looked at Dillon and asked: "My place ok?"

The taxi drew up outside Charlotte's flat and they both got out. Dillon turned as if to pay the taxi driver through the window, but instead asked him to wait. He turned to Charlotte and before she could say a word, he kissed her on the cheek. "Charlotte, I've had a great evening. I would love to see you again, but for now I had better go home before I make any mistakes. Is that ok with you?"

Charlotte was a little bemused but went along with what Dillon had said. She kissed him on the lips and said "That is fine with me. Until the next time" and repeated the kiss as if to make sure Dillon had got the right message.

Dillon watched Charlotte open her flat door and then got back into the taxi. On the drive to the nearest tube station he reflected on a great evening. He wanted to have a proper girlfriend, a long term relationship, and decided Charlotte was the one.

13 THE LETTER

Most letters and briefs arriving in chambers were addressed to "the clerk to….." rather than counsel personally, and anything addressed to the clerks could therefore be opened by the clerks. So any personal mail went straight into counsel's pigeon hole.

That morning Dillon had sorted the mail. He spotted one which looked a bit official addressed personally to the head of chambers. He showed it to Jack who took a careful look at the envelope and said "Leave that with me Dillon. Thanks."

A short time after Charles Wadsworth popped his head round the clerks' room door with his usual introduction of "Morning all" and carried on to his room. The clerks all stopped and looked at Jack. He picked up the envelope and left the room. The air of anticipation was on high alert.

Jack went into Charles's room and approached his desk. "I thought you might like to see this straight away, sir."

Charles Wadsworth read the letter twice to be sure of its content and then passed it to Jack.

The letter displayed the Lord Chancellor's seal and the House of Lords address. At the top it started with the words: "From the Right Honourable the Lord….." It read:

"Dear Mr Wadsworth,

I am pleased to inform you that I am minded to recommend you to the Queen for appointment to the Circuit Bench, with a view to being assigned to the Northern Circuit to sit in the Crown and County Courts as required."

The letter concluded "In the meantime, please treat this offer of appointment as strictly confidential and not to be mentioned outside your close family. Yours" and then a hand written signature by the

Lord Chancellor.

Jack looked up and said "Congratulations, dare I say, your Honour?"

"Thank you Jack, but leave the title out for now. We must be patient. There is a lot to organise. As the letter points out, there are formal procedures to follow. I will get the acceptance sorted today, but I must first ring my wife."

"Indeed, but well done sir." As Jack walked down the stairs his mind started to race with matters which he could now progress. It was going to be a very exciting few weeks to come.

Jack re-entered the clerks' room which fell silent. He took up his seat at the head of the group of desks and opened a brief which he had been working on. Jason broke the silence and asked Jack "Good news then?" Jack nodded approval. Everyone smiled and carried on and the silence prevailed.

They all knew what Jack meant and so started to think through the consequences of the judicial appointment. They also understood the news was not public yet and had to remain confidential until Jack said otherwise. Jack did not say a word on the subject so he could, if asked, confirm he had told nobody.

The following day Jack and Jason met for breakfast at the Crown Café Bar on the Strand. They ordered their usual full meal and after the big mug of tea arrived, started to discuss the news of the appointment of Charles Wadsworth QC as a judge.

"Just in time, eh Jack?" Jack replied "Too true, Jason. Just in time. Now what are we going to do about his replacement?"

There was a lull in the conversation as they thought through the options within Barcourt chambers. Jason spoke first. "There are one or two obvious candidates, but they are by seniority rather than choice by quality, if you get my meaning".

"I agree" said Jack. "There has been enough mediocracy in recent times. It is high time chambers took a bold step and appointed a rising star, and if that means going further afield, then so be it."

"That won't go down well with the old school who see dead men's shoes as their entitled way up the ladder. Jack, to swim against the tide is a risky option. It could cost you personally."

"I appreciate the warning Jason, but if we stay as we are with just the next in line to the throne, there is nothing to stop the junior members throwing their toys out of the cot in six months' time and chambers imploding. Then we all lose out big time."

Jason reflected on Jack's words. "So what do you have in mind?"

"Jason, you recall your list of quality rising stars in the personal injury field. Take another look and update it. A top ten should be plenty as they won't all be available. In the meantime, I have got a couple of meetings to organise to get the ball rolling."

Jason was inquisitive as breakfast arrived. "Can you tell me any names?" "Not yet, Jason, but I will as soon as I can. Now you get stuck into the eggs and bacon. We will need all the energy we can get over the coming days and weeks!"

On arrival in chambers that morning Jack noticed a buzz about his team in the clerks' room. He decided it was more in anticipation of positive change rather than any actual knowledge of what was afoot.

In his own mind there was only one place to start and that was with Nicola Mortimer. Jack looked up the secret number for her on his mobile and drafted a text message to her which read:

"Hope we can meet very soon to discuss planning matter. Regards J."

He read the message again to make sure it was sufficiently secretive, paused, and then pressed the send button.

For the rest of the day Jack kept looking at his phone to the point that the rest of the clerks noticed his behaviour. This just added fuel to the mood of excitement, but nobody dared to ask Jack anything. He concluded by the time he left chambers in the evening that Nicola Mortimer wanted to sleep on his text message. They both knew that once the ball started to roll events would happen quickly and could easily get out of control. So reluctantly Jack decided to be patient.

The next morning Jack came out of the tube station at Chancery Lane into the bright sunlight. He felt his mobile vibrate against him through his jacket pocket.

He had a text message which simply read: "Available as before. Today." Jack smiled and looked forward to a gin and tonic at the Russell Hotel at 7.00pm that evening. He thought to himself: "So far so good but early days".

On his arrival in Chambers, Jack mentioned to Jason that he needed to be away promptly at the end of the day. "I'm meeting you know who for a drink." Jason nodded to indicate he understood the importance but said nothing.

After an hour or so had passed, Jack realised that Dillon was missing from the clerks' room. He called out to the team: "Has anyone seen Mr Dillon?"

Nobody answered except there were several heads shaking their negative answer. Jack muttered more to himself than the others. "Give me strength! What is he playing at?"

At that moment Dillon was minding his own business walking along the Strand pushing his now empty trolley back to chambers. He had delivered Mr Wallace to court 38 in the RCJ with his ten lever arch files and made a mental note to collect him, or just the papers, at 4.30 later that day.

His iPod blasted his eardrums with his favourite Oasis tracks as he admired his trolley. It was mark two, a new design as his mark one had finally lost its wheels on the back stairs entrance to the RCJ in Carey Street. The new mark two was capable of carrying twenty lever arch files with the new wider straps. He felt he was the envy of the junior clerks in the Temple.

Suddenly Dillon felt the left earphone being ripped from his ear with such ferocity that he thought it had taken his entire ear off with it. He swiftly turned as he screamed out to see the member of chambers Nathan Blake holding his earphone.

"Dillon, we don't pay you to listen to trash. Where are you going?"

"Oh, Mr Blake, I am on my way back to chambers." Blake decided otherwise.

"I need you to go immediately to the Red Lion and recover by brief case and bring it to the robing room now. I need the contents for my hearing in half an hour."

Dillon understood his instructions and the urgency. "What does the bag look like Mr Blake?"

"It's a large black captain's pilot case with the initials NB on the top. I'll leave my mobile on in case you can't find it. Text when you are on your way to the robing room."

Dillon worked out that if he took a short detour he could drop the trolley back at chambers on his way to the Red Lion and let the clerks know what he was up to. He broke into a trot to save time.

Jack was about to scream at Dillon as he rushed into the clerks' room and announced. "Nathan Blake has left his briefcase in the Red Lion. I have to collect it now and take it to the robing room."

Jack immediately changed his mind. "Christian, ring the RCJ listing officer and ask him to put Blake's case at the bottom of the list. That will buy Dillon a bit more time." Dillon stopped as if waiting for approval. Jack looked at him. "What are you waiting for? Go! And take your mobile with you."

Dillon searched the Red Lion tap room and the rest of the pub. He could not see Blake's brief case anywhere. He asked the staff if anything had been handed in since last evening, but no joy. He rang chambers.

Jason recognised Dillon's mobile number on the display screen and took the call. He relayed Dillon's bad news to Jack who responded with his own choice words.

"Unbelievable. This grown man makes school boy errors, shits on you and then expects you to wipe his ass! Unbelievable."

Jack felt better for his little outburst. He picked up his phone as he checked the diary to see who the instructing solicitor was in Nathan Blake's case. He rang the solicitor and told him that Mr Blake had had an accident spilling coffee over the brief and could the solicitor please fax a new brief immediately. "I am sorry for the inconvenience and of course your help will be reflected in the fee note for today."

At the end of the short silence Jack concluded the call. "Many thanks. Your understanding is appreciated."

Five minutes later the fax machine started printing out the seventy five page brief which he handed to Dillon. "Off you go and tell Blake what has happened, and that I want him in chambers immediately the case has finished."

Dillon picked up the bundle of papers, tidied them up with pink ribbon to hold them together as a brief, and flew out of chambers.

A couple of hours later Nathan Blake came into the clerks' room carrying the now disheveled brief. "Jack, any news of my brief case?"

"No Mr Blake, unfortunately not. How did the case go?" Blake put the brief down on Jack's desk. "Fine. Judgement for our client and costs. No problem in the end."

Jack needed a few answers from Blake. "What else was in your brief case apart from the brief?" Blake paused for thought.

"Well, my conference papers for this afternoon which I need to read, papers for a couple of opinions, and a few private matters. I do really need to find the case ASAP."

"Ok" said Jack. "Where else have you been since leaving the Red Lion last night?"

"Nowhere really" replied Blake. "I was pretty tired and just took a cab back to my flat." "Black cab?" asked Jack. "Yes" said Blake.

Jason, who had heard the full conversation, picked up his phone as he knew exactly what to do. He knew a guy named Paul who worked at the London black cab main office. It was not the first time counsel had left a brief in a taxi. The cab company knew that there would be a reward for papers and other possessions likely to belong to barristers and left in taxis so would put them to one side.

After a short conversation, Jason said to the person on the other end of the call "NB" referring to Nathan Blake's initials on the briefcase, and waited. The other end responded again to which Jason replied "Brilliant. You're a star!"

Jack took one hundred pounds out of his wallet and handed it to Dillon. "Dillon, Black cab main office. Ask for Paul. Give him the ton in exchange for Mr Blake's brief case. Be sharp about it."

Blake heard all of this, but before he could say a word Jack spoke.

"You will find a miscellaneous item on your chamber's expenses for this month £70 for the cabbie who handed your bag in and £30 for their office admin. Your fee note for today will be reduced to reflect the inconvenience your solicitor was put to when having to fax seventy five pages to chambers as a matter of urgency. Is that ok?"

Nathan Blake knew he had cocked up and once again Jack had got him out of a pickle. "Thanks Jack, you're a star."

As Blake left the clerk's room, Jack spoke under his breath but loud enough for the other clerks to hear him. "Not a star, just a bloody nanny!"

A subdued ripple of laughter went round the clerks' room in case Blake heard. "Now can we get some proper work done today?"

Jack was about twenty minutes early arriving at the Russell Hotel for his evening meeting with Nicola Mortimer QC. After he sat down with his gin and tonic he had time to reflect on the issues of the day. He had focused on one stupid member of chambers who had taken up a disproportionate amount of time.

As Nicola Mortimer arrived Jack thought "the day when everything goes according to plan will be the day I get bored!"

Nicola raised her glass to Jack and before she took her first sip of gin and tonic, asked Jack: "Should there be a toast, or do we just drink?"

"Cheers" was Jack's reply. He did not want to get carried away just yet.

"So, Jack Temple, what news do you have for me?" Jack saw little point in being cagey or defensive. He knew he had a hard pitch to make.

"Ok. I said I would only contact you if I had taken matters further. In the strictest confidence, I can tell you that Charles Wadsworth has had his appointment letter from the Lord Chancellor. I expect to go with him to the House of Lords in about two weeks' time. So we have little time to put our plan into action, if that is what you decide."

Nicola returned to the same issue she had raised at their initial meeting. "And what authority do you have from your chambers' management committee?"

Jack took no time to reply. "I thought you would ask. I have spoken in confidence to a main player on the management committee. He is aware I have a plan to get the committee to consider an external application from a worthy silk, but no more than that. He knows I will only go back to him with your name if you are in agreement."

Nicola thought before replying. "Can you tell me who you are dealing with? I accept that may be difficult for you, but I need to weigh up the chances of him wanting to go forward."

Jack did not want to show any reluctance or hesitation. "James Campbell."

Nicola raised an eyebrow. "Good. I know of James but we have not met. He has a good reputation and some serious work. I would welcome leading him."

They talked around the subject, including the possibility of Nicola bringing one or two quality counsel with her. Jack suggested that would improve the chances of success whilst not being critical.

After about an hour, Nicola drew the conversation to a close. "So, Jack, what is the next step for you to take if I give you an amber light?"

"I would like you to meet James Campbell off the record. Would you be willing to meet him on that basis? I would be happy to attend to make the introduction and stay if that is what you both wish."

"Ok" replied Nicola. "There is one more thing I should mention. I have mentored a few junior counsel who are personal injury specialists. I think at least one or two would move with me, and that would be made easier if you took on my first junior clerk. That might give counsel, and me, an extra degree of confidence. She is a first rate clerk, and she compliments my work brilliantly. That would give you a second female clerk. Would you be happy with that, Jack?"

"Very much so. I have a mind to add more female counsel and as you say, another female clerk would strengthen that cause. So are we agreed to go to the next step?"

Nicola raised her glass. "Oh, I think so, Jack. Cheers!"

Going home on the tube Jack's head was full of ideas for the future of Barcourt chambers. He was in a new scenario now and it would take some careful planning to execute properly. He spent little time reflecting on what he had told Nicola Mortimer QC or on what might happen if it all went wrong. That was a scenario he did not wish to contemplate.

That evening at home his wife Barbara knew Jack was preoccupied with what was going on in chambers and she did not press him to disclose anything he was not willing to tell. As she curled up beside him in bed, she spoke softly.

"I can tell your mind is elsewhere, Jack, and I don't suppose you are going to sleep much."

Jack leaned over and kissed her on the forehead. "You know me too well" he said and put the bedside light out.

14 THE ESCORT

Jack was in early as usual to witness the junior clerks opening the post and DX. Christian Bennet was leading the banter, most of which was aimed at the romantic pastimes of Dillon. "Come on Dillon. You are always punching above your weight. Then you get so drunk you let yourself down. You want to drop a division and settle for someone who will appreciate you for what you are. You don't need to get hammered and you just might enjoy an evening in female company. What do you say Jenny?"

Jenny was not interested. "Oh no you don't "She replied. "You're not involving me in your little drama to wind Dillon up."

By then Christian had a big lever arch files worth of papers open on his desk. He was looking for the back sheet with the solicitor details on and the fees marked. Unfortunately in the post the parcel had broken open and the bundle was no longer in order. "What a mess. It looks like someone has tried to shuffle the pack."

Before he could get the bundle sorted and back into looking like a brief again, Tom Wallace came into the clerks' room and asked him to help get some papers from his room and take them over to court. Christian was away for about half an hour before he could resume what he was doing, and by then several other sets of papers had been dumped on his desk. He muttered to the other clerks looking at his now covered desk "More shit from a great height!"

Dillon had no sympathy in view of Christian's attempts to interfere in his love life. "Stop moaning. Gordon Bennett, anyone would think you didn't love the job really."

It took Christian the rest of the morning to clear most of the papers. As he got to the original set he had been working on several hours earlier, he realised that not all of the brief was there. He panicked and immediately went to check the paper bins they all used for empty envelopes and packaging material along the corridor. Nothing. He paused to retrace his steps and came to what he saw was the only conclusion. He had mixed two or more sets of papers up. He had broken a golden rule: never open more than one set of papers at a time. So only ever take one pink ribbon off one brief at a time.

The blood drained from Christian's face as he returned to the clerks' room. He went over and over in his mind how such a mistake could have happened. At lunchtime, when the others had left the clerks' room, he spoke to Jack.

"Jack, can I have a word?" "Sure, what is it, Christian?"

"I've messed up big time, Jack." He went on to explain what had happened to his day from the moment he sat down at his desk that morning up to the moment he realised his error. Before addressing the problem, Jack told Christian "You were right to tell me straight away. Good lad."

Together they went to the pigeon holes of all the barristers which Christian had put briefs in that day, and took them all to the main conference room. One by one jack opened each brief and checked to make sure they only had the papers relating to the correct case. Eventually he found a couple of small bundles which belonged to the set Christian had left on his desk before going to help Tom Wallace earlier in the day.

"Ok, Christian, I think we have found the missing bundles. Now put all the briefs back in the correct pigeon holes, and we will say no more about it. I am sure you have learnt your lesson so there is no need for me to say more. Am I right?"

Christian nodded. "Thank you Jack. I am so sorry. It will never happen again."

Jack was content for now that the problem had passed. He would use the story to teach the others in the clerks' room.

Two weeks later Peter Livingstone came storming into the clerks' room holding a medical report which he threw onto Jack's desk. "I found this in my set of papers for tomorrow. It has come from another set which are not mine. I want to know how it got there and who it belongs to."

All the clerks looked puzzled and bemused by Livingstone's reactions. That included Christian who did not initially put two and two together.

Jack replied. "Certainly Mr Livingstone." He picked up the medical report and read the name at the top. He spoke to Jason. "See who is dealing with the case of Michael Benson will you Jason."

Jason did as he was asked and replied. "It is one of Tom Wallace's cases. Accident claim for the Union. The case is listed for trial next month"

Jack shook his head. "Oh it would have to be Wallace wouldn't it! Christian, go and see if you can find the brief in Wallace's pigeon hole or in his room. If it is there, add this medial report to it."

Christian came back into the clerks' room without the medical report. "It was in his room. It doesn't look like he has opened it yet. I have added the medial report to it."

Jack went to see Peter Livingstone and explained what had happened a couple of weeks before and how he thought he had put everything in the correct briefs. Livingstone was not satisfied. "So you have now swept the issue under the carpet and expect to get away with it. Well that is not good enough."

Jack was not going to lose a good clerk over this simple error, and Christian had come to him straight away. "Mr Livingstone, the lad told me immediately he realised he had made a mistake. I took steps to rectify the error and so I take full responsibility for what has happened."

Livingstone calmed a little but was determined to make trouble for Jack. "Well we will have to see what the management committee have to say on the subject."

Sure enough Livingstone raised the matter at the next committee meeting under "Any Other Business". Whilst there was general condemnation of the mistake, nobody had the stomach for a full committee fight and Jack just ate a manageable slice of humble pie. As he left the meeting, he resolved to add more training to the clerks' room menu to eliminate as best he could any repartition. As he explained to Jason that evening over a pint of Guinness, "eating humble pie is not good for my indigestion!"

On the tube home that evening, Jack's thoughts turned to his wish list for new members he wanted to get into Barcourt chambers. He considered a few more potential recruits could be lined up if the Nicola Mortimer QC application to join chambers was successful and she became head of chambers.

Jack's thoughts turned to Sarah Ryman and how he could approach her to re-join chambers once there had been a successful hand over to Nicola Mortimer QC. Sarah would feel comfortable with a woman running the show.

He always thought that the outgoing head of chambers had conspired with a person or persons unknown to get Sarah her tenancy. Chambers had been going to appoint just one new tenant as was the usual practice, and that year that person was Nathan Blake.

Jack was right to be sceptical. He had had the opportunity at the last summer charity garden party to speak to the District Judge he believed to be part of the conspiracy. Jack had spotted him enjoying the company of several female barristers during the afternoon. He had already taken several glasses of champagne on an empty stomach.

At a quiet moment, Jack had approached the District Judge carrying a bottle of champagne in one hand and a cold bottle of Chablis in the other. This was Jack's usual networking technique which he used to full advantage.

"Good to see you here sir. Can I top you up? I'm Jack Temple from Barcourt Chambers." The District Judge was momentarily off guard, and then placed Jack as the senior clerk to Sarah Ryman at the time she left Barcourt.

"Yes Jack. Thanks. You certainly can. I know Charles Wadsworth very well. We were old university pals." The usual pleasantries about the day followed, but both then appeared to be struggling to continue the conversation, and as nobody came to rescue either of them, Jack felt the door was open to ask about Sarah.

"Not many of our members seem to come before you these days. These things go in cycles, bit like the buses. None for ages and then loads all at once!" Jack waited for the laughter and reply. He was not disappointed.

The District Judge replied. "Oh yes indeed. I am not sure who you have got at the junior end who might cross the threshold of my courtroom. Give me a few names." By now the District Judge was ready to move on, but felt he should do so tactfully.

Jack reeled off three or four names that got no response from the District Judge. Then he added: "I think Sarah Ryman was probably the last, but she has moved on."

"Oh Sarah. Yes she still comes in from time to time. A bright girl. She seems to be doing very well. I know several firms of solicitors that think very highly of her. Johnson Mann are particularly keen to use her. Now I'll have a drop more from you but I cannot hog the drinks man!"

With a full glass the District Judge moved on and Jack went in search of his deputy senior clerk Jason.

"Are there any partners here from Johnson Mann that we know to have a quiet chat with?"

"Not sure. What about?" asked the clerk. "That is for me to know and you to forget I even asked!" replied Jack.

Jason had pointed out a young partner at Johnson Mann who looked as pissed as Jack needed him to be with an empty glass. The waiters probably felt he had drunk enough, but Jack had decided one more glass should do the trick. He approached.

"Looks like you need one for the road. Here let me fill you up." Jack proceeded to pour before the reply came. "How very kind of you. Have we met before? Your face looks familiar." Right now Jack thought Genghis Khan would have looked familiar to this guy.

"I'm Jack Temple, senior clerk at Barcourt chambers. You must be a partner at Johnson Mann. Good to meet you at last." Jack didn't actually know his name, but it did not matter.

"Gosh I am honoured! Being served by none less than the senior clerk at Barcourt. Well there's a first."

Jack carried on focused on his mission. "We don't see enough of you at Barcourt chambers. My deputy Jason was only saying this morning that your firm have dropped below the radar recently, and we should do something about that."

Keen not to take any blame for such a state of affairs, the young solicitor replied. "I do send in a few sets of papers, but I am dictated to by the counsel instructing policy laid down by the senior partner, you know, the "She who must be obeyed!" one. She decides who gets what work in which chambers. She can be a bit, how shall I say, precious and tends to support friends of friends she wants favours from herself"

The young man then drew close to Jack as if about to whisper in his ear the secret codes for the nuclear detonators. "She's having a bit of a do, you know, fling with a member of the judiciary. It's all hush hush – nobody is supposed to know but everyone in the office does. What a laugh!"

"Oh I see." Jack replied. "I'm not sure you do" came the response. Jack looked puzzled and waited for more information.

"You have just been talking to the very District Judge. He is here which is why she is not!"

Back in chambers later that day Jack went straight for the Solicitors' Directory for the previous year. It was not on the shelf where Jack kept the clerks' volume. It was one of his "bibles" like the Bar Directory, the definitive list of all barristers. He turned to see Jason was already reading it open at the page for the solicitors listed at Johnson Mann. Jason spoke first.

"Who are we looking for Boss?" Jack ignored the question as he did not know himself. It was just a hunch, and Jason had shown sharp skills in reading what Jack was doing, albeit not the full picture.

Jack glanced down the list of names, most of whom meant nothing to him, until he shouted: "Bingo! Thanks – now put the book back where you found it." Jason did as he was told and asked Jack. "So go on – what did you find out?"

Jack digested the information from the Directory for a couple of moments, and then went into full speech.

"I think I have sussed out why the head of chambers backed Sarah Ryman in her tenancy application, and why she moved to Carey Street after the drugs scandal. Follow this one!

Sarah's uncle was a solicitor, but she never talked about him. She said he was off limits for looking for work for her and anyway did not do the type of work she was interested in doing anyway. He is a partner at Johnson Mann. The person who does have the work is the female senior partner, and I am reliably informed she is having an affair with a District Judge.

Apparently most of their office know, so Sarah's uncle will too. My bet is that he got his senior partner, in return for a blind eye to her affair, to bend the District Judge's ear on the pillow to help secure the vote for Sarah. The District Judge knows our head of chambers from university days and when he was an instructing solicitor years ago. There you go. It all comes home to Jack eventually!"

Jason looked unimpressed. "That's a bit farfetched isn't it?"

Jack replied. "Not in our world. Anyway, if you can find a better more likely link, let me know." They both reflected. Jack broke the silence. "The fact remains, Wadsworth should have stood up to the District Judge and let the members elect Nathan Blake on his own which is what they were going to do in the first place."

That was all in the past as far as Jack was concerned. He had seen what Sarah had to offer and she was definitely a rising star. He knew the solicitors who instructed her liked what she did. She delivered and was approachable. That was half the battle the clerks had every day. Jack also knew she had been hard done by at the time of the drugs scandal and her premature departure from Barcourt chambers.

As Jack's train slowed down for his stop, Jack decided that tomorrow he would meet Sarah Ryman and bring her up to speed. He sent her a text message which read: "Can I buy you breakfast tomorrow at the Crown Café Bar. 7.30am?"

As he put the key into his front door, he got a reply from Sarah. It just said: "Confirmed."

Sarah and Jack arrived almost simultaneously at the Crown Café Bar.

Jack ordered his usual and asked Sarah what she would like. "Poached eggs on toast please, and a black coffee." They sat round the corner out of sight from the Strand passers-by. "Ok Jack, what news?"

He did not want to launch straight in, but preferred to hear about Sarah's leaving chambers and not attending the ECM which would have expelled her anyway. She explained that at the time she thought there was another reason they were considering her position. She decided to tell Jack the full story of an incident in chambers during her second six months of pupillage, the period when she was allowed to take cases into court.

"I was so chuffed to get work and at last do the job I had waited so long for. Anyway, I had a conference in chambers for one of those early cases. I went to the waiting room to collect my solicitor and lay client. Sat behind a newspaper in the corner was someone I vaguely recognised, another solicitor. I think he was also waiting for a conference, but nobody else was with him."

Sarah paused and then proceeded. "He smiled at me, and then I remembered where I had seen him before. You recall I told you I had done a little escort agency work while at Oxford University?"

Jack nodded. "Well, I used to travel to Birmingham for the work so no one would know me, and there would be little fear of meeting them again."

Jack nodded again to indicate his understanding so Sarah continued. "Ok, in all the time I did the work, which was for about a year, I never had any problem. I was taken out to functions and for meals, I acted like a trophy wife but more glamorous, and the men behaved. There was no expectation for more, and no pressure on me to offer more. If I chose to sleep with anyone, it was because I fancied them, and never for money."

Jack interrupted her. "Sarah, you don't have to justify your actions to me." She carried on.

"I know, but you have to understand the context. You could count on one hand the number of times that happened. The vast majority involved just a good square meal and drinks in exchange for my company and conversation. Except one occasion. A solicitor from the North Midlands got too interested in me. He became possessive, and demanded I sleep with him or else he would complain to the agency. I told him where to go, and when he went to the agency, they told him where to go as well. I think if he had ever found out where I was from, he would have stalked me around Oxford."

"What happened?" asked Jack.

Sarah continued her story. "I never heard from or saw him again, until that day in the waiting room. I thought if he remembered me in chambers, and I was sure he would have, then he had decided to go to the head of chambers. That would have been so humiliating. He was seriously pissed off at the time he got banned by the agency"

"Why didn't you come to me? I could have helped."

"That's easy to say, but I thought it had gone too far. It was better to move on and keep my reputation in tack."

"Did you ever bump into him again?" asked Jack. "No. If I met him now, I am so much older and wiser I would not let him get to me. I can forget he exists, which is what I should have done before."

"Do you recall his name?" Sarah smiled. "Oh yes, I will never forget it!"

Jack saw a positive outcome. "Then if things go according to plan, and you return to Barcourt, I will make sure he never sets foot in chambers again. Got it?"

Sarah smiled and continued. "To attend the ECM was impossible for me. It would have been too humiliating for words to have my past life exposed. It would have been like being stripped bare in front of the entire membership. No, I could not go through that."

Breakfast arrived but Sarah was keen to hear what Jack had to say. "But you didn't offer me breakfast just to rake up the past. What are you up to?"

Jack threw into the ring his best line first. "Ok, how do you fancy being led by Nicola Mortimer QC?" Sarah raised an eyebrow. "Wow, I did not expect that question which has an obvious answer."

"Then how about Nicola as your head of chambers at Barcourt?"

Sarah put her knife and fork down and looked Jack in the eyes. "Seriously?" she asked. Jack replied. "Seriously!"

"Ok Jack, which particular box of tricks are you opening to make that happen?"

Jack took a more serious tone. "I cannot tell you any more for now, but let me say, wheels are in motion to make it happen and I need to know if you are interested in returning. It will be up to you to meet the management committee and explain not only why you did not attend the ECM, but also your version of events that led to your leaving. The difference this time is that you would get a fair hearing with Nicola Mortimer in the chair."

Sarah finished her breakfast in silence, her mind full of ideas for the future mixed with how she would handle the major obstacle of the management committee.

"Jack, I have a lot of respect for you and your team, and I would be crazy not to take your offer seriously. But I cannot get involved until everything is in place at Barcourt. Do you understand?"

Jack nodded. "Of course, I would not expect anything different. I just need to know that you are on the list when the time comes."

Sarah was inquisitive. "So who else is on the list?" This time Jack shook his head. He did not need to say anything and Sarah understood.

On his arrival in chambers that morning Jack went to the clerks' room and immediately picked up the solicitors directory and looked for the solicitor who had caused Sarah the problem. He then found the case in Sarah's diary which she had referred to, and on the same day the conference in chambers which the solicitor had attended.

The date was the last time that solicitor's firm had instructed anyone in chambers. He concluded that the solicitor had indeed recognised Sarah and decided he did not want to open an old wound. Perhaps he was now married, or always had been, and did not want his sordid past raking up.

He marked the case management system with a note to the effect that he should be told if the solicitor or his firm contacted chambers again. There was no need to be any more specific than that, and he could re-assure Sarah she was quite safe in his hands.

Jack and Jason met in the WI for an early doors drink to reflect on progress with potential recruits and Jack told him of his breakfast meeting with Sarah.

"Jason, you cannot underestimate the impact we will have with two female stars joining Barcourt. A quality silk and top junior makes a really powerful statement." Jason agreed. "My list would have several more names on it if that happens."

They sat for what seemed ages in the pub staring into the future like two loved up lads. In the end Jack snapped out of it and spoke. "Come on, Jason, finish your drink. It's your lucky night. You can buy me a ruby. Your treat!"

Jason smiled. "Thanks a bunch!"

15 COINTREAU ON ICE

Several days passed and the visit to the House of Lords for Charles Wadsworth QC to be sworn in as a Circuit Judge was looming on the near horizon. Jack's plan for chambers was underway, but progress was slow. He wanted all the ducks in a row before he went with his head of chambers to see the Lord Chancellor for the official swearing in of the new Circuit judge. It was a very fine line between success and failure as so much of what Jack wanted was not down to him. It needed others to make bold decisions.

Jack felt the time was right to confide in James Campbell and bring him up to speed.

That lunchtime he asked Campbell if he was staying in chambers. "Yes, I am having an admin day today, doing my VAT return." Jack knew all counsel hated that task as it not only meant they were not earning any money, it also meant it was time to shell out a stack of money they had probably already spent.

"Can I get you a sandwich?" asked Jack. "Thanks Jack that would be great."

Jack returned twenty minutes later armed with a tuna salad ciabatta roll, crisps and a bottle of diet coke for James and his own similar lunch bag. Campbell sensed Jack had something to say so invited him to join him for lunch.

A couple of mouthfuls in Jack said "I was hoping to have a word." Campbell replied. "I thought as much. What is on your mind Jack?"

Jack told him all about the head of chambers appointment to the Northern Circuit, his two meetings with Nicola Mortimer QC and Sarah Ryman and the prospect of getting them both in chambers.

At first Campbell was not sure about the moves. "I think you would have some resistance from the old guard who are expecting the next in line to succeed. You could split chambers if it went wrong. And Sarah Ryman has got some explaining to do around the incident with the powder in the toilet. I'm not sure I could support you based on what I know now."

Jack was not too pleased with Campbell's response but was not going to give up that easily. "I appreciate there is more to be done, but I am telling you now as you asked me to keep you informed."

Campbell softened his remarks. "Jack, I can see where you are going and yes there is merit in your plan. I am just warning you that it needs to be water tight if it is going to stand any chance of success."

After lunch, Jack took a coffee into the main conference room with a few old briefs on which he needed to work the fees out. He jotted down a few names, folded the piece of paper and put it in his jacket pocket. He was joined by Jason carrying two cups of coffee.

"Can I join you, Jack? I brought you an extra coffee as I think you are going to need it."

Jason only attended listing meetings when an important case needed fixing and there was a potential diary problem if it went wrong. He left most of the mundane case listings to Christian or Jenny. That day Jason had spotted potential danger so went to the meeting himself.

The case for Tom Wallace to be fixed for trial that morning was for one of Wallace's best firms and would be a high profile case involving a guy with multiple lasting injuries when he fell off faulty scaffolding. His opponent was a similar senior barrister from Carey Street, so Jason was expecting to do battle with his opposite number there Barry Nicholson.

Just as Jason anticipated, he had got into a blazing row with Barry. As a result, the listing officer sided with Barry as they were good mates in the same football team. So Tom Wallace ended up being double booking and having to decide which case he would return.

Jason knew he would have to take the blame for what had happened at the listing meeting but the first thing was to report the incident to Jack. He told the full story to Jack.

"The trouble is Barry had been clearly sent by Richard Murray to screw me over at the listing meeting. This cannot go on, Jack. Your feud with Murray is costing us our reputation with our own governors. What am I going to tell Wallace? I got shafted because of a personal vendetta between two senior clerks?"

"You're right Jason, it is time for me to put Richard Murray in his rightful place, once and for all. Leave it with me."

Jack had a plan but decided he had to pick the right moment to ensure maximum impact on Murray. No more was said but Jack knew that Jason did not appreciate taking the blame and resolved to make it up to him in due course.

Jack had more pressing issues he wanted to discuss with Jason as they both sat in silence. He thought then was a good moment to bring Jason up to speed on the Sarah Ryman matter. They sat drinking their coffee, both deep in thought.

"Jason, I've been thinking. If Sarah Ryman is going to stand any chance of convincing the management committee, let alone the members of chambers at another ECM, she is going to have to get over the hurdle of the picture Nathan Blake took on his mobile of her in the toilet and the two lines of white powder. And the problem there is that she has never seen the picture. So how can she prepare her defence?"

Jason did not have any answer to Jack's question so he went on. "It's too late now to ask Blake for a copy as he would be very suspicious of why we wanted it."

Jason pondered the problem whilst sipping his coffee. "I have an idea. I could borrow his phone while he is at court and send the image to my phone, then delete the message so he will never know it was sent."

Jack absorbed what Jason has suggested. "Sometimes, Jason Middleton, you're a genius!"

The idea sounded good, but lacked a plan for how Jason was going to get hold of Nathan Blake's mobile phone. All the clerks were into the new technology, especially the new mobile phones with built-in cameras. Jason was not put off by the apparent problem of relieving Nathan Blake of his toy for long enough to get the offending image so decided to sleep on the issue.

"Leave that to me. The less you know Jack the better." For once Jack, who normally wanted to know everything there was to know about life in chambers, agreed with Jason.

The next day Jack felt he needed to make more progress with touting new members, so he approached Stuart Brookes in the robing room. They discreetly adjourned to an unused conference room in the RCJ and Jack laid out what he could in confidence.

"Jack, I have got to say I think your plan is brilliant. Everyone is aware there are more female counsel at the bar, and to have a woman lead chambers who is approaching the top of her game can only invite quality work. So yes you can count me in, but I must issue the usual health warning. I will deny everything until Nicola is appointed as your new head of chambers."

"Fully understood Stuart."

Jack of course had been a little economical with the truth as he had not disclosed the full story about Sarah Ryman's departure from Barcourt chambers, but he decided it was not necessary and may never become necessary as far as Stuart Brookes was concerned. He was on board if Nicola Mortimer QC became head of chambers. That was all Jack needed.

Back in chambers, Jack found a quiet moment at the end of the day to fill Jason in with his meeting with Stuart Brookes. "Jack, we are going to have to make a few more approaches. This is such a good team you are putting together, we need to milk it for all it's worth."

Jack was in less of a rush. "The more we approach the greater the risk the story will leak out, and that could kill the whole plan before it gets under way. Once our new head of chambers is appointed, and that is going to happen very soon now, we can talk more openly to prospective candidates. They in turn will make instant decisions and move very quickly as well."

Jason listened intently. "You're probably right Jack. It just seems we have gone so far and the others need to catch us up."

"I know. Think of us as the scouts for a wagon train driving across the prairies. We have been ahead and looked over the hill to the green pastures beyond. We know the right direction to get to those lush green fields and want the wagons to follow us quickly. And all the cowboys want to do is circle the wagons and put the beans on!"

The following day Jack got a call from Charles Wadsworth to confirm the appointment day had been fixed. It would be the following Thursday, so they had a week to get everything arranged.

Jack spoke to Tom Wallace and Peter Livingstone on when they wanted to have a management committee meeting to consider the appointment of a new head of chambers. They were the two most senior and influential members of chambers, and if there were no outsiders to consider, then one of them would likely be appointed.

Both counsel were keen to hold the meeting before Charles Wadsworth had gone to the Bench. As Jack told Jason later, "It could be a difficult vote, and neither wants to lose. So better to get the succession sorted before the old head of chambers is out of the door."

So the management meeting was arranged for the following Monday with a chambers meeting on the next day to formally vote on the new head of chambers.

James Campbell called Jack into his room. "We need to keep in close contact over the coming days. I will want a full list of those you have approached, those you want me to speak to, and those who are likely to be a soft touch once the word is out that Nicola has been appointed head of chambers."

Jack decided now was a good time to mention Nicola's request to bring her first junior clerk with her. "I would not say it was a deal-breaker, but it would help cement Nicola's position in chambers and provide continuity for her solicitor clients we want to attract. We will need another clerk to cope with the new added work-load. The girl she is suggesting has a solid reputation in the clerking world, and I will vouch for her. She will be a good addition."

"Jack, that is fine with me. The clerking team is your responsibility and if you think we will need another clerk that is your call. Put it to the management committee for approval."

Jack left the room feeling that one more box had been ticked. Jason was pleased too when Jack told him, along with lots of other information, over a pint of Guinness that evening in the Wiltshire Inn.

"Jack, we are getting there slowly. But can I remind you that Richard Murray at Carey Street is going to go bananas when he finds out what you are up to."

Jack took on board Jason's timely reminder. "I know, but by the time he tries to do anything about it, I expect he will be so preoccupied with his own problems to be incapable of any revenge."

Jason had another warning to add. "And if Sarah Ryman comes back, Nathan Blake may not survive in chambers, especially if he is seen to have been the instigator of her departure."

Jack had already worked that issue out. "That's fine by me. Richard can have him at Carey Street. When you are shuffling the pack at Barcourt for a new game, you want to spit out the joker you don't need!"

Jason regarded Jack's comment as harsh but true. "So it's watch this space then?" asked Jason. Jack just smiled.

On his way to the tube station, Jack send a text message to Nicola Mortimer QC. It read: "Appointment next Thursday. Can you meet Campbell ASAP?" Five minutes later his mobile rang. It was Nicola Mortimer.

"Let's meet at the Russell Hotel as usual tomorrow evening. Can you fix that Jack?"

"Sure. Regard it as arranged. By the way, I have Peter Campbell's agreement to your first junior clerk coming with you. He is leaving it to me to arrange approval with the management committee so I will need her CV to present if asked at next Monday's meeting. The full chambers meeting is scheduled for the day after."

"Excellent. See you tomorrow." Nicola hung up.

Jack skipped down the steps at Chancery Lane tube station thinking "Additional clerk sorted. That's another duck in position!"

The following morning shortly after all counsel had left for court and Barcourt chambers was quiet except for the busy clerks' room, Jack called for the attention of his team.

"Ok everyone, listen up." The clerks' room ground to a halt as the team waited for Jack to make the expected announcement.

"As I am sure you will have all guessed, Charles Wadsworth is to be appointed a Circuit Judge. He will be joining the Northern Circuit and the swearing in ceremony at the House of Lords is fixed for Thursday next week. So we have got some extra work to do between now and then. The news goes public this morning when Wadsworth sends out an email to the members of chambers."

"I am going to be heavily involved in organising his departure which will culminate in a celebration party in chambers on the Friday evening, the day after the appointment."

Jack turned to face James Dunn. "James, can you organise the caterers and make all the usual arrangements for the party. Jason, can you speak to Wadsworth and get his guest list sorted and invitations sent out."

"Christian, get on to the florist and ask for a quote for the usual floral displays, and then get Wadsworth to approve. We are spending his money on the party, so he gets to agree all quotes."

Christian looked puzzled. "But won't Jenny deal with the flowers?"

"No. Who usually deals with the florist, Christian? You do, so stop being sexist and do as you are told."

Christian replied. "I just thought" but was interrupted by Dillon. "Don't think Christian, you know it's dangerous!"

Jack carried on. "Jenny, there is a list in the party file for drinks, glasses and the like. What's on the list is your job." Jenny nodded her agreement.

He continued speaking to the team. "There will be extra meetings next week for the management committee on Monday plus an ECM on Tuesday to elect a new head of chambers, so make sure the main conference room is available and check the diary to make sure those who want or need to be freed up are available for those meetings. Any questions?"

Jason piped up. "What do we say if asked about who will be the new head of chambers?" Jack responded quickly. "It is a matter for the members to decide and you have no comment. Don't get drawn into speculation. Stay neutral, understood?"

The clerks all indicated their understanding of the situation and the roles they were asked to play. Everyone knew Jack would be under a lot of pressure for the next week or so, and wanted to help him as best they could. The phones started ringing and work resumed for what was another hectic day at Barcourt chambers.

Jack took Jason aside just before lunch and told him of his planned meeting to introduce James Campbell to Nicola Mortimer that evening. "So I will be leaving a little early this evening, Jason."

"No worries, I'll put the diary to bed. Hope it all goes well."

Jack decided to keep out of the way of as many of the other senior clerks for the time being. He did not want to be dragged into a conversation about who would be his next head of chambers, and besides, he had plenty to think about without a load of small talk.

James Campbell made his own way to the Russell Hotel that evening. He had agreed with Jack that they should not be seen out together as it would only lead to speculation which they could do without. Jack was there first and had his now customary gin and tonic in hand. Nicola Mortimer QC followed moments later ahead James Campbell.

Jack made the formal introduction and they all sat down with identical drinks. Nicola raised her glass. "Cheers gentlemen. Here's to a successful week next week." "Indeed, cheers" responded James Campbell. Jack joined in with "Yes, cheers everyone."

The conversation turned to Nicola's career to date, and then to James's position in chambers. The questions flew backwards and forwards between the two barristers as if they were sparing in court, but with a professional respect afforded to colleagues.

Jack was pleased they were getting on without trying to be best buddies. They acknowledged each other's high standing in the personal injury world, and were surprised their paths had not crossed before. Curiously Jack felt that was a good thing. There was no bad feeling from a previous encounter.

As they neared the end of their drinks, there was a pause in the conversation whilst the two counsel reflected on what they had heard. Nicola broke the silence.

"So where do we go from here?" James spoke up first. "Well, I don't know about you, but I'm going home. Thank you for coming Nicola. It has been a very worthwhile meeting and there is plenty to reflect on. I don't think there is any more we can achieve this evening. May I ring you in the morning and we can decide how we want to handle next week?"

"Please do, James. I need to sleep on it too. Jack, if I think of anything else to add, such as a list of those who might want to join me at Barcourt, I will text you."

"That is fine, and can you email me your first junior clerks' CV?" replied Jack.

"Of course." Nicola left the bar and James finished the last sip of his gin and tonic. Jack wanted to get his first reaction. "So what do you think?"

"Jack, first impressions were very good. I need to think through how we handle what some will see as a female takeover in Barcourt. That aspect needs to be carefully managed otherwise it could all go pear-shaped. We'll talk further tomorrow. But for now, I need to get home."

The next day both Peter Livingstone and Tom Wallace wanted private discussions with Jack. They each wanted to know about the clerking team and what could be done to increase the work in chambers. Jack understood from their respective lines of questioning that they were both preparing themselves for a bid to become the new head of chambers and wanted to be up to speed with what was going on in the clerks' room. Each would come up with a strategy to be presented to the management committee, and then to the membership at the ECM.

Jack went along with the questioning without giving any clue to either counsel about his plan with Peter Campbell and Nicola Mortimer QC.

Later that morning over coffee with Jason, he did admit there could be trouble ahead. "The shit could hit the fan big time when they realise I have been plotting to bring a woman in over their heads. It feels like I have been in the tap room at the Red Lion playing them at their own plotting game!" Jason laughed as he could see the irony in Jack's comments.

Mid-afternoon Jack got a call from Margaret on reception. "Jack I have a message for you from Elizabeth Richardson. She was about to go into court but wanted you to know she was settling her case this afternoon."

Jack smiled as he thanked Margaret for the message.

Jack usually took the day's events in his stride. He had coped with most scenarios before, but this time the wait overnight for James Campbell and Nicola Mortimer QC to reach the right decision for the future of Barcourt chambers was different. His whole plan could fall at the first major hurdle if either of them chose to take the proposal no further.

So Jack had thought he would be in for a sleepless night until Margaret's message changed his plans. He rang Michael the landlord at the Wiltshire Inn.

"Michael, its Jack. Is my room available tonight?" There was a pause whilst Michael consulted the pub diary. "Yes Jack. Your usual double room is now booked for you. See you later."

That evening Jack and Beth enjoyed each other's company, rounding the evening off with a double Cointreau on ice in their room at the WI. Jack had wanted to tell her what was going on but realised that if he did it could place her in a very difficult position within her own firm. She would know soon enough anyway.

Beth sensed a tension in Jack who seemed more preoccupied with chambers than usual. "Come on Jack, what are you up to? You know you will tell me in the end, so why not spill the beans now. A problem shared is a problem halved."

Jack took Beth in his arms. "Right now, life is not that straight forward, and I don't want you distracted from a night of passion by my mundane chambers' matters." He kissed her on the lips. "So why don't you focus on what is in front of you right now and sod tomorrow?"

Beth kissed Jack with more passion than Jack had expected. "Well, after all, it is why I am here!"

16 THE CANDIDATES

As he had stayed in London overnight, Jack was first into chambers the next morning. He busied himself with the early morning routines that got the clerks' room under way.

James Campbell would not be in chambers for a couple of hours, so Jack turned his attention to his promise to Richard Murray, senior clerk at Carey Street chambers. He tossed around ideas for how and when he would confront him with the DVD of his nephew having sex with a solicitor whilst he was working in Manchester.

Jack wanted to maximise the effect on Richard. But it was more than that to Jack. He wanted to make sure Richard was no longer a threat to Barcourt chambers or Jack personally.

As James Dunn arrived at work Jack took him to one side in reception. "James, can you make me a copy of the DVD, the one you found from the Manchester conference?" James wanted to make sure they were talking about the same sex DVD. "You mean the one…"

"Yes James, that one." James nodded and said it would be with Jack the following day. He needed to make the copy on equipment he had at home. Jack was pleased. "Excellent, James. Thank you."

James Campbell walked into the clerks' room half way through the lunchtime adjournment in his case. "Jack, a word please in my room."

They both sat down in Campbell's room. "Jack, I have spoken to Nicola Mortimer a few minutes ago. She has given me her approval to go ahead and I have agreed with her that we will present her application to join Barcourt and become head of chambers to the management committee this evening. She will send you a private and confidential envelope containing her CV and application, along with the CV of her junior clerk plus the names of counsel whom she believes would follow her to Barcourt chambers in the event she is elected head of chambers."

Jack was so relieved but did not show it. "Understood" was all he replied.

"Now we have to decide how to make her pitch at the meeting. I want you to raise her application and explain why you first approached Nicola. If it requires my assistance then I will join in." That much seemed sensible to Jack.

"If, on the other hand, Nicola's application looks to be going to split the committee and possibly chambers, then you are on your own Jack. I will have to align with the will of the members. Do you understand? I cannot put my position in Barcourt chambers at risk."

"Of course, I fully understand."

Jack left the room and picked up Jason on the way out of chambers to grab a sandwich. "The spineless, gutless piece of shit. He expects me to take the blame if it all goes tits-up."

Jason sympathised. "Jack, what did you expect? A clerk is expendable so long as counsel's career is preserved. At least you get to take the plan to the next level."

Once Jack had eaten he calmed down so Jason continued. "Campbell is the good guy in this scenario, but only for so long as it suits his purpose. That's life at the bar, Jack, and you know it."

Jack shrugged his shoulders and turned to Jason. "Listen, if it does all go tits-up for me, I want you to promise me here and now that you will stop Richard Murray taking over as senior clerk."

Jason was happy to oblige. "Now that is a promise I can keep!"

The following Monday back in chambers, Jack composed himself ready for the management committee meeting that evening. An envelope addressed to him and marked "Private and confidential" arrived about an hour before the meeting was due to begin. It contained everything Jack was expecting from Nicola Mortimer.

The full committee attended except for Charles Wadsworth QC, the outgoing head of chambers. He agreed not to attend as the members did not want him involved in the discussions. He was not concerned and indeed was delighted not to be present. Tom Wallace took the chair.

"It seems to me that this committee, which will have to put itself up for re-election once a new head of chambers is elected, must make a clear recommendation to the membership at the ECM tomorrow. As the senior counsel in Barcourt, we must make a choice and present a united front behind a single candidate."

Not to be left out, Peter Livingstone piped up. "Cutting to the chase, you have a choice between Tom and myself. I propose we both put our cases to the committee now, and then we vote on who to recommend to chambers tomorrow."

Jack thought now was the right time to intervene. "May I at this point raise another potential candidate with the committee?"

For a few moments there was a stunned silence. Who on earth did Jack have in mind, and how could they possibly lay any claim to the role of head of chambers ahead of the two present applicants?

Tom Wallace regained his composure first. "Who are you talking about Jack?"

"Nicola Mortimer QC" Jack paused to let his words sink in. The members of the committee now focused on the bundle of papers in front of Jack which contained evidence of his proposal. He went on.

"I have here the application and CV of Nicola Mortimer QC, along with an application from her first junior clerk, and a short list of counsel she expects would wish to follow her to join Barcourt chambers in the event of her being elected head of chambers. I have copies for your inspection."

Jack passed round the table in silence the various copies of the CVs and list of names and everyone present including James Campbell read the contents for the first time cover to cover.

Afterwards, Tom Wallace was furious. "Jack, explain yourself. How has this come about? Did anyone know or expect such an application? It's one thing to apply to join a set, quite another to apply to become its head of chambers."

Jack took the committee through the events since the news of Charles Wadsworth's appointment went public, leaving out any mention of James Campbell, or his own earlier conversations with Nicola.

Peter Livingstone wanted to know more. "Jack, let me get this straight. You approached Nicola Mortimer a few days ago to invite her to apply to become our head of chambers, without consulting anyone here or obtaining this committee's approval to do so. Am I right?"

Jack responded. "There is no easy straightforward way to invite a rising star to join chambers. To get a quality silk and the opportunity to attract the quality work she would bring meant going out on a limb, so I did it for chambers. And it was apparent from the outset that the only way to encourage her application was to offer the prospect of leading chambers."

"I would urge you to look at the long term benefits for Barcourt chambers, the message such an appointment would send out to solicitors and the bar if we could attract a rising star in the field we claim to lead in."

Peter Livingstone was having none of Jack's flannel. "No, Jack, answer the question. Did you, yes or no, approach Nicola Mortimer without any prior consultation or authority to do so?"

James Campbell intervened before Jack could reply. "No he did not. Jack came to me and I met Nicola Mortimer with him last Friday evening at the Russell Hotel. I did not know she was going to go ahead with her application until now, although I thought it highly likely she would.

"I too have read her CV for the first time just now, and I have to say it is impressive. She fills a gap we have at the senior end of chambers for a top silk in personal injury work, and I see her very much as the future. We would all benefit from her high profile position as the head of Barcourt chambers."

Tom Wallace had another go at Jack. "Apart from the obvious kudos at becoming a head of chambers, what is in it for Nicola Mortimer?"

Jack was ready with the answer to that question as it had been part of the argument he put forward to Nicola Mortimer when he first met her.

"She has about ten or so years to go in private practice before she may apply for a High Court appointment, which in turn may lead to higher office. She would have to wait too long for dead men's shoes where she is now to become a head of chambers, and she sees a move to Barcourt as raising her profile and the opportunity comes at the right time for her."

"It is worth adding that once on the High Court bench, she may be able to help the careers of those who helped her at this time."

Jack sensed the mood of the meeting was changing until Tom Wallace spoke again.

"This is an outrage and without precedent. We have never looked to an outsider to run our chambers, and certainly never appointed a woman in the post. To bounce this on us with no notice, no time to fully consider the ramifications, is frankly unacceptable."

Campbell knew he had to stop that approach being adopted by the other committee members immediately. "Tom, you know how these things work when someone moves chambers. It is all done behind closed doors and happens quickly, sometimes overnight."

Tom Wallace was having none of it. "That's no excuse. I, we, should have been consulted first."

The row went on for the best part of an hour. Jack thought the body language soon made it clear that several members liked the third option which Jack had presented to them, but nobody actually came out and said so for fear of upsetting either Tom Wallace or Peter Livingstone.

Eventually James Campbell realised that a vote was not going to happen. "Listen, it is obvious we are not going to be able to offer the membership a single recommended candidate. I suggest we all sleep on it, and let chambers make the decision tomorrow."

Nobody spoke out against Campbell's proposal, so he concluded. "I trust the committee will keep the information we have discussed confidential, and I suggest we leave all copies of the documents we have before us with Jack until the ECM tomorrow."

There was silence as the committee members departed. After they had all left the conference room, Jack asked James Campbell why he had spoken out when he did.

"Jack, you made the pitch, and it is still your call. But it was obvious to me that if I did not step in when I did, you would had said yes in answer to Livingstone's question. Not only was that wrong, you would have been dead in the water before the consideration of Nicola Mortimer had even begun."

Jack conceded to himself that Campbell's intervention was well timed, but still felt he could be hung out to dry if the vote went against Nicola Mortimer tomorrow. "Shall I call Nicola to let her know where we are up to?"

"Yes please Jack, and ask her to be available tomorrow to come in at short notice if we need her."

His message to Nicola Mortimer was just as brief but not so graphic. "Application going to ECM tomorrow. Be available close by."

It was too late to let Jason know what had happened, so he just sent him a text message which read; "Going to the ECM for decision tomorrow. Blood on the walls!"

James Dunn was in early the next morning. He had a small jiffy bag for Jack. "I have the original and copy DVD as you asked. Where do you want me to leave them?"

Jack looked into the bag and replied. "Pop them in separate bags in the top draw of your desk after you have sealed each bag with some binder tape. I will collect them later."

As soon as Jason arrived, he wanted to know from Jack how the management committee meeting had gone. They left the clerks' room and picked up a coffee before heading to an empty conference room.

"It is in the balance Jason. No decision to recommend anyone to chambers, so there is the real prospect that their egos will take control of their tempers at the ECM this evening, and bingo, chambers could be split right down the middle. So if you are not a gambling man, you should dust off your CV."

Jason winced. "Ouch, that bad eh?" "I'm afraid so" replied Jack. "Look, I really don't know which way it will go this evening. Can you hold the fort for the rest of today, and possibly into tomorrow? We will just have to play the whole thing by ear."

Jason was happy to take the responsibility. "Sure Jack, I have got your back. Do what has to be done and we can talk later. Ring if you need anything."

"Thanks Jason. I hope you never have to go through this!" Jason was sure in his own mind that he would never have taken the bold steps Jack had taken, but then reflected to himself that maybe he would if it was in the best interest of his chambers. "Jack, you are a walking advert for why so few can do your job!"

"Are you referring to the theatrical agent, the nanny and the pimp again?" asked Jack. "Absolutely!" replied Jason.

"Ok, now can we address the issue of Richard Murray? I want him put in his box before the news breaks. I need a pretext to get him into the main conference room to watch the video without him realising why he has been asked to come in. Any ideas?"

Jason thought for a few moments. "How about a meeting to discuss video conferencing facilities and the charges to be passed on to clients and professional bodies. I can suggest it will be a pre-senior clerks meeting for us to get our ducks in a row with Carey Street first as they are a main user. I can suggest we meet here as we have the kit. What do you think?"

"He just might buy that. Get James Dunn to ring him to explain the meeting, and that several senior clerks will attend. We need that meeting to be this afternoon. Murray will know we have had an ECM tonight so will be eager to pick up any gossip. Let me know how it goes."

Jack still kept his cards close to his chest about exactly what he was going to do or say to Richard Murray. Jason wanted to be in the room when they met but accepted that it needed to be a private conversation just for the two senior clerks.

Jason told the rest of the clerks what was happening later when James Dunn had fixed the meeting for that afternoon.

Dillon added: "We could sell front row seats for the Temple fight of the year. It could go down in history as a blockbuster!"

Jason left a text message on Jack's mobile phone to confirm the arrangements for the meeting with Richard Murray and told the rest of the team to "maintain radio silence throughout on this matter or risk the wrath of Jack Temple".

Christian tried to lighten the mood with a characteristically bad joke that he felt he could make as Jack was absent from the clerks' room. "Ah the wrath of Shirley Temple. Hell hath no…"

Jason interrupted him. "Gordon Bennett, don't go there, all right, just don't go there!"

Jack decided to go to the conference room for his meeting with Richard Murray fifteen minutes early as he wanted to make sure the DVD was working properly and set to start at the right moment in the short video of Murray's nephew having sex.

Richard Murray strode into the main conference room at Barcourt expecting to see several of his senior clerk colleagues seated round the table. Instead he just saw Jack seated at the head of the table with the video screen switched on but not playing anything. "Oh where is everyone. Have I got the right time?"

"You have the right time but it is just you and me, Richard." Richard sat down opposite Jack looking a little puzzled. "Ok, is the video a snuff movie? That's what you like to watch, isn't it Jack?"

Jack did not rise to the bait. "You're right we have a video to watch, but it is more of a porn film than snuff. I think you will appreciate this much more."

Richard's blood pressure began to rise. "I don't have time for your childish pranks, Jack. If there is no meeting then I'm off, and don't waste my time in future." He started to get up from his chair.

Jack spoke in a dominant tone. "Sit down and watch." He pressed the play button on the remote control and the video started.

Richard Murray sank back into his chair with a look of total disbelief on his face. He watched his nephew having sex on a conference room table with a woman several years his senior. At the end, he just stared at the screen with his mouth wide open. He did not hear Jack's words.

"Close your mouth Richard, I can see your fillings." It took Richard a few moments to recover his composure. "Where did you get this?"

"Right here, Richard. Good isn't it? Your nephew has another career in the porn industry if he ever wants to leave clerking."

Richard knew there would be a reason for Jack showing this video to him now. "Ok Jack, what do you want?"

"Nothing Richard. From you, absolutely nothing." "What do you mean, nothing" responded Richard.

"Just that. Nothing at all. You can have the DVD, it's a copy. This is just one senior clerk looking out for another, as you would expect."

Richard was still expecting the worst was to come, and he was right.

"Today, you will hear breaking news about exciting developments at Barcourt chambers, and more news in the coming days and weeks, some of which will effect Carey Street. I don't expect to hear a single word from your lips to interfere with what you learn, no attempts to block any action any of your governors may take, and no getting your clerks to say a bad word about Barcourt chambers. Do you understand?"

For a moment Richard went on the offensive. "Are you trying to blackmail me?" "Of course not Richard. I am merely seeking your support for events out of your control, and giving you a copy of a very sensitive video, as a work colleague would do."

Jack took the DVD out of the machine and handed it to Richard as he started to leave the room. Jack went ahead of him and opened the door.

As Richard walked alongside him, Jack leant forward and whispered into his ear. "And no more silly nicknames. I told you I would fuck you, Richard. Now you know how it feels"

Richard did not reply but stormed off out of Barcourt chambers. The clerks saw him go through reception. Jason was the first to speak. "I don't think we will have any problems with Carey Street. Dillon, not a word to anyone. The same goes for you all, understood?"

As he finished speaking, he looked up to see Jack enter the clerks' room with a smile on his face. He knew he had just met Richard Murray. "Good meeting, Jack?" "Oh yes, very satisfactory!" Nothing further was said on the topic.

Members of chambers started arriving for the ECM as soon as the courts rose for the day. There were no conferences with solicitors or lay clients so most of the members gathered in their rooms to await the appointed time of six o'clock.

It looked like a full turnout of the membership which involve Dillon and James Dunn moving lots of chairs into the main conference room. Dillon put the last in place and surveyed the room. "It is going to be cozy, that's for sure."

Eventually Jack arrived with about ten minutes to spare. He had not wanted to be in chambers so nobody could collar him before the meeting started. This meant he avoided lying to anyone. He had asked Jason to confidentially make extra copies of the paperwork supplied by Nicola Mortimer to hand out if required. As Jason handed the copies to him, Jack left instructions for the clerks to go home on time once the diary was put to bed, and for them all to meet for breakfast at the Crown Café Bar at 7.30 am for a breakfast briefing. "Until then, total silence. Understood?" Jason nodded.

Tom Wallace and Peter Livingstone arrived in the main conference room for the ECM with a minute and two minutes to spare respectively. They did not acknowledge each other's presence. James Campbell nodded towards Jack, feeling that any more contact would not help their mutual cause.

The top table in the main conference room consisted of Tom Wallace and Peter Livingstone, flanked by James Campbell on one side and Jack Temple on the other.

Tom Wallace again assumed the role of master of ceremonies. He rose to his feet.

"Well as the clock has just passed into happy hour, it seems appropriate to call the meeting to order. As the most senior member of chambers, it falls to me to call this ECM. Thank you all for coming at such short notice. I know we would normally have this meeting to elect the new head of chambers after Charles has been sworn in, but in the circumstances, we had no alternative but to call the meeting for today."

"Before we start I would like on behalf of chambers to thank Charles Wadsworth for his sterling work as our head of chambers for the past few years. He has applied himself to looking after our interests and promoting Barcourt across the legal landscape with his usual diligence and attention to detail. We wish him every success in his new role on the bench."

"There is only one item on the agenda, namely the election of a new head of chambers.

Jack kept his head down looking at the bundle of copy documents in front of him. They comprised the CV of Nicola Mortimer QC, the CV of her junior clerk, and a short list comprising the names of counsel who might follow her to Barcourt if she won the election.

Wallace carried on. "So there are three nominations. They are myself, Peter Livingstone, and Nicola Mortimer QC." Jack could feel the sharp intake of breath around the conference room as the surprise third name was revealed. As nobody spoke, Wallace continued.

"As neither I nor any member of the management committee, except James Campbell who can speak later, were made aware of the third applicant until late yesterday, I feel we should hear from the instigator Jack Temple so we may all make an informed judgement on the outside applicant. Jack"

Jack rose to his feet. He was very careful to set out exactly what he had told the management committee the night before. He realised any inconsistency would be seized upon by the opponents to Nicola Mortimer.

Wallace then invited James Campbell to address the meeting and tell what he knew of the last minute application by an outsider. Campbell described his involvement without giving away his feelings or the likely direction of his vote when the time came. He sat down and Wallace resumed.

"So ladies and gentlemen, there you have this extraordinary turn of events. For our part, Peter and I are available to questions, and the floor is open for debate. Start us where you will."

Wallace took a moment to reflect on his own words, and as nobody spoke up, he chose to carry on. "Oh dear that sounds rather like the words of an auctioneer at a public auction. Sorry. Please let us have your views."

Jack realised nobody was keen to stick their head above the parapet. If they did they ran the risk of offending which could hinder their career. He felt the members lacked a passion to fight for a candidate, and although the debate rumbled on for the best part of an hour, no clear result appeared in sight.

James Campbell, sensing the same level of inertia around the room, picked his moment to speak again, and this time weighed in with all the arguments for chambers being dynamic and taking a bold decision. He sounded as if he was addressing the Court of Appeal on a topic he was passionate about. Jack, who had never seen him in action in court before was seriously impressed.

Campbell summed up the situation. "Yes, we can follow the traditional route and elect from within our own ranks, but here we have a chance to put Barcourt chambers well and truly on the map. I believe we will all individually and collectively benefit, so my vote will go to Nicola Mortimer QC."

Campbell's words broke the ice and a proper debate followed. After another half an hour Nathan Blake, who was seated at the back, decided now was the right time for him to speak. "Dear colleagues, may I suggest a show of hands for each candidate, or perhaps a secret ballot?"

Wary that his opportunity of a successful outcome might be about to slip through his fingers, Peter Livingstone interrupted. "You have all had the opportunity to put questions to two out of the three candidates, yet the third, who is hardly known to you, has not been heard at all. So either Nicola Mortimer should be invited to join out meeting to be interviewed, or disregarded from any vote."

Wallace agreed as Campbell looked at Jack who knew what Campbell wanted to know. He nodded his confirmation at the same time as getting his mobile phone out of his pocket.

Campbell spoke. "In anticipation of your request, I asked Jack to make sure Nicola was close by to attend at short notice. Jack, would you please ring Nicola Mortimer and ask her to join us in ten minutes. In the meantime I suggest we have a short comfort break."

17 BREAKING NEWS

For most top Queen's Counsel, appearing before the House of Lords was the pinnacle of their career. It did not get much better. Many eminent QCs never got to appear before the five law Lords who represented the most challenging panel of inquisitors.

Their Lordships would allow counsel a few minutes of opening remarks to get into their stride and then launch into a debate amongst themselves and counsel on the law surrounding the case as each of them saw it. Consequently counsel, whose well-rehearsed speech would go out of the window, was left flying by the seat of their pants. The questions came from five different highly intelligent lawyers who often argued amongst themselves as counsel was trying to hold their case together.

Nicola Mortimer QC strode into the main conference room at Barcourt chambers with the confidence expected of a highly respected silk who had appeared in the House of Lords. She was smartly dressed in her court clothing of black suit and white open-necked blouse, and Jack saw the striking similarity with how Elizabeth Richardson looked the first time he had seen her. Nicola had that certain star quality that got her noticed. Whatever it was, she had it in spades.

Tom Wallace greeted Nicola and invited her to sit alongside the main top table. Jack watched as the members of chambers politely asked questions of Nicola ranging from her formal qualifications to her two appearances in the House of Lords. It was all very friendly, nothing like the bloodletting he was expecting.

Nicola didn't just play every question with a straight bat, she positively knocked them out of the ground. As James Campbell put it to Jack later, "You don't get to become a silk unless you are a very good advocate. It is those advocacy skills that set you apart from the rest."

Peter Livingstone became resigned to the fate of his application to become head of chambers and looked forward to the chance to be led by her. He had not appeared in the House of Lords, and fancied such a trip, even as junior counsel being led by a female QC, would enhance his prospects of judicial appointment one day.

As the questioning became less aggressive, Jack's confidence in the outcome grew. He thought if he just kept his head down, focusing on the CVs in front of him, he might not have to speak.

A large pregnant pause became a little uncomfortable for Tom Wallace who turned to Jack and glared at him with a look that would have killed lesser mortals. "Jack, do you have anything to say?"

Jack composed himself and thought for a moment or two, and then replied. "Well at this stage in a tenancy application I am normally asked if I feel I can sell the candidate to our solicitor clients. All I can say on this occasion is that the prospects excite me enormously, and I am confident chambers as well as counsel will benefit hugely from taking such a bold step."

Tom Wallace had heard enough. His chances of being elected were receding, and he realised that he had better play the sycophant card while he had the opportunity. He would have another day to get his own back on Jack, the man he saw as responsible for him not becoming head of chambers.

"I think we have all heard enough. Nicola, would you like to wait in reception for a few minutes. I don't think we will be too long. Jack, would you please escort Nicola to reception and stay with her? Thank you."

Nicola sat in the big arm chair in reception and reflected with Jack on the events of the last hour. "Well, I thought that went well. I would love to be a fly on the wall in there now. My ears are burning alright!"

Jack was calm on the outside but in turmoil on the inside. "This is worse than sitting outside the headmaster's office."

"Jack, if I don't get in we will have to make sure nothing gets out. Whoever is elected will need to assure me that nothing will go public." Jack nodded his understanding, although just at that moment he did not want to contemplate failure. The ramifications were too horrendous.

After what felt like a lifetime to Jack that was actually about fifteen minutes, Nathan Blake walked into reception and asked both Jack and Nicola Mortimer to return to the conference room. They both resumed their former seats as Tom Wallace rose to his feet and turned towards Nicola.

"Nicola, I am pleased to announce that after a show of hands and a unanimous decision, your application to join chambers has been accepted. You are now the new head of Barcourt Chambers. Congratulations!"

There followed an enthusiastic round of applause. Jack rose to his feet with the others as Nicola moved to centre stage and shook the hands of the others on the top table.

Wallace asked her. "Would you like to say a few words Nicola?" The room fell silent.

"Well, let me start by thanking you all for the confidence you have placed in me. I am truly honoured to accept the role as your head of chambers."

As Nicola went through her short acceptance speech that would have graced any new incumbent at ten Downing Street, Jack's mind raced ahead to the tasks in front of him. Getting the new head of chambers he wanted was a massive step, but still only one step in the right direction.

The next day Jack strode down the Strand towards his breakfast meeting with the clerks at Crown Café Bar. Despite it being nearly an hour before any of them usually arrived in chambers, that morning there was a hunger for food and information.

Jack did not disappoint on either count. "Fernando, your finest full English all round please, and a bottomless coffee pot!" he exclaimed walking past the counter to the assembled clerks sitting at the back of the café. "Morning all. It is time to put you all out of your misery. I can confirm that we have a new head of chambers."

He turned to speak directly to Jenny. "She is Nicola Mortimer QC"

Jason watched his colleagues absorb the news with varying degrees of surprise and excitement. He broke the silence. "How did Tom Wallace and Peter Livingstone take it?"

"As well as could be expected, really Jason. To begin with they fought for what they thought was theirs, but in the end I think even they could see it was a bold and exciting move for Barcourt chambers. It was a unanimous decision, although one or two did abstain. But there were no votes against Nicola Mortimer, which was good."

Dillon asked the next question. "When does she move in? When will we meet her? According to gossip, she's a bit of a hottie." "Way out of your league Dillon" said Christian. Jack continued.

"She is bringing her first junior clerk with her. I have not met her yet, but she sounds a good strong addition to our clerks' room." Dillon picked up on the gender of the new clerk.

"Jack, you said "she". So we will have another female in the clerks' room?" "You're sharp this morning Dillon" said Christian.

"Great" said Jenny. "It will be good to have some female banter for a change. Will you cope Dillon?"

Jack took control again. "That's enough wise-cracks over breakfast, you are putting me off my eggs. I expect Nicola Mortimer will move over the coming weekend. She is going to tell her chambers this morning. James, you make sure all her cases are on the system next Tuesday, and Jason you bring our diary up to speed with the new clerk. I am sure she will bring a print-out of Nicola Mortimer's diary. She will need some training on how we do things here, so you can show her the ropes. Any questions?"

Christian spoke again. "Are you going to eat that spare sausage on your plate Jack?" "No Christian, it's all yours."

As soon as Jack had announced that Nicola Mortimer QC was to be the new head of chambers, Dillon's heart sank. It plummeted further when Jack then announced that she was bringing her first junior female clerk Charlotte with her.

He realised his relationship with Charlotte could not continue once she joined chambers with Nicola Mortimer QC. Even if Jack could be persuaded to allow them to continue, the members of chambers would not allow any mixing of work and pleasure within their clerks' room.

Dillon realised what was even worse for him. Charlotte would be seated in the same clerks' room with him every day. He would not be able to forget her which made the situation hard to bear.

But Dillon did not want to forget her. Normally he would say to Christian: "Just my luck. Still, plenty more fish in the sea!"

This time he did not want to say anything of the sort. For once in his life he felt sad, and it showed on his troubled face. Jason spotted it first.

"What's up Mr Dillon? Don't you want a new lady QC to dream about? Maybe her clerk will be a stunner too!"

Dillon put on a brave face but did not reply. He was deep in thought of how his weekend would pan out with Charlotte.

After the chambers' meeting had folded the previous evening, Tom Wallace and Peter Livingstone adjourned to Tom Wallace's flat in the Temple, to lick their mutual wounds. Each felt hard done by in not becoming head of chambers. They debated long into the night over two bottles of claret what had happened, choosing not to accept it might have been their own lack of leadership qualities that had led Jack to approach an outsider.

Having realised that it was Jack who must have laid the ground work for Nicola Mortimer's application to join chambers, they speculated on how he would have gone about making an approach to her in the first place.

"Peter, for Nicola Mortimer to even contemplate moving to Barcourt, she would have had to know there was a vacancy, so Jack must have told her about Wadsworth's appointment, which would involve disclosing the contents of the Lord Chancellor's letter of appointment to Charles Wadsworth before it was public knowledge."

Livingstone picked up on where Wallace was going with his train of thought. "They both knew that the letter and its contents were only to be disclosed to immediate family."

"Exactly" said Wallace. "Jack has flagrantly disregarded the Lord Chancellor's specific instruction. That could place any future application for a judicial post from a member of Barcourt chambers in jeopardy if it ever got out."

Livingstone, who regarded himself as next in line to apply to become a judge, agreed entirely. "Jack is a loose cannon. He has to be stopped. His tactics in the clerks' room are unacceptable. Work allocation has gone to pot, and he is out drinking far too much instead of working the phones to get the business in."

The pair of them concluded the evening vowing to have Jack's blood, especially as they each now blamed Jack for one of them not becoming head of chambers. Wallace outlined their tactics. "We attack Jack's behaviour and have him sacked. That way Nicola Mortimer will be embarrassed and may well stand down, leaving the way clear for chambers to go down the correct and traditional path in its election of a new head of chambers."

They both arrived late into Barcourt chambers the following morning and went straight to their respective rooms bypassing the clerks' room. Neither could face confronting Jack as it was neither the time nor the place for such action. They had decided to rally support for a vote of no confidence in the senior clerk before introducing it as an item in the "Any Other Business" category at the next chambers management committee meeting.

Jack and the clerks had been in chambers after their breakfast meeting and were busy on the pre-court morning routines. They did not see Wallace and Livingstone walk past reception.

Jason was deep in thought about whom Jack would next approach to join chambers once the news of Nicola Mortimer's election became public. He was hoping to get to make a few initial contacts himself as he wanted the experience. Now the news was in the public domain, Jack felt more comfortable discussing his plans in the clerks' room.

Jason got out his list. "So where do we start Jack?"

Jack got out his list too. "We will have to wait for Nicola to see how her colleagues react to her move, so we can pick up with those next week. I will speak to Sarah Ryman today, and then we can look at the guys that left us over Sarah's departure. Before then, I must also speak to Stuart Brookes. I think he will be interested in returning to us."

"I think you should put a few feelers out for those on your list, but only one at a time. The momentum has to build, and we don't want any farmers. We've got enough of those as it is."

The next day Jason told Jack that he would be out at lunchtime and he would be late back in the afternoon.

"Are we likely to have any trouble with Carey Street chambers when the shit hits their fan?" Jack responded in a positive mode. "Oh, I don't think so. Their senior clerk now knows when he has been shafted big time. I doubt he has any stomach for a fight."

"Excellent!" said Jason as he left the clerks' room.

He did not return until around three o'clock, which was very late for him. Just before he left, Nathan Blake had rung into chambers and left a message with Margaret to the effect that his case would go on all afternoon in the RCJ, so Jason had gone over to the robing room to check it out and make sure Nathan Blake would finish before the end of the day. It meant counsel would be available for his case the following day.

Jason had an ulterior motive for going to the RCJ. At 2.15pm promptly, all the courts resumed and Nathan Blake left the robing room along with all the other barristers. As was his custom, He put his mobile phone on charge and left it on the table next to his wig box.

Jason had been prepared to rummage through Blake's bag to find his mobile, but he spotted it on the table. "Thank you Nathan, very kind of you" thought Jason as he picked the phone up. He hoped it was still unlocked, but he was out of luck. He punched in the factory default password "1234" and the mobile opened. He smiled to himself as he quickly found the image of the toilet seat showing the two lines of white powder and sent a copy of it to his own mobile number.

Once it had arrived on his mobile, and he could see the image, Jason deleted the sent message off Blake's phone. He then put the mobile back where he had found it and went back to chambers.

On his return he whispered to Jack. "I have the image you wanted on my mobile. Shall I send it to your mobile?"

"Yes please, Jason. That would be kind" replied Jack.

As soon as the image arrived on Jack's phone, he forwarded it to Sarah Ryman with the text message: "Urgent. News. Jack."

Sarah sent an immediate reply. "Sure. My flat 7.00pm"

Jack rang the bell exactly on time and Sarah let him in. "Jack, have a seat. Can I get you a drink? A beer or a glass of wine. I'm having a chilled glass of Chablis."

Jack was partial to a glass of Chablis. "I'll have the same as you please. Have you heard any news yet about Barcourt chambers?"

"No" replied Sarah. "What has happened?"

Jack brought Sarah up to speed on the appointment of Nicola Mortimer as head of chambers, and that she was probably going to move in over the weekend and bring her female first junior clerk with her.

"So if you want to come back to Barcourt, now would be a good time. It makes a big statement to the legal world if we can attract two rising female stars in our specialist area of expertise."

Sarah thought for a few moments. "God, I think Richard Murray will be spitting chips when he finds out."

"I don't think you have anything to worry about Richard. He knows when he is beaten. So will you rejoin us?"

Sarah hesitated again. "It is a big step, and I am going to have to deal with an appearance before your management committee to explain the picture you sent me. It could go wrong."

"Sarah, I have to ask you to trust me. I will speak before hand to Nicola Mortimer and pave the way as best I can."

"Jack, let me sleep on it and I will text you first thing in the morning. Is that soon enough for you?"

Jack accepted it was a very important move for Sarah, and there was still a big hurdle to overcome in the form of the management committee.

As Sarah held the flat door open for Jack to leave, she had a thought. "You do realise that if I do come to Barcourt, there is every chance Nathan Blake will leave?"

Jack smiled. "I do hope so. Leave him to me!"

As he walked towards Holborn tube station he rang Stuart Brookes.

"Stuart, sorry to be ringing so late. Is it convenient to talk?" Stuart confirmed he was free so Jack carried on. "Good, I wanted to let you know that the plans I outlined to you recently have happened."

"Jack, that's great news. When does it all happen? I have been out of town all day and not spoken to anyone."

"Charles Wadsworth going to the House of Lords to be sworn in as a circuit judge, Nicola Mortimer was elected head of chambers yesterday and moves in over the weekend, and I am expecting Sarah Ryman to re-join chambers within the next week. Are you still interested?"

Stuart Brookes was ecstatic. "Jack, you had me at the House of Lords. The rest is the icing on the cake. What do you want me to do?"

"I will get Jason to ring you on this number tomorrow afternoon and make the arrangements. I would do it myself but I am having tea with the Lord Chancellor!"

18 HOUSE OF LORDS

The next day, Jack sat on the tube travelling into London for what he knew would be another action packed day at the coal face. He imagined life under a new head of chambers which he found stimulating.

As he came out of the underground station his mobile phone pinged to tell him he had a message. It was from Sarah Ryman and read: "Happy to go ahead but we need a careful plan. Speak soon. Sarah"

Jack was pleased with her decision and would think through the steps once he had got Wadsworth off his back. As he sat down at his desk, Jason handed him a copy of the Times newspaper for that day. It was folded open at the announcement page, and the top box advert read:

"Barcourt Chambers congratulates His Honour Judge Charles Wadsworth QC on his appointment to the Northern Circuit. We wish him well in his new career."

The announcement brought home to Jack the importance of Wadsworth's judicial appointment and the trip to the House of Lords was the beginning of a new chapter for Jack and Barcourt chambers.

Jack had breakfast brought into chambers for the clerks plus two bottles of champagne to wash down the croissant filled with scrambled egg and crispy bacon plus pastries and the other delicacies supplied by the Crown Café Bar.

Jack's team stood around in the clerks' room enjoying the special moment with some lively banter, mostly aimed at Jack who cut a dashing figure in his morning suit hired for the day from Ede and Ravenscroft.

The lads warned him not to spill tomato ketchup on his black morning coat that matched the cashmere striped trousers and dove grey double breasted waistcoat hiding a plain white shirt. Jason felt a word of warning was due.

"Bright red sauce on a white shirt would suggest blood on the walls in chambers." James Dunn chipped in as well. "That was at the chambers ECM to appoint the new head of chambers. Should I call the paramedics?"

Jenny joined in. "Wow, what a handsome senior clerk we have!"

Christian Bennett weighed in with a caution. "Steady on now guys, the bodyguard is falling for the boss. And we all know what happened when the boss fell for the bodyguard. Jack, watch out."

Dillon was seriously impressed. "Looking quite the part, Mr Chaplin. Where's your walking stick?" Jack obliged with a Charlie Chaplin waddle round the clerks' room twirling an umbrella.

Charles Wadsworth was in his room with his wife putting the final touches to his formal attire. Jack would traditionally have helped him dress for the occasion, but he left it to his wife who clearly was enjoying her moment as well as her new outfit that would have graced Royal Ascot.

Jack got the nod from Margaret in reception that the car was outside chambers so Jack went up to the head of chambers' room for the last time.

"Quite a day, don't you think Jack? Are we ready to go?" Jack nodded and held the door open as Mrs. Wadsworth lead the way.

Photographs were taken on the steps of chambers before Jack, Charles Wadsworth and his wife climbed into the waiting black limousine for the short drive to the House of Lords

The three of them were seated waiting outside the Lord Chancellor's office admiring the grandeur around them and soaking up the history of the place. Charles broke the silence. "So this is the head master's study we see before us."

The door opened and Charles Wadsworth led the way into the Lord Chancellor's office, followed by his wife with Jack bringing up the rear thinking to himself that the atmosphere was about as tense as it gets in the Court of Appeal.

After the formal swearing in, the Lord Chancellor turned to Jack. "I suppose you have a large void to fill now you have lost your head of chambers. No doubt you will work some magic behind the throne as all good senior clerks do."

Jack nodded in agreement but felt he should be both complimentary and non-committal at the same time. "The end of an era for Barcourt chambers, that is for sure, but we will have to see what the future holds."

The Lord Chancellor decided that was enough small talk and suggested tea with his wife in their flat above. "The view across the Thames is worth a look."

The limousine took the new judge, his wife and Jack to the Savoy Hotel where Jack had arranged a small reception and meal for the new judge plus his close family and friends to celebrate the occasion. On the way most of the conversation was dominated by the décor of the flat where they had tea.

"Did you take in that fabulous wallpaper?" asked Mrs. Wadsworth. "I bet it cost more than £4 a roll at B & Q!"

Her husband replied. "I think you can add a couple of noughts on that figure, and don't get any ideas. I'm on a judge's salary now so we will have to pull our belts in."

The usual chambers' party to celebrate the appointment was arranged for the following evening in Chambers. Wadsworth had been pleased the occasion fell on at the start of a weekend as some of those invited would be away on holiday and others would not stick around as they would be on a three line whip to get away. "I'll save a fortune on drink!" had been his comment to Jack in the car on the way to the Savoy Hotel.

The turnout at the party in chambers was much higher than anyone expected. Nicola Mortimer and several of her colleagues made an early entrance and exit, not wishing to steal the limelight from the new judge.

The hot topic of conversation was the Lord Chancellor's flat. Everyone wanted to know about the infamous wallpaper which had been in the news when the flat had been renovated.

In his address to his guests, Charles Wadsworth reminded everyone of his new boss's words. "As the Lord Chancellor was reported as saying, the residence is part of the Palace of Westminster. This palace is the mother of parliaments. It is a Grade I listed building. It should be refurbished to the highest possible standards because it is part of our national heritage."

Most of the current members of chambers turned out to wish their former colleague well in his new role. Many spent the rest of the time huddled in small groups winding each other up, or being wallflowers, standing alone. The art of working a room and getting stuck in with their solicitor guests was alien to many of them.

Despite all the back stabbing, sycophantic behaviour was in abundance at the party. Plenty was aimed at the new circuit judge and the new head of chambers whilst she was briefly there. Nobody wanted to miss the opportunity to put a good word in for themselves, but most failed to do so with the many solicitors present. They were the ones who had been loyal to chambers for many years and had new colleagues of their own who needed to be chatted up.

This lack of marketing skills annoyed Jack. Yes it was his job, but not his alone. He picked up two full bottles of wine and handed them to one of his junior barristers engaged in light banter with fellow members of chambers near the door. "Are these for me?" laughed the barrister.

"No" replied Jack. "They are for your guests. Go and work the room and get yourself some new clients. Can you do that, sir? Off you go"

One of the other barristers in the group asked Jack for a couple of bottles, but the rest carried on as if nothing had been said. Jack returned to Jason who understood Jack's anger.

"They just don't get it. The world is changing but they think they are immune."

The caterers helped clear up the mess after the last guest had left, and Jason and Jack retired to the clerks' room with a fresh bottle of champagne.

They reflected on what had been a good day for Barcourt chambers.

Jason was on form. "Yes it is the end of an era, but it is most definitely the beginning of a new exciting chapter in the history of this fine chambers."

Jack's thoughts turned to the now old head of chambers. "I'm not sorry to see the back of Wadsworth. He was a fine example of the wrong man given the reins to run chambers at the wrong time. The sad thing is he knew it but still carried on. He did not like the post. Much more of his antics and chambers could have imploded."

Sarah Ryman walked into the clerks' room carrying a bottle of red wine. "Hello gentlemen. I thought I'd come and keep you company and refresh my memory of the bridge on the good ship Barcourt!"

"And why would you want to do that Sarah?" asked Jack.

"Well it would be the sensible thing to do if I was going to become a tenant at Barcourt, again."

Jack and Jason smiled and got up for a group hug which seemed the right reaction to Sarah's remarks and as they were all approaching the state of drunkenness where they could no longer stand independently.

Sarah sat in the chair normally occupied by Dillon. "This is the first time I have sat in the clerks' room. It is very cozy in here."

Next to walk in was Beth Richardson. "Oh, am I interrupting anything?"

Jack got to his feet slowly. "No no, please come in. Do try out a clerk's chair. It is all the rage, you know." Jack offered her his glass of champagne and he drank from the bottle. As it was getting late, Jason realised why Beth had turned up.

"Miss Ryman, would you like a personal guided tour of chambers? There are some fascinating rooms available for new occupants."

Sarah, even in her inebriated state, had spotted the looks between Jack and Beth and thought something was going to happen that night between them, if it had not already done so previously. She did not want to play gooseberry either.

"Why thank you kind clerk. Lead the way!"

As Jason and Sarah stumbled out of chambers into the night air, Beth took a close look at Jack.

"So Jack Temple, this was what you were plotting and looked so worried about a while ago was it?"

Jack tried to play it cool. "I don't know what you mean, who was plotting what?"

"Jack you are such a terrible liar. I am talking about the last time we stayed at the Wiltshire Inn. You were engrossed in something, I could tell. But I did not press you for the reason, so now is the time to come clean."

Jack poured Beth another drink which finished the bottle. Beth continued her cross examination in the face of Jack's silence.

"Ok, then what about your questions on who was a good female silk. That was no coincidence was it?"

Jack decided it was safe to talk. "Ok, yes. You're right, but I couldn't tell you for fear of compromising your position at Crompton & Ashdown. Geoffrey Ashdown would not take kindly to our relationship at the best of times, especially if you got caught up in the cross fire and accused of siding with the senior clerk in a bitter chambers struggle. It was wrong to involve you, so I didn't. Anyway, it is not all over yet, so the less you know the better."

Beth downed the remains of her glass of champagne, got up and walked round the clerks' desks and put her arms round Jack's neck. She passionately kissed Jack again and again. She could tell he was more than interested. "Come on lover boy, let's get to the WI and not waste this special night."

19 THE AGENDA

The following Monday morning was special for Jack and Barcourt chambers. A new head of chambers had been installed over the weekend and Jack was excited to start the process of adding more barristers.

All the clerks were in by eight o'clock to share his enthusiasm and to pick up any further developments. They were all refreshed from the weekend off, including Charlotte who arrived with her boss Nicola Mortimer. She introduced Charlotte to Jack and his team. Everyone was unaware that Dillon and Charlotte were an item and they had no idea of how they planned to end or continue their relationship.

Dillon had spent the weekend at Charlotte's flat, neither of them wanting to discuss what would be happening at work the next week. On the Sunday, they walked together hand in hand all the way around Victoria Park, trying to decide how they would play it once Charlotte started at Barcourt chambers. Neither wanted to end their blossoming relationship and Dillon did not want to leave Barcourt. He loved his job, just as much as Charlotte loved clerking for Nicola Mortimer.

By the end of the day, they had decided that they would not tell anyone about their affair. Dillon was more bullish. "It's nobody else's business, and we can carry on as normal during working hours and at the Wiltshire Inn. We can spend the weekends together so no one need know."

Charlotte was content to give it a go but knew Dillon's plan would not work out long term.

That morning Jack wanted to get started on his plans but had to get the week under way first. "Dillon, will you give Charlotte a guided tour of chambers and get her settled in. She can have the spare desk next to you. Make sure she has everything she needs."

"Of course Jack." Dillon took Charlotte out of the clerks' room and along the corridor to the main conference room. Once inside he shut the door.

"I don't know if I can do this. Sitting next to you for eight hours a day and not able to give you a kiss or a hug. What am I going to do?"

Charlotte took a different approach. "But we are together. Think of all those couples where one partner is miles away on the other side of London and they only see each other at the weekend. It won't be so bad." She squeezed his hand. "Now show me how to use the video conferencing kit."

Back in the clerks' room, Jack and Jason were busy comparing their lists of potential recruits to Barcourt chambers. Jack summed up.

"So apart from Stuart Brookes, I need to focus on Sarah Ryman first as the intro to the other three, Stephen Savage, Monty Evans and Tim Shaw."

Jason interrupted. "Why do you want those three back? They chose to leave, they are more farmers than hunters, and if they were capable of plotting once, they can do it again."

Jack agreed. "You're absolutely right Jason, but I have two compelling reasons. Firstly, I don't want to leave Richard Murray with any of my counsel. He did not deserve them in the first place. And secondly, we will need more counsel to service the extra work we are going to get and better the devil you know. Besides, they will be grateful for being welcomed back. I won't have any trouble with them."

Jason accepted Jack's arguments for the time being as he as more interested in getting to work on his list. "There are a few interesting names on the list Nicola gave us. She has kindly put them in the order we should approach them which helps. Shall I just work my way through them? There are five in total."

"Fine. I will ask Nicola if she wants to deal with applications herself or within the management committee. I would expect her to deal with most herself unless she feels there is any conflict. Let's meet up at the end of the day and see where we are up to."

Jack set about his next mission to get Sarah Ryman back into chambers. She had agreed to try to clear her name, so Jack's first step was to tell the full sorry tale to Nicola Mortimer in her new capacity as head of chambers.

To begin with she was reluctant. "Jack, if I had been here for even just one year, I might consider her application on my own. But to take the responsibility within days of my appointment is risky to say the least. Mind you, what I know of Sarah as an advocate is all good. She does remind me of myself in the early days."

Jack felt she was not going to take the decision on her own, so offered a solution. "May I suggest you invite the management committee to interview her? That way it will come across as democracy in action, and set the tone for good leadership. You can open the item at the meeting along the lines of inviting the committee, if they so conclude, to put right a serious injustice against a fellow member of the bar."

Nicola agreed with Jack's plan which he relayed to Sarah, who in turn agreed to represent herself. Two days later, Jack went to the management committee. Nicola was in the chair along with most of the committee, including Tom Wallace, Peter Livingstone, James Campbell and one newly elected member Nathan Blake. After dealing with several mundane matters, Nicola got to the matter of Sarah Ryman.

"Next item on the agenda – new members – Jack, this is one you asked for."

"Yes. I have been approached by a small group of practitioners who may wish to be make applications to join chambers. They only wish to be considered as a group, not individually, as they will only move together. This is mainly because they have a lot of work which they share for specific solicitors who will remain loyal to them."

"How do we know that?" piped up Nathan Blake who had until then remained silent at the table. He was interested to protect his own position in chambers rather than have more competition for his work.

"Because I have spoken in confidence to each firm and they all confirmed without hesitation they would follow counsel here."

"Well that sounds very positive. Who are they?" asked Tom Wallace.

"At this stage, I am not authorised to disclose any names save for one."

Tom Wallace saw the opportunity to kick off at Jack. "What do you mean, not authorised? This committee cannot deal with any applications or proposals without knowing who we are dealing with. Who are they?"

Jack had rehearsed his response. "The one person who I can name is well known to you, but if that person is unsuccessful in their application, then none of the others will apply. They do not wish to rock the boat they are currently sailing in."

Nicola Mortimer decided now was the right moment for Jack to disclose the one name. "Jack, who is the person you can give us?"

Jack paused for effect. "Sarah Ryman."

At once everyone else in the room except Nicola expressed an opinion in varying degrees of disapproval. Jack explained his argument about rectifying a possible injustice, and Nicola said she had heard good things about Sarah's advocacy, trying to appear objective.

Jack looked as if he wanted to say more, and Nicola picked up on his expression. She said: "Jack, is there more to tell us?"

Jack launched into his prepared speech. "Thank you – yes. I have worked out the financial implications for the members of chambers if four or more new members are elected, taking into account the changes already made with the loss of Charles Wadsworth and the arrival of the new head of chambers."

Jack deliberately omitted to say that Nicola Mortimer earned in her last year significantly more than Charles Wadsworth ever did, and was worth potentially a lot more to chambers income if several of her friends joined as well.

"The added fees income and so contributions to chambers' expenses would result in the committee being able to reduce the monthly charges to members by a full 1%. Over a year, even allowing for one additional clerk which would be necessary for such an increase that would reduce each member's fees payable to chambers by about £1,200 per annum."

This information brought a calming silence to the room. Nicola took over again.

"Thank you Jack. Most helpful. I don't think we can ignore such a benefit and the members should be the ones to decide this."

Peter Livingstone decided it was time for him to support his new head of chambers. "I for one would welcome such a reduction, but I don't see how Sarah can be considered in view of how she left."

Jack responded. "I have spoken to Sarah and she has indicated that she would welcome the opportunity to clear her name before this committee. If she fails to do so then that will be an end to it, and no applications will be made. On the other hand, if she succeeds, then the way is open for you to consider the joint applications."

Jack sat back while a frenzied debate took place before him. Not once did anyone suggest it was right to hear Sarah. They all focused on the potential work and new solicitors, and the reduction in chambers' rent they would each benefit from.

As the debate seemed to be fizzling out without any clear conclusion, James Campbell spoke for the first time on the subject of Sarah Ryman.

"If you talk to counsel outside chambers, the overwhelming feedback is very positive. She has come on as a junior and developed quality advocacy skills. I would expect her to take silk in the coming years."

The head of chambers had heard enough and so summed up the meeting. "So we are agreed then, we will reconvene to hear Sarah's submissions at a venue to be agreed outside chambers. Jack, make the arrangements."

Jack nodded. "Of course. I would suggest the Russell Hotel tomorrow evening at 6.00pm unless that is a problem for anyone." Nobody responded so Jack confirmed. "Six o'clock tomorrow it is then."

James Campbell drew Jack to one side as he picked up his papers. "Jack, good financial preparation work. I am sure you can improve on the figures should we get a few of Nicola's colleagues on board as well. Well done."

Jack was pleased to be given credit where he felt it was due. "Thank you, sir" he replied.

Jack felt the moment warranted a little humility hence his reference to "sir". Actually he did not approve of such titles unless he was dealing with an actual lord. He had been pulled up by a QC he once called "sir". He got short measure by the QC's swift reply: "Jack, as far as I am aware I have not been knighted, and I don't think I ever shall. So don't call me "sir". Use my christian name in private, and surname in public. Got it?"

Jack had agreed and usually followed that rule, unless it was to his advantage. And what had just happened was certainly, in Jack's eyes, to his advantage.

The following evening the secret chambers management meeting was duly convened in a private room at the Russell Hotel. Assembled were the members of the chambers management committee including Jack. Whilst he never had a vote, he always attended such meetings and would leave if they ever wanted to discuss him. The head of chambers started. "Jack, ask Sarah Ryman to join us will you? Let's get this meeting under way."

Most of the committee were intrigued to her what Sarah had to say for herself. She came in and sat at the last empty chair at one end of the long table. The head of chambers sat at the other end, with her deputy Tom Wallace by her side.

There was a full turnout of the members of the management committee with one notable exception. Nobody wanted to miss out on hearing Sarah's version of events which they had been denied at the ECM she did not attend on the day she left chambers.

The only member of the committee who was not present was Nathan Blake. Jack felt it might be difficult for Sarah to get a fair hearing if he was there. So he arranged for him to be in court out of town that day. Jack gave him a quality brief with a quality marked fee that he could not refuse. It also meant Jack would not be questioned by Nathan Blake on how Sarah got hold of a copy of the image he had on his mobile phone.

Jack pressed home his main argument for Nathan taking the case. "I know you will miss the management meeting, but this case offers a chance to meet a new solicitor client and earn a good fee."

Nathan accepted Jack's advice, partly because he did not fancy a confrontation with Sarah in front of the senior members of chambers, and so gave his proxy vote to the Head of chambers. A typical sycophantic gesture thought Jack.

Sarah Ryman sat in the only remaining empty chair. Nicola Mortimer opened the meeting. "Sarah, good of you to join us at such short notice. I gather you wish to address this committee. The floor is open to you. Prey continue."

Her opening remarks were music to some ears, but not Sarah's. She felt herself bite her lip as she rose to address. Nicola quickly added: "Oh do stay seated Sarah. No need for court formality here." Better thought Jack but hardly amongst friends.

Sarah began. "I gather you have heard about a picture produced by Nathan Blake on his mobile phone, and his version of events in the basement toilet on the day in question." They all nodded approval so she carried on.

"It is my submission that he misinterpreted what he saw, and that there is a much simpler explanation. It was well known in chambers that I used to go to the gym a lot, and that I frequently changed in the basement toilets so as to attend functions without the need to go home first.

On the day in question I did just that. However I do often suffer from athlete's foot, especially in the summer months. One remedy to ease the condition is to cover my toes, especially the top two, with a white powder called "Mycil". It is in common use for sports people, it is not perfumed but does have an odd smell. One or two of the lady members of the bar were aware of my condition at that time as I have occasionally remarked on the irritability when wearing court shoes, but it is not something I have mentioned often. I regard it as a personal matter.

When confronted later with the drugs allegation by the former head of chambers I have to confess such an explanation never occurred to me. The events that followed happened so quickly, it is only recently that I have realised what may have happened."

Sarah paused to allow her words to be absorbed, then continued.

"Now you may well ask: But what about the photograph? That puzzled me too until I decided to re-enact what happened on the day in question."

Sarah produced a photograph with a couple of copies from her bag and passed them round the table. "Would this be the photograph you have all seen?"

Sarah paused whilst the image was viewed by everyone around the table. There were nods of confirmation until the picture ended up with Tom Wallace. "Well it certainly looks like it."

At this point Sarah produced another picture which she passed round in similar fashion. This too ended up with Tom Wallace. He asked Sarah "Are these one and the same images?"

"No." replied Sarah. "The first is one I took last week at home. It is a reconstruction in my own bathroom of the events that happened in the chambers' toilet. The second is a copy of the original image taken by Nathan Blake."

Several members of the committee looked closely at both pictures and were struggling to spot any difference, especially Tom Wallace. "They do appear to be identical. When did you first see the one taken by Nathan Blake?"

"That was only shown to me for the first time by Jack a few days ago when we discussed by wish to address this meeting.

James Campbell then asked. "Did Charles Wadsworth show you Nathan's picture?"

"No" replied Sarah. "I wanted to accurately reconstruct what I had done in the toilet without seeing the image. I did exactly as I had done separating my toes to allow the powder to pass through."

The head of chambers interrupted her. "Jack, is this correct? Sarah only saw Nathan's image for the first time a few days ago?"

Jack had his answer prepared and said:" Yes it is. When I spoke to Miss Ryman about attending this meeting, we agreed that it would be necessary to prove her innocence. We further decided that if there was no or insufficient similarity between the images, she would not address you today and applications would be withdrawn. However, when we both saw both the pictures, Miss Ryman agreed to continue."

You could hear a pin drop. Several of the committee compared again the two images and finally all agreed they were too close to call which one was taken by Nathan Blake.

Tom Wallace decided it was time for a little cross examination. "That does not get round the unanswered question. Why didn't you attend the ECM and defend yourself?"

Sarah wanted to be aggressive, but bit her lip again. "Because I did not know the image existed. In my one short meeting with the head of chambers the night before he made it quite clear that if I wanted a reference I had to go quietly. I was left in no doubt that had I attended the ECM I would have been kicked out of chambers without a reference."

Nicola Mortimer had heard enough. "Thank you Sarah, you have been most helpful. Unless anyone has any further questions, I think we have enough to go on. Sarah, please let us have a few minutes to reflect on what you have said. Would you be good enough to wait outside and we'll call you back in should we need your assistance any further."

Sarah withdrew in silence and sat outside down the corridor. She could not hear what was being said or whether there was a heated debate. After about ten minutes, Jack came out of the meeting. His expression gave nothing away.

"Ok, they have decided to hear the other applications for tenancies as soon as possible, and asked that we both keep everything confidential for now."

"What does that mean Jack?" asked Sarah who had not understood a word Jack had said. "It means they accept your version of events on that day are the more likely to be correct, so there is no reason to stop you or anyone in your team applying to join chambers."

Sarah concluded: "So we have won?!"

Jack calmed her down. "Miss, we have won a battle, a pretty big one admittedly, but not the war. There is more to be done. Can we meet the other applicants as soon as possible?"

At a separate meeting later that evening in the tap room of the Red Lion Nathan Blake listened as Tom Wallace and Peter Livingstone went on about Jack's behaviour.

They did not like his tactics and the way he ran the clerks' room which they were sure would eventually bring chambers into disrepute. More importantly for them, Jack was responsible for the new order with a female head of chambers. They had lost the chambers vote when Nicola Mortimer QC was elected, and as far as they were concerned, chambers would not be the same ever again.

So they listened with great interest to the speculations offered by

Nathan Blake as they tucked into their second bottle of their favourite Saint-Emilion tipple, a Château Grand Corbin-Despagne fine red, on the behaviour of Jack prior to that election night.

"Think about it gentlemen" suggested Nathan. "Nobody knew that Charles Wadsworth QC had applied for a judicial appointment, and certainly nobody outside chambers knew of his appointment. And of those in chambers, the only person Charles confided in was Jack."

Tom Wallace took the suggestion further. "Wadsworth was not interested in who would succeed him as head of chambers. So the only one who could have tipped Nicola Mortimer off that there was going to be a vacancy at Barcourt chambers was Jack Temple."

Peter Livingstone joined in. "So he plotted with Nicola even before Charles was appointed. The scheming little weasel!" "Peter, I can think of far worse names to call him!" said Tom.

Nathan chose to add a little more oil on troubled waters. "You are all familiar with the Lord Chancellor's specific instructions contained in his letter of appointment to Charles Wadsworth. I quote:" treat this offer of appointment as strictly confidential and not to be mentioned outside your close family." Since when has counsel from another chambers been classed as close family?"

Tom summed up the situation. "Well as I see it, Jack faces instant dismissal for a clear breach of the clerking code of conduct regarding confidential information, never mind a possible dressing down by the Lord Chancellor's department. Such conduct brings chambers' reputation into disrepute."

Peter Livingstone emptied the dregs of the second bottle of red wine into Nathan's glass and concluded. "Thank you, Nathan, for bringing these matters to our attention. You can rest assured we will take them further."

Tom agreed. "Yes indeed. I am not sure of the consequences for our new head of chambers, but Jack is in serious difficulty. He has a lot of explaining to do."

Peter thought for a few moments before speaking again. "Tom, you do realise we cannot confront Nicola Mortimer with this. She would have to defend herself first, and that would involve defending Jack. We cannot go to anyone else for now. I think we are going to have to put it on the agenda of the next management committee meeting under "Any Other Business". That way there is no time for anyone to concoct their story."

20 CAUSE FOR CONCERN

Nathan Blake was in his room in chambers the next day when Jack told him the news of Sarah's triumph at the management meeting the previous evening. He was gutted. He held his head in his hands and although he felt like crying out, he controlled his emotion in front of Jack.

He had contemplated this outcome ever since he was told of the proposed chambers meeting to discuss Sarah, but still had no idea that she had won the day by producing his photographic evidence to support her version of events. He asked: "What happened? What did she say? And how did she get hold of the photo that was on my mobile phone when I have never sent it to anyone?"

Jack relayed the full story, leaving out the bit about Jason going to the robing room while he was in court and sending himself a copy of the image. As he listened Nathan felt his heart sink further and further. There was nothing he could do to save his day.

"Jack, I'm going to have to leave chambers. I can't stay here. Once the full story gets out, and I have to assume it will, I will be ostracised, a Billy no mates. I could not face being in the same room as Sarah. It will be hard enough continuing to practice at the Bar. I could be finished!"

"With respect, you are overdramatising the situation. I agree staying at Barcourt might be difficult to begin with, but as time passes…" Nathan cut in: "What do I say to Sarah? No, she will not forgive me, and neither will the others accept me. No I will have to go. Can you help Jack?"

Of course Jack could help. He already had a plan but it still needed flushing out in the detail, and Nathan's agreement. Nathan's move would take a little time to secure, but in the end Jack knew Nathan had no option but to go along with it.

Sarah arranged for Jack to meet the others who would return to Barcourt chambers with her at her flat that evening. Stephen Savage, Monty Evans and Tim Shaw all arrived late. Jack was the first and on time.

Sarah opened her flat door for Jack to enter and shut the door behind him. Just for a moment she lost control and flung her arms around Jack's neck. She kissed him on the lips. "Oh Jack, right now I want your babies!" Jack pushed her away to arms' length. "I don't think so Miss. We can do without any more complications, but the idea is not without merit!"

They both laughed. Just for once Jack restrained himself despite his split second imagination of a picture of Sarah naked and willing. "Best not on my own doorstep" he thought.

The doorbell rang. Sarah let Jack go and turned to open the door saying "Saved by the bell Jack!"

Stephen Savage, Monty Evans and Tim Shaw trouped into Sarah's living room and grabbed a glass of wine each which Sarah had already poured.

"Are we celebrating?" asked Tim Shaw.

"Not yet" replied Jack. "But hopefully soon. Sarah has taken the first steps and has been cleared by the management committee to apply to re-join Barcourt chambers. They have also confirmed that under the leadership of Nicola Mortimer QC they will look at a group application from yourselves."

"Do they know about the drugs incident involving Sarah?" asked Savage who was nervous in case what he had known at the time came out.

A jubilant Sarah stepped forward. "Oh yes, and it was all the fault of that stupid Nathan Blake. If he had not jumped to the wrong conclusion, none of it would have happened."

Jack felt a little explanation would help as the cronies would likely pass the information around the Temple as soon as they could. "The substance was Mycil foot powder, not cocaine."

"You are kidding?" exclaimed Monty. "Athlete's foot powder?"

"Yes, and what's more" said Sarah in a highly excited laugh, "It will cost the idiot his place in Barcourt chambers. Justice at last!"

Jack thought her comment a little harsh as Nathan had only been guilty of jealousy, although he could have gone about the incident differently.

The three cronies expressed their delight and planned with Jack their applications to re-join Barcourt chambers. Jack gave them no idea that there would be others who might apply at the same time as he knew they were not trustworthy to keep any such information confidential. As it was he imagined the gossip at the Red Lion tap room would go into overdrive with the news about Sarah Ryman.

Sarah's comments about Nathan Blake served to emphasise to Jack that he had to help Nathan find a new home and quickly. He preferred to get him out of London if possible for his own reasons, but also because Nathan's attitude and brittle personality meant he would not be comfortable amongst his peers in the London robing rooms. So it was time to give Richard Murray a call.

Jack had gone to the main conference room in chambers to make the call in private. He thought how ironic it was that he should be calling in a favour from the man he crushed in that very room.

"Richard, I trust you are well?" Murray was in no mood for pleasantries, especially not with Jack. "What do you want Temple?" Jack did not take the same tone.

"Yes thanks Richard, I'm fine. Just wondered if the Manchester chambers your nephew had been clerking in would like a new experienced civil practitioner. Only I have a member of chambers who would like to move to Manchester."

"Who is it?" barked Murray. "Nathan Blake." That got Murray's attention.

"Why on earth does Blake want to go to Manchester? I thought he was wedded to Barcourt."

"Well" replied Jack. "He was, but now he wants a fresh start and Manchester seems as good a place as any."

Murray was sceptical. "What have you done to him Jack?"

"Nothing" replied Jack. "He has done it all himself. I would appreciate you making the introduction to your friends in Manchester in our new spirit of co-operation, Richard, it you get my drift."

Murray knew exactly where Jack was coming from and although he did not like having to help Jack, did not see it would cost him in any way. The Manchester chambers were grateful he had taken the thorn that was his nephew out of their side without any scandal getting out.

"I'll see what I can do."

"Thanks Richard. I'll tell Nathan to expect a call from Manchester to get him moved this week if possible." As there was no comment from the other end of the call, Jack put the phone down and commented to himself "We love you too Richard!"

Jack went straight to Nathan Blake's room and told him the good news and that he should expect a call from Manchester later that day. "I suggest they are told that you are looking to move north for personal reasons, and they have an exclusive one time only opportunity to get you into their chambers, but they have to move quickly."

"Thanks Nathan, I won't ask how many favours you have had to call in to get me this chance. I am truly grateful."

Jack felt like adding that he was just pleased to no longer get stupid phone calls in the early hours of the morning to pay his restaurant bills for him, but thought better of the idea.

With Nathan Blake about to leave Barcourt chambers for good Jack felt more secure in his own position, especially as the risk of chambers imploding was gradually receding with the new head of chambers and the imminent return of Sarah Ryman and the three cronies.

But Jack had made enemies along the way. The main two, Tom Wallace and Peter Livingstone, did not like the way Jack operated and blamed him for one of them not becoming head of chambers.

Nathan Blake would also be in the anti-Jack camp as he entirely blamed Jack for what happening to him even though Jack was helping him to find new chambers.

And there was Richard Murray senior clerk at Carey Street. Since day one as far as Richard was concerned Jack was an unscrupulous scoundrel who had no place running the chambers he should have got.

The following day Richard Murray spotted Nathan Blake getting ready for court in the robing room at the RCJ and went over for a quiet word.

Nathan, I gather you are off to sunny Manchester at the end of the week. I hope it all goes well for you."

Blake was mystified as to how Murray knew he was leaving Barcourt chambers, let alone that he was going to Manchester. Murray saw the puzzled look on his face. "Oh I had a word with Manchester at Jack's request." The penny dropped for Blake.

"Thank you Richard. Yes it is a new challenge, I am sure." Richard leant forward towards Blake. "Before you go, there is a little information you might like to know, just in case you feel able to use it at some point in the future."

Blake finished straightening his wig and turned to Murray. "Go on" he said. Richard Murray launched into the gossip which he had started about Jack having an affair with a solicitor client.

"I am reliably informed by a member of my chambers that Jack Temple has been seen at the Wiltshire Inn late in the evening on several occasions by counsel who witnessed him kissing a woman that he recognised as a solicitor client of Barcourt chambers. Apparently on more than one of these meetings Jack and the woman disappeared upstairs together, not to return before closing time."

"How very interesting Richard" said Blake as he pondered on how he might use the information to his advantage, and whether it was too late to influence his own destiny.

"I thank you for telling me. Does anyone else at Barcourt know about this?" "Not yet" replied Murray. "I thought you should know before you go to Manchester."

"Thank you Richard. Very thoughtful. I'm obliged." They parted company and Nathan Blake went into court, his mind barely focused on the case he was dealing with. All he could think about was engineering a meeting with Tom Wallace. He would have to leave it up to Tom to decide what to do with the information.

Nathan convinced himself that getting the story to a member of the management committee at Barcourt chambers was the best move he could make. They were mostly old school and not in favour of Jack's tactics and the introduction of a female head of chambers. For some, having one female clerk was bad enough. Now they had two.

That evening after he had packed his personal possessions into the customary storage box often used by those leaving a job, Nathan knocked on the door of Tom Wallace's room. It was gone eight o'clock so he was surprised to see a light still on under the door.

Nathan gave Tom every detail he had been told by Richard Murray about Jack's affair with Elizabeth Richardson. Wallace made a couple of notes so as not to forget any detail and said he would add it to his growing list of complaints about Jack and the way he was running chambers, all to be raised at the next management committee meeting.

As Nathan Blake left Barcourt chambers for the last time, he half-dreamt of the possibility that Jack and Nicola Mortimer could be ousted from his now former chambers, and Tom Wallace elected as the new head of chambers would repay Nathan by inviting him to re-join. He went home concluding that was a possible outcome although a bit of a pipe dream, but that stranger things had happened in chambers.

Jack's team all knew about his relationship with Elizabeth Richardson and thought it was very risky. Jason in particular was worried if Jack's conduct became an issue before the management committee, they could decide to go to a vote at a full chambers meeting which under the chambers' constitution was the only way Jack could be ousted from chambers. He told Jack of his views.

"If Wallace and Livingstone get their knives out, you could be having to defend yourself at a full chambers meeting. Once the momentum gets under way, your affair with Beth could split chambers and then we are all in trouble."

Jack refused to talk to anyone about these issues. Jason could not get him to open up, or at least discuss how to defend himself. Jack refused all attempts to help, even from Sarah Ryman who had realised the relationship with Beth after the chambers party. She and Jason had discussed Jack's intransigence on more than one occasion since. Sarah spoke more forthrightly than Jason as she was someone who had benefitted from Jack's help more recently.

"Jack is burying his head in the sand. One day it will come out and he will be fighting for his position as senior clerk. Even worse, he could drag chambers down with him. The old guard still has some fight left in it."

"Sarah, you are preaching to the converted. I have known Jack for over a decade now, and he can be so stubborn when it suits him. What are we going to do? Have you heard any mutterings of discontent amongst the members?"

"No" replied Sarah. "But it is early days yet after the new head of chambers was elected. We are still in the honeymoon period for Nicola and the membership. But give it time, and there will be a few huddled meetings in the tap room at the Red Lion no doubt. Mark my words.

Nicola Mortimer QC would not want to see Jack leave, but she would be concerned for her own position if chambers was to be split over the senior clerk. She had invested her remaining years in private practice with Barcourt largely because of what Jack offered her both in chambers and helping to get her on the High Court Bench.

However Nicola knew she could not be seen to condone Jack's behaviour with a solicitor client. It would not be enough to even be seen to slap his wrists for such behaviour."

Jason added to the debate. "Then there is the possibility of the older members of the management committee deciding to put it to a chambers ECM and forcing a vote to have Jack kicked out."

Neither Jason nor Sarah relished the possible outcomes but felt helpless without Jack accepting there was a problem. "I will have a quiet word with Nicola to see what can be done. At the very least she should be given the heads up on a dangerous situation which may be on the horizon."

Nicola met Sarah Ryman at the restaurant Chez Lamps for lunch that day and discussed the several cases they both had which would merit two female counsel. They were excited at the prospect of working together.

"I feel we could work well as a team on some of these more high profile Union cases" said Nicola.

Sarah responded. "I agree. And it will be good to have someone of your experience to discuss points of law with in chambers, a luxury I have not had before."

She chose her moment to mention the discontent amongst some of the senior members of chambers at the way Nicola had been brought in and Jack's role in the matter. She was still finding her own feet with Nicola, so decided to tread carefully.

"I am sure you are aware of one or two of the senior members of chambers being a bit miffed at the election process and your arrival in chambers, irrespective of the way the vote was unanimous."

"Yes I am" replied Nicola. "I guess it was bound to be the case. I know I have to win a few doubters over."

"Indeed" said Sarah. "I am told a few of them may turn their attention towards Jack more than you to vent their anger. I think he needs to be careful, especially if his conduct can be called into question."

Afterwards Sarah wished she had told Nicola the full story about Jack but in the end decided she had done enough. Her relationship with the head of chambers was more important to her.

Nicola Mortimer decided it was best to confront Jack at a meeting in her room. She decided it was for him to tell her about any matter she should be aware of and she would provide every opportunity for him to do so.

The main concern was the potential rebellion by Tom Wallace, supported by Peter Livingstone, which could topple her new leadership.

"I was going to suggest we met at the Russell Hotel as a timely reminder to you Jack of what you offered originally. I hope you haven't lost your focus on the main issues?

I would expect it to take time to win over those who had hoped to become head of chambers. I would feel the same if the boot was on the other foot. But of more concern would be if they harbour any grudge against the senior clerk which might cause a rift in chambers. Do you understand what I am saying, Jack?"

"Yes I do, and as far as I am concerned, there is no reason for any member of chambers to harbour any grudge against me. I have always acted in the best interests of chambers." Nicola pressed Jack further. "You are quite sure there is nothing I need to know? Now would be the time to tell me."

Jack was not entirely sure what Nicola was getting at, but in any event was not going to delve into his private life and certainly not get Beth Richardson into trouble with her partners at her firm.

"I am not aware of any matter within chambers which would give you cause for concern. I have no doubt that one or two members are unhappy with some of what goes on in the clerks' room, but it goes on in every clerks' room in the Temple. That's life at the bar."

Nicola understood and chose not to pry any further. "A need-to-know basis is fine with me" said Nicola. "Let's leave it there for now." Jack hoped that would be good enough to keep her support at the management committee meetings, especially as there were all the applications to increase the membership coming up. He did not wish to see all that hard work undone.

21 THE GIRLFRIEND

"Right listen up you miserable bunch. I'm only going to say this once. Christian, put the phone down. Whoever you were going to ring can wait. James, shut the door."

Once Jack was sure he had everyone's attention he spoke to the packed clerks' room. Everyone was sat at their correct seats, including Dillon next to the new clerk Charlotte.

"It will come as some surprise to you all to learn that Mr Dillon here has a girlfriend. God knows what she sees in him, but so far she has failed to see the error of his ways. But it is what it is and I for one hope she will be a better influence on him than I have been."

The clerks laughed at Jack's remarks as well as the prospect that Dillon had a girlfriend.

Christian opened the questioning after the ripple of laughter died down. "Does she have a guide dog then Dillon?"

Jack chose to answer for Dillon by speaking directly to Charlotte. "You don't need a guide dog do you Charlotte?" "Of course not Jack" she replied.

"What?" exclaimed Christian, looking at Dillon "You are going out with Charlotte? And I didn't know!"

Dillon raised his eyebrows and looked at Charlotte, and she at him with a romantic smile on her face. Jack decided he should nip any more wise cracks in the bud.

"That's right Christian. They have been an item for some months now, and I understand have moved in together this last weekend. And before anyone asks, they started dating well before Nicola Mortimer became head of chambers."

Jason was as surprised as the rest of the team at Jack's

announcement. "Does this cause a problem, a relationship between two clerks in the same chambers?"

"Why should it?" suggested Jack. "Nicola Mortimer specifically asked Charlotte to come with her to Barcourt. Anyway, would you rather lose a good clerk to another set and have the risk of trade secrets being stolen, or at least the governors thinking they were being stolen. No, I believe the modern way is to allow their existing relationship to develop within this clerks' room. That way, we can all keep an eye on Dillon, don't you agree Charlotte?"

Charlotte smiled. "I am sure I can manage, but a little extra help is always welcome!"

Jenny and Charlotte smiled to each other as Jack spoke again. "A word of warning, folks. I intend to advise the management meeting of the relationship but until then keep it within these four walls. We don't want anyone, particularly the senior members, getting the wrong end of the stick. Understood?"

Everyone agreed. "OK, James, let's have the door open and get on with some work."

Later in the morning Jason and Jack took their coffees into the main conference room. "I hope Charlotte knows what she is letting herself in for" said Jason. "It could be the making of Dillon, or leave her with a dilemma. If, or when they finish, does she leave chambers and her great job with Nicola Mortimer, or just what does Dillon do? Does he have to leave chambers?"

"Jason, let them be. We can cross that bridge with them if it happens. Until then, they have every right to enjoy their time together."

Jack relayed the story of the two clerks meeting and starting to date to Jason who could not quite believe what he was hearing about Dillon. "You know what, Dillon can be serious when he feels he needs to be taken seriously. Charlotte will be the making of him."

Jenny thought so too when she had lunch with Charlotte shortly after Nicola Mortimer had told Charlotte that she was going to Barcourt chambers and asked if she would go with her. She confided in Jenny on a promise to say nothing until she found out officially.

"Wow that's quite a compliment coming from a top silk" said Jenny. "Did you tell her about Dillon?"

"No" replied Charlotte. "Now I wished I had, but at the time I did not want to jeopardize moving with her, or give her more to worry about when making her own decision.

That is why Dillon and I went to see Jack at his home last Saturday morning to tell him what we were doing and hoped he would understand."

"And did he?" asked Jenny.

"Oh yes, he was wonderful. He told us to get on with our lives and leave chambers to him. We wanted him to know when we first started seeing each other and it was not just a mad fling. We both have strong feelings for each other, and who knows?"

"Exactly!" exclaimed Jenny. "Can you throw the bouquet to me please?!" They both laughed. "Seriously though Jenny, we could not go on working in the same room together without everyone knowing. And then there was the risk that the wrong version would get back to the management committee."

"Have they been told yet?" asked Jenny.

"I think Jack is going to raise it at the next meeting."

Jack had already decided he should tell the head of chambers in advance of the meeting for two reasons. He did not want her to be caught unawares at the meeting, and secondly she should be aware of what her own clerk was up to with Dillon in case she had a different view on the matter.

So Jack went to see her an hour before the meeting to run through a few matters that were going to be raised. "Ok Jack, what's on the agenda apart from the various applications to join chambers?"

"There is a small matter I was going to raise under the heading of any other business" replied Jack.

"I see, and what is that matter?" asked Nicola.

"Well, it concerns your clerk Charlotte." Jack paused as Nicola would have expected to know everything about her clerk. She looked concerned. "She's not leaving is she, or pregnant, or both?"

"No" replied Jack. "At least not at present, in answer to both questions."

"Thank God for that. I could not cope without her. So what is it?"

"Well, it also concerns one of my clerks, Dillon."

"Really!" replied Nicola. "I thought he was a lads' lad. What have they been up to?"

Jack then brought Nicola up to speed with the Dillon and Charlotte relationship, including their moving in together and that they had confided in him shortly after.

"What have you told them, Jack, from chambers' point of view?"

"I have given them my blessing as their senior clerk as the relationship was well established before your move to Barcourt, and I expect neither of us want to lose a good clerk."

Nicola thought for a moment. "I entirely agree. They are sensible youngsters and we should not interfere. Raise it at the meeting and I will support you."

Jack liked the positive and immediate style of his new head of chambers. He had confidence in her decision making. All he had to do now was persuade the senior members to see the modern approach.

The next management committee meeting started on time. Nicola Mortimer's appointment as head of chambers had resulted in more items on the agenda than had been the case under the reign of Charles Wadsworth, or at least Jack thought so. He wanted to see much more progress with his grand plan for Barcourt chambers, and was keen to get cracking on the implementation.

Not only did the agenda contain the usual reports by Jack on the financial state of play for chambers as a whole, and the building repairs which were much needed including the refurbishment of reception and the waiting area, there were the applications to re-join chambers by Sarah Ryman and the three cronies Stephen Savage, Monty Evans and Tim Shaw. There was the application by Stuart Brookes as well. Five new members plus a possible further five from Nicola Mortimer's old chambers would make a massive difference to Barcourt, and boost Jack's income substantially.

There was also the matter of the vote of no confidence in the senior clerk proposed by Tom Wallace and Peter Livingstone.

Nicola Mortimer could see that sparks were going to fly at this meeting, and although she did not want to lose the man mainly responsible for her being at Barcourt, she could not be seen to be siding with him if he had done wrong. She chose to alter the order of business to allow for all the applications and other business to be dealt with first, leaving Tom Wallace and Peter Livingstone to wait until the end to have their go at Jack.

Nicola opened the meeting. "Shall we deal with all the applications to join chambers first? They will all be eagerly waiting to hear their respective fates. You have a list of them on the agenda. Does anyone wish to comment on any particular applicant?"

To begin with nobody wanted to get the ball rolling and as Jack knew he had some explaining to do regarding Sarah Ryman he decided to speak first.

"May I assist the committee regarding Sarah Ryman's application?"

Nicola was relieved someone had spoken to break the uneasy silence. She nodded her approval so Jack reminded the meeting about Sarah's earlier meeting with the management committee but again left out how Nathan Blake's mobile phone image of the toilet seat had been copied without his knowledge.

The general consensus was to blame the former head of chambers for what had happened. That was the easy option as he was no longer a member of chambers and so could not defend his actions.

Nicola looked around the room for comment and as nobody seemed willing to step up, decided to move on.

"Shall we move on to consider the rest of the applicants? Are there any objections?"

For the next forty five minutes Jack watched and listened as the senior members played against the junior members of the committee, with the latter wanting all applicants to be welcomed with open arms, whilst the senior members did not see the need for a single one of them. They argued there was not enough work to go round so it should not be diluted any further.

Eventually Nicola brought Jack into the conversation. "Jack, what is your view on the likely increase in work to satisfy a larger membership?"

Tom Wallace interrupted before Jack could open his mouth. "It's no good asking him. This is all his idea anyway. He is just lining his own pockets, and to hell with the consequences for those of us who have stayed loyal to these chambers through thick and thin."

Jack ignored the outburst by Tom and instead attempted to answer Nicola's question.

"We have to set our stall out to show to the solicitors in our specialist field that we are going forward and have available some of the finest legal minds. By taking on the list of names before you, we are telling the market precisely that. To do nothing in the face of these opportunities would be a backwards step, in my submission."

After another rant from Tom Wallace, supported by Peter Livingstone, Nicola called for a vote. "To save time, you each have a copy of the list which we can treat as a ballot paper. So I suggest you put a tick or a cross next to each name, fold your ballot paper and hand it to Jack. Is everyone happy doing the voting that way?"

Nicola felt a little more clarification was necessary to avoid further squabbles later. "And for the avoidance of doubt, a simple majority means I will approve each application."

Nicola turned to Jack and whispered "I thought by now they would be tired of fighting. Let's hope so for the other issues coming up!"

Jack smiled and nodded his agreement with Nicola's sentiments. He collected the ballot papers and handed them all to Nicola without opening any.

Nicola read each one then addressed the meeting. "Well, after a healthy debate, which I am grateful for, I am pleased to announce that all the applicants have each acquired over seventy five percent of the votes cast, and so I will duly elect them all into chambers. Thank you all for such a clear mandate. I think we have all earned a short comfort break. Back in ten minutes please."

Nicola again lent over to speak to Jack. "Well that was a good result. I will phone each one after the meeting is over to welcome them aboard. You can sort the clerking out tomorrow."

Jack was thrilled. It was the culmination of a lot of hard work and planning. He could not wait to tell everyone.

Once the meeting was reconvened, Nicola suggested they deal with a matter Jack wanted to raise under any other business. Jack spoke in a now more bullish mood.

"Yes, I would like to raise the matter of the relationship between two of our clerks, Dillon and Charlotte." He then went through events from the start, and at the end got the support he was expecting from Nicola.

The same support did not come from the senior members, most notably Tom Wallace who realised that if he condoned such behaviour between clerks in his own chambers, it would be much harder to be heavy handed on Jack concerning his affair with Beth Richardson. So he weighed in.

"No, I cannot condone such behaviour. If a member of chambers was involved, either they or the clerk would have to leave. It should be no different when the relationship is between two clerks."

"I agree" said peter Livingstone. "Not the sort of behaviour we want to encourage."

Nicola Mortimer was furious. "As the sole representative of the female gender in this room, I am appalled at the outdated attitude on display. If it was a fling between two clerks, a one night stand, I might understand your view. But this relationship started well before my arrival in chambers, and their relationship has blossomed to the point where they are living together. The only item missing which would legitimize them is a piece of paper containing the words marriage certificate."

Jack entered the debate. "I have spoken to them both, and it is a serious relationship. I would not want to lose either of them in the clerks' room."

Tom Wallace sensed he was losing the battle. "Well you would condone such behaviour, wouldn't you Jack? Mark my words, it will bring Barcourt chambers into disrepute. Mark my words."

Nicola brought the debate to a close and asked if a vote was necessary. Wallace finally gave in. "No, go ahead and sanction this affair. I have had my say on the matter, for now."

"Jack" said Nicola, "Please let Dillon and Charlotte know we are behind them and no action will be taken." Jack nodded his confirmation.

She continued. "Now are we done for the day, or is there any other business we need to attend to. It is getting late."

Tom Wallace pulled from his jacket pocket a piece of paper which appeared to have several notes on it. "Yes. There is the matter of the conduct of our senior clerk. This committee should be aware of his behaviour in several respects, none of which I find acceptable from someone representing us to the legal world."

He laid into Jack. "I have a long list of complaints, any one of which would be sufficient for instant dismissal in any other walk of life. Where do I begin?"

Wallace started with the time Christian had broken the Brief rule – only ever take the pink ribbon off one set of papers at a time, and always tie it back before you open another. Jack got it wrong when the medical report from Peter Livingstone's case was found by Tom Wallace in his set of papers. Jack had taken responsibility and a bollocking from the committee at the time. He had eaten a large slice of humble pie already, but Wallace and Livingstone still wanted to use it against Jack, quoting it as an example of Jack's poor leadership.

Jack felt he rightly took the blame for Christian Bennet because he told Jack as soon as he realised his error. He responded: "I did not seek to cover it up. I dealt with the issue as I saw correctly at the time. Christian knows he made a mistake, and I have used it to teach the others.

One or two committee members wanted to side with Jack, but it was not the right time to do so.

Wallace pressed on with his attack. "Next, there is the constant gambling on trials collapsing and double booking of counsel.

He has little control over his staff. I lost a major case because of clerking errors. I was double booked at a listing meeting by his deputy. That was unacceptable. He has fallen out completely with at least one other senior clerk in the Temple. These are people and their counsel we have to deal with every day in cases and in court."

Wallace paused to take a breather, and then continued.

"Then there is his affair with a female partner in a leading firm of solicitors who instruct chambers, one Elizabeth Richardson. That is totally unacceptable behaviour which brings chambers into disrepute."

Peter Livingstone weighed in at this point. "As they say, it will end in tears, and chambers will lose a substantial client. We will all suffer just because Jack cannot control himself with the ladies."

Before any of the committee members could absorb fully what they were being told, Wallace reached what he regarded as his main argument.

"Worst of all, Jack is guilty of leaking confidential material regarding the former head of chambers' appointment letter in which the Lord Chancellor specifically wrote that only Charles's immediate family were to be told, but nobody else. Apart from his wife and Jack, Charles has confirmed to me that he told no one."

At this point Wallace looked Nicola Mortimer in the eyes. "So how would anyone, especially outside chambers at the time, know about the letter of appointment and subsequent vacancy for a new head of chambers before the Charles Wadsworth's appointment became public knowledge?"

Nicola Mortimer knew where the line of questioning was going and it was embarrassing for her. James Campbell realised as well and intervened.

"I don't think any useful purpose would be gained by going down that road, Tom. It is history now."

Wallace was like the proverbial dog with a bone. "I could not disagree more. Our professional reputation is on the line with the judiciary and the bar because of a lack of judgement on the part of the one person we are supposed to trust with all confidential matters."

Livingstone had a go next. "Some of his tricks may not be known to this committee, but they are leading our chambers into areas of disrepute in the Temple."

"Jack" said Nicola who looked distinctly uncomfortable at the way the questioning was going. "Would you like to respond to these matters raised by senior members of chambers?"

Jack collected his thoughts before he replied. "Well, what can I say? As for mistakes I or the clerks have made, they are infrequent, we always apologise to whoever is the victim, and yes we are human.

The introduction of females into the clerks' room was inevitable as more and more women qualify as both solicitors and barristers, and so relationships will inevitably occur between clerks. So long as chambers is not compromised, I see no harm.

And as for my personal life, that is for me and my family to judge."

Jack decided that going on the offensive was his best form of defence.

"Now might be a good time to remind everyone in this room and within chambers that everyone benefits from my work. Nobody can question my loyalty nor motivation to always act in the best interest of those I look after.

Yes there are other chambers which have recognised my unique skill set and would love to tap into it and benefit, but not once, not for a single second, have I ever entertained such a move."

"Whilst some of what you have seen here may not at this moment be acceptable or appear to make sense, I know that there is always a game plan, a long view to benefit chambers. And if something does not come off, which is rare but not impossible, I have never swept anything under the carpet as the former Head of chambers knew. What he chose to put into the chamber's domain was his call."

Jack then asked "So just what am I supposed to be guilty of?" Before anyone could answer, Jack continued.

"I have always looked after chambers for which chambers has looked after me. And in exercise of that duty, I have protected each and every member and my clerks from all sorts of challenges and conspiracies. I have never gone after anyone who did not throw the first punch, and when they do, sometimes the gloves have to come off to better fight your corner.

So if the charge is protecting something I care about, then yes – I'm guilty as charged!"

Nicola did not allow any pause to develop. "Thank you Jack. Unless you or anyone else has anything further to add, would you leave us please so we can consider the right way forward?"

Jack went back to the clerks' room and sat mulling over the way Wallace had attacked him. He confessed to himself it did not look good.

Nicola called Jack back in after the rest of the management committee had left the meeting.

"Jack, there is to be an ECM and chambers will be asked to vote on a motion of no confidence in the senior clerk. As I am sure you already know, the chambers' constitution says you can only be dismissed by a majority vote of the members. The vote to go to an ECM was carried on my casting vote."

Jack could not believe what he had just heard, and Nicola knew she needed to explain herself. "I had no choice, Jack. I had to support the motion. If I had not then I could be charged with a conspiracy to get elected to chambers and to the post of head of chamber."

Jack's initial reaction was disbelief that Nicola Mortimer could turn on him so soon after he got her elected. She could see the look in his eyes.

"Jack, right now you probably think I am Judas. But think about the situation and the long term. Every member of chambers needs to decide on how they want chambers to be run. It is democracy in action. We can come out of this with a clear mandate for the future. I have every confidence in the will of the majority being whole heartedly in your support, and it is up to us to make sure everyone with a vote exercises their right in the best interests of chambers as a whole."

Jack did not appear convinced so Nicola went on. "If I had voted to close the matter there and then, chambers would be divided into two camps and likely it would lead to a serious split. That would undo all the great work you have done for so many. Instead you have the chance to set the record straight once and for all."

"I have told the meeting we will have the ECM just as soon as possible. I will select a date that uses the minimum notice period under the constitution."

22 THE VERDICT

Two days before the ECM to determine whether Jack still had a future at Barcourt chambers, Nicola Mortimer QC was in the main conference room at Barcourt chambers waiting for her four thirty conference to arrive. She was reading again her instructions from Geoffrey Ashdown at Crompton Ashdown.

She had been asked to advise in a claim for a potential class action following a major incident at a clothing factory involving a collapsed roof injuring some fifty or more female factory workers, some seriously.

It was the first time Crompton Ashdown had briefed Nicola, and she was aware that Jack had been trying to get Geoffrey Ashdown to use Barcourt chambers more for some time. The instructions told her that if her advice was positive then the Trade Union which was backing their injured members at the factory would authorise Nicola to select a junior counsel to assist. She had already in her mind decided that she would ask Sarah Ryman. This was the kind of high profile case Nicola reveled in, and provided an opportunity to work with Sarah.

The conference room door opened and Jenny allowed Elizabeth Richardson to walk past her. Beth spoke in a confident mood. "Hello Nicola, I'm Beth Richardson, pleased to meet you."

Nicola rose to her feet and extended a hand of welcome towards Beth. They smiled and shook hands. Nicola was immediately impressed and could see why Jack had become involved with Beth who she thought was a stunner.

Today Beth had gone the extra mile on clothing and make-up. She would have wowed the Court of Appeal in her court attire.

"Beth, do sit down. Is Geoffrey coming along too?"

"No, it's just me. The Union is Geoffrey's client but they decided as all of their injured members are female that they wanted a female team to handle the cases. So Geoffrey arranged this preliminary conference for us to meet and decide if we could work together.

The case is very important for the Union. Their membership has been dwindling and they want a good public win in a high profile class action to bolster membership numbers."

Nicola took in what Beth had said. "I see. Are you acting for all those injured at the factory when the roof collapsed?"

Beth replied "Yes. The Union have made sure via their shop stewards."

There was a pause as Nicola reminded herself of the ECM in two days' time to determine Jack's fate and his relationship with Beth.

Beth instinctively knew what Nicola was thinking behind her perplexed expression, so she continued. "Before we discuss liability issues, there is another matter which I think we should mention."

Nicola looked up and straight into Beth's eyes. "Oh yes, fire away." Both ladies were now on the same wavelength.

"Nicola, I have been made aware that your chambers has an ECM scheduled in a couple of days to consider Jack's conduct, and whilst that is a matter for chambers and of no direct concern of mine, I and my firm could be affected by the outcome."

Nicola did not appreciate Beth's interference in a chambers matter and was about to say as much when Beth continued. "I am also aware that the main reason for the potential vote of no confidence in Jack stems from my private relationship with him. If that were the case, then I believe you should hear me out."

The head of chambers sat back in her chair, her body language suggesting to Beth that she should continue.

"Jack and I have a special relationship which has grown over the years. I am single and want to remain so, and both of us fulfil roles for each other which suit us both, if you get my meaning." Nicola nodded her understanding.

"I like the way Jack runs your chambers, and he is probably in the top ten senior clerks in the country. He has been after all my firm's work for as long as I can remember, and at last Geoffrey Ashdown is coming round to that idea. Otherwise I would not be seated here now."

"Beth, I appreciate what you say, but this has to be a matter for chambers to decide. There can be no outside influences."

"Indeed, I understand and respect that Nicola. But equally I must make you aware of my firm's response should your vote go against Jack. And I can tell you that our response would most certainly not be in your best interests, nor those of your colleagues here. Do I make myself clear?"

Thoughts of her first meeting with Jack in the Russell Hotel and his vision for the future flashed through Nicola's mind and on to the ECM. "Beth, I cannot predict the outcome of our meeting. It is up to the members to decide Jack's fate."

Beth responded. "Of course, but I came today to make sure you have all the facts you need to make an informed decision with your colleagues in chambers."

Beth went on. "As for me personally, if my relationship with Jack ends as it surely will one day, I will not throw all my toys out of the cot and take my firm's work away from Barcourt chambers. But if my relationship with him results in Jack losing his job, well then I would not like to be the cause of such an outcome. I and my firm would stay loyal to Jack, and not to Barcourt Chambers.

For Jack it is not just any job. He lives and breathes Barcourt chambers. He does what it takes to get the work and protect his barristers. He has your back, and in my book you should have his."

Both women reflected on their conversation. Beth spoke first. "This is your chambers and from what I hear you run it your way. I would not dream of trying to interfere, but it is right you should know the consequences."

Nicola thought further about Beth's words. "I hear what you say and will consider the best way forward with my members. As a matter of interest, who told you about the ECM?"

Beth answered. "It was Jenny. She gave me a call last week. Actually it was the day before I decided to send in your instructions in this case. Jenny knew Jack would not tell me about the vote of no confidence in him, but once I knew I felt we ladies should take control of the situation."

Nicola did not see the need to discuss the situation any further. Beth had made her case.

Beth picked up her case notes. "Now shall we consider liability for a collapsed roof?"

Nicola looked at Beth with a smile on her face and replied "Indeed. Jenny James certainly lives up to her nickname."

The same day, Jack went for breakfast with Jason at the Crown Café Bar on the Strand.

"Well, Jason, this could be our last breakfast together."

Jason was not happy at the suggestion. "Don't talk like that Jack. We will always have our breakfast meetings here whatever happens. You will get another senior clerks' job in the Temple, no problem. There are several sets who would welcome you with open arms.

But you are going to win at the ECM, and the old guard are going to lose out big time. Nicola will come through, I am sure of it"

Jack looked worried. He had hardly slept since the last management committee meeting, and whilst he appreciated Jason's loyalty, he did not share his view of the situation.

"I'm not so sure. Nicola has to look after her own position. She took the biggest gamble by joining Barcourt chambers and stands to lose the most if it goes wrong. No, I think she will revert to type and look after number one. I would do the same if I were in her position."

Jack changed the subject. "Do you remember your promise to me about Richard Murray?"

"Yes" replied Jason. "But I am not sure I can do much to stop him if he is chosen by chambers to succeed you. Apparently it was a close vote last time when you won and were appointed, but if there is a next time, he will fancy his chances of winning."

Jack looked Jason in the eye. "As soon as the vacancy for senior clerk is advertised, just remind Richard I have the original video of his nephew which will get put on the desk of the head of chambers if he so much as thinks about applying for my job."

"Does Richard know you have a copy?" asked Jason.

"Oh yes" replied Jack. "You can remind him of that fact if he ever steps out of line again. Understood?"

They both raised their coffee cups and exclaimed "Cheers!"

On the afternoon of the day of the ECM the clerks' room was in sombre mood. Only Jason and Jack knew the exact nature of the meeting and why it had been called at such short notice. The rest of the team were inquisitive but neither Jack nor Jason gave any clues, and instinctively the others knew not to ask.

"You will just have to be patient" remarked Jason to Dillon. "You can do it."

Jack's patience was pretty thin and he felt he was on a short fuse. Jason could see the tension in his face and so did his best to deal with the day's business on Jack's behalf.

Jack was entitled under the chambers' constitution to have a representative with him at any meeting to consider his dismissal from chambers. He had thought about who he might turn to in his hour of need. He did not want to go to anyone outside chambers for fear of it getting out, whatever the outcome. He could see chambers being damaged.

Inside chambers, there were only the members, and none of them would want to have been seen to support a dismissed senior clerk. Jason had offered but Jack did not want him involved. If he lost the vote, Jason would want to apply for Jack's job himself.

Jack's only other option was to instruct a solicitor. He had considered asking Beth to represent him as she knew chambers and the people he was dealing with, but he did not want her involved especially as one of the main allegations involved his relationship with Beth.

In the end, Jack resolved to go it alone. He told Jason "I have no choice. I will fly solo. It's for the best."

Normally when Jack wanted something from chambers as a whole, or from a group of barristers, even the management committee, he made his notes of what he wanted to say and ran through the list.

The one thing Jack could be sure of was that they would all pull in different directions at different times depending on their own agenda. "You cannot herd cats" was one of Jack's favourite expressions and today was no exception. He knew the nature of the beasts he was dealing with, just not how to handle them when it came down to defending himself.

Nicola opened the chambers meeting in the main conference room. Normally the room was not big enough to seat all the members of chambers. As a result the conference room was packed with standing room only at the back.

"Thank you all for attending at such short notice. You all know why we are here. I will ask Tom Wallace to address the meeting first, and then anyone who wishes to raise points on the matter to be considered. Finally Jack will have the opportunity to respond on his own behalf, and I will then ask him to leave us whilst we consider and vote on the matter before us. Any questions?"

The room remained silent as Tom Wallace repeated all the issues he had raised at the management committee meeting. Peter Livingstone chipped in, more for his own gratification than to offer anything new to the debate.

Jack listened to everything said about him and admitted to himself it was a compelling argument. He too went through his fighting speech to the management committee meeting only tempered this time with a little more humility.

He left the meeting to determine his future satisfied he had given it his best shot. He returned to the clerks' room which was empty save for Jason to await the outcome. Jason did his best to rally Jack's morale, but could say little to help.

"I now know what it feels like to be an accused waiting for the jury to return. It is hell" commented Jack to Jason.

After what seemed like an eternity to Jack but was actually forty minutes, the head of chambers walked into the clerks' room. Both Jack and Jason rose to their feet. "Jason, could you give us a minute?" asked Nicola.

"Of course" replied Jason, thinking as he left the clerks' room shutting the door behind him that it was bad news. The head of chambers never came into the clerks' room.

Nicola sat in Jason's chair and looked straight at Jack.

"Jack, I am pleased to report that the vote of no confidence in you was defeated by an eighty percent majority. Indeed it was a massive vote of confidence in what you do here, and I for one am delighted with the outcome."

For once Jack was speechless and emotional. Nicola could see that in his eyes and there was no point in saying any more at that moment. "Jack, chambers are leaving now and after they have gone, in say ten minutes, I would like to see you in my room to tell you the detail of what happened. Will you come up shortly?"

Jack nodded. Nicola opened the door and walked past Jason who went into the clerks' room. He looked at Jack's drained face and blank expression, fearing the worst.

As Jason approached his own chair still focused on Jack's face, he saw the blank look slowly turn to a big smile.

Jack uttered just two words. "Eighty percent!" His expression told Jason it was good news. "What?" exclaimed Jason "You're kidding? Eighty percent! That's ridiculous. Nobody scores eighty percent. It's one hell of a pass mark!"

Jack got up and gave Jason a hug for the first time ever. "Not a word to anyone tonight. I'm going up to see Nicola for the full details. I'll see you in the morning, ok?"

Nicola's door to her room was wide open so she saw Jack approaching. "Come in Jack and take a seat. You have earned it." She could see Jack's composure had returned so launched into what had happened at the meeting.

"Now, some of what was said must remain confidential to the members, but I am able to tell you that you have some powerful friends in chambers. They include in particular Sarah Ryman who had clearly rallied support for you amongst the youngsters. I think the old guard had misread the mood of chambers.

But you should take heart from a massive endorsement of what you do for us, Jack, and I am so pleased for you."

"Thank you" replied Jack. "I had not expected such a positive response. It is very encouraging. How did Wallace and Livingstone take it?"

"Livingstone was fine" said Nicola. "But Wallace won't accept it. However he now knows he will not win the day, meaning he won't ever be head of chambers. Once he comes to terms with that, I expect him to get back to work. Just look after him as best he will let you."

"Should I still be concerned about the confidentiality issue and the Lord Chancellor's letter to Wadsworth?" asked Jack.

"No" replied Nicola. "That has passed, but we have parked your affair with Beth for the time being. It all depends on how that pans out in the future, and if her firm continue to support chambers. That will be up to you."

"Understood" said Jack. "Is that all for now?"

Nicola smiled. "I think so. It's quite enough for one day."

Jack took the tube train straight home and was just in time to read his son a story in bed before opening a bottle of red and pouring a glass for himself and one for Barbara.

"Good day, was it Jack? She asked. They cuddled up on the sofa and Jack broke off from his thoughts. "You could say that. Now, what is for supper, I'm starving!"

The next morning, Sarah Ryman popped her head into the clerks' room and greeted the team with a cheery smile. Jack rose and followed her out and up to her room, closing the door behind him.

"I am told by the head of chambers that you played a big part in the outcome of the chambers' meeting last night."

Sarah carried on with taking her coat off and sorting her pile of papers for court that morning. "Oh, not really" she said. "Most of chambers did not want to see you leave."

"That's not how Nicola put it. She said you had canvassed support and were particularly supportive."

Sarah stopped what she was doing and looked at Jack. "Do you really think I was going to let all your efforts to get me back into chambers come to nothing, which is what would have happened if we had let you go?"

Jack smiled. "Thank you." Sarah was not finished.

"Jenny should take a lot of the credit for her work behind the scenes. Anyway, at least one of your expressions has come home for you."

Jack was puzzled. "Which one, there are so many?"

Sarah obliged. "Look after the company, and the company will look after you. So we did!"

On his return to the clerks' room, Jason spoke to everyone, including his senior clerk. "Jack I have told everyone what happened last night at the meeting, and so there is no need to say anything except that you are available for a drink in the WI after work this evening."

"Sure" said Jack sitting down at his chair at the head of the clerks' table. "Now can we get some work done in here?"

The Wiltshire Inn was packed shortly after six o'clock that evening. The whole clerking team were in attendance with a few of the younger members of chambers, including Sarah Ryman. She put her arms round Jack's neck and gave him a diplomatic peck on the cheek.

Jack whispered in her ear. "So is the offer to have my children on the table still?"

Sarah whispered back. "On the table, in the shower, anywhere you like Jack!"

Dillon who was holding Charlotte's hand, broke them up. "Come on, none of that in chambers. You know what Wallace will say."

Everyone was in good spirits until Richard Murray from Carey Street and his deputy Barry Nicholson walked in. Jack called them over and offered them a glass of champagne.

"What are we celebrating Jack? It's a bit early for Christmas."

"Nothing really, Richard, just another good day at Barcourt." Jack leant forward and said "Nice try Richard. Just remember, you've fired all your bullets now. All you've got is an empty gun and no ammunition to fire at me any more, loser."

Richard put his glass down on the bar. "Come on Barry, the company is off in here." Richard and Barry left to a round of applause from Jack's team.

As the evening progressed, Jack thought he was not going to make it home so had a word with the landlord Michael. "Don't suppose you have a room free for tonight? I think I may need one."

"Sorry Jack" replied Michael. "I'm full tonight."

Twenty minutes later Beth Richardson walked in carrying her overnight bag. She walked up to Jack and gave him a big kiss on the lips. Jack was happy with her sign of affection in front of his staff as they now all knew about their relationship, but did not understand how she knew it was alright.

"Jack" said Beth "a little bird told me you were celebrating tonight so I thought I would pop in. Can I have a drink?"

From Jack's point of view, the evening just got better, but he hit on a practical problem. "I'm afraid there are no rooms left here tonight" he told Beth.

"Good job I booked us a room earlier today then, wasn't it?"

Jenny came over to them with a spare glass of champagne and handed it to Beth. They smiled to each other.

"Thanks Jenny." Turning to Jack, Beth said "Do you know what Jack, this woman certainly lives up to her nickname."

Jack was not sure what Beth meant so asked her "How come?"

Beth smiled. "Well, because when you were in difficulty, Jenny had your back, even though you did not know it at the time."

The clerks had all heard what Beth had said. Jason felt a little emotional so to combat any potential for a breakdown, he raised his glass. "I feel a toast coming on. Are we ready?"

As everyone raised their glass to Jenny James, Jason called out at the top of his voice.

"To the bodyguard!"

ABOUT THE AUTHOR

Bob Moss have been a practising Solicitor, a senior clerk / practice manager in barristers' chambers, a notary public, a trained mediator and a magazine publisher.

Bob first had the idea for Jack Temple about 20 years ago but he never seemed to enough time to write. Only in "retirement" has he been able to focus on writing, an empowering experience he can thoroughly recommend.

Educated at St Edward's School Oxford as a Barclays Bank scholar, Bob started work at 18 in a solicitors' office. He was taken on to do five years as an articled clerk rather than go to university, a route into the profession which meant his training had a greater focus on office management.

This would help Bob enormously when it came to becoming the managing equity partner in his firm of solicitors and later as a chambers' senior clerk / practice manager in both London and Liverpool.

For more than a decade he produced and edited *Clerksroom Magazine* for staff in chambers. He ran a buying group for chambers and law firms, and designed and produced products for the legal profession.

Bob is a fair weather golfer, preferring to play abroad whenever possible. His hobbies now include watching rather than playing sport generally and Liverpool FC in particular.

Printed in Great Britain
by Amazon